RESTLESS SOUL

Emily Tipton Williams

ISBN 0-7414-2541-6

Cover photo by Emily Tipton Williams

Published by:

INFINITY
PUBLISHING.COM

1094 New DeHaven Street, Suite 100
West Conshohocken, PA 19428-2713
Info@buybooksontheweb.com
www.buybooksontheweb.com
Toll-free (877) BUY BOOK
Local Phone (610) 941-9999
Fax (610) 941-9959

Printed in the United States of America

Printed on Recycled Paper

Published June 2005

DEDICATION

To Julie and Nell, my soul sisters.

Thanks

This novel grew from a short story I told one afternoon several years ago when I facilitated an Advent Quiet Day at a church in Fort Worth, Texas. At times the characters took on a life of their own, leading me across the inspiring countryside of England and Wales.

As I wrote I would often glance at pictures of my mother and father, who I am sure, are amused at their violin-playing daughter in her attempts to write a novel. I want to thank those dear ones who are no longer with me on "this fragile earth, our island home." I am deeply indebted to family and friends for their love, support and encouragement, especially my husband, Mike.

Thanks to my "readers," Julie Cochran, Nell Noonan, Mike Williams, Joan Dennis, Marion Pearl, Ruth Bridge, Jean Frick, and The Rev. Pip Short. Thanks to book doctor, Robyn Conley, who prescribed the right medicine for the ailments of my written words. Blessings to my "priestly" friends, both ordained and lay, who ministered to me in inspiring and unsuspecting ways.

And a big hug to the members of Fort Worth Freelance Writers Network critique group who welcomed "The Church Lady" into their midst.

"Our souls are restless until they rest in you, O Lord."

St. Augustine of Hippo

Chapter One

One letter can change a life.

The stark white envelope lay on a weathered table by the front door. Pursing her lips and tapping her foot in indecision Elizabeth Ann Davies regarded the return address on the envelope. No mistaking the prominent seal of the Bishop of Chester.

"Why open it? I know the answer. No!"

Beside the letter lay a novel. On impulse, Beth scooped up the book on her way toward the back of the house. The smell of cooking bacon hung in the home. She heard her parents' voices rising and falling in animated conversation as they shared their first cups of tea.

Beth paused for a moment in the doorway of the kitchen, enjoying the familiar scene. An old oak table dominated the center of the kitchen. A small bay window with faded, curtains offered a vista to the outdoors. Clouds flowing in from the Irish Sea hid the early morning sun over northwest England.

Her mother, a short robust woman in a tattered apron covcring hcr simplc drcss, stood at thc stovc turning bacon. Sitting at the table Charles Davies held a steaming mug of tea with ruddy working hands. He looked up smiling with emerald eyes matched by his daughter. Beth walked into the room.

"Going out before I catch the train to London," Beth informed her parents.

"Beth, just what did Mr. High and Mighty over in Chester have to say? Am I going to have a minister for a daughter?"

"Mum, I haven't opened it yet. I'll do it when I get back."

Grabbing a couple of scones from a plate, Beth wrapped them in a napkin and put them in her jacket pocket.

"Daughter, I'm almost at the end of my tether. You march back and get that letter!"

Beth and her father exchanged a knowing smile as Beth walked out of the kitchen.

At the front door, she turned and shouted, "I'll do my marching as soon as I get back."

A large white dog with wagging tail stood on the front porch. The two set out on their usual morning adventure. Manna ran ahead. No need to follow. She knew the destination. Engulfed in light fog, a deserted footpath led to the Gately estate grounds.

"One of those velvet mornings. The best for being out," Beth whispered.

Dressed in jeans and wellies she climbed a fence with a weathered sign, "Gately Estate. No Trespassing." The dampness on her hair was of no worry. Dark brown curls always fell into place, no matter how she brushed it. Her long stride was silent on the damp leaves. Trees, the oldest in this part of northern England lined the path with branches intertwined far above Beth's head.

Walking into the deep forest, she stopped at a familiar moss-covered, flat stone that was twice as long as she was tall. The Gatelys had allowed experts to examine it several years back. They determined it was the same type stone as found at Stonehenge, but had no other information.

Putting her hands on her hips Beth reflected for a few moments. *What were you used for centuries ago? An altar to a Druid god?*

Scraped clean, it would be a perfect place for a picnic. But it had to stay, hidden from most, with mushrooms as its companions.

On the path ahead, an archaic stone bridge hid the ever-flowing stream below. Passing over with a smile on her face, not daring to look right or left, Beth remembered the childhood words of her mother.

"Leprechauns and fairies live under the bridge in the woods. If a wee child should look down and see them, that wee one belongs to them. The old crone will gather them up at midnight of the next full moon, never to be seen again."

Beth knew it was just a story to keep young children out of the woods without their parents, but still, she never looked down.

Massive rhododendrons of vibrant pink greeted her as she came out of the woods. Hesitating for a moment, she looked back at the stream. The overhanging fronds of ferns danced in the water. Walking on, she glanced up the hill to her favorite spot.

"Must be the best place in all the world," she told Manna. "So peaceful. My kind of church."

She hurried up the incline at a half run, trying to race past Manna, but as usual the mass of white fur stood waiting at the top. Reaching the summit, she turned around to survey the scene before her. In the east the sun struggled to peek through the clouds. The fog pulled back, leaving dampness on the surrounding vegetation. She filled her lungs with the fresh air. Birds chattered from distant trees, while white boulder-like objects dotting the hillside started moving. The lambs bleated, signaling an empty stomach.

Beth settled comfortably on a log, taking her breakfast from her pocket. The scones filled with currants melted in her mouth, reminding Beth of the bakery in Oxford during her university years. She devoured the pastry, wiping her hands on her jeans. Taking the book out of her pocket, she opened it at random.

"The choice must be made," the passage began. "It would affect the lives of countless others for years to come. After listening to all his advisors, the prime minister left the room and retreated to his private office."

Closing the book, Beth put it back in her jacket. *Why am I reading this? Trying to escape from the real world into the world of fiction?*

Beth felt she knew these characters better than she knew herself. This afternoon she'd meet the author, the real Bala Foresight.

As Beth sat thinking of the trip to London, she studied the stirrings of life in the valley below. The sheep had fully awakened and assembled in a loose flock. A dog worked the fringe, a constant reminder to those who dared to stray.

Her thoughts turned to the unopened letter waiting back home and the labyrinthine circumstances that had shaped her life to this point. She was now at a crossroads. Her eyes closed tightly as she opened her heart for an answer.

Chapter Two

"Now the house of Israel called its name manna."
(Exodus 16:31)

Beth remembered vividly that Sunday five years ago. Spring in Chester. The advance and retreat of warm and cold had settled on warm. A glorious morning, the type that bonds mankind to nature and God.

After the service at St. John's, Beth joined Rev. Gareth Sloan for tea in the Prior's Hall. They chose a table in the far corner. The subject, though not unexpected, left Beth nonplussed and at a loss for words.

"The ministry, Vicar? Not me."

"I've known you and your family for many years. I've watched you grow up. I believe the Lord has blessed you in a special way."

Beth listened with a slight smile, shaking her head.

"But your whole life has been leading you in that direction. I've seen it happening."

Rev. Sloan put his hands together as though in prayer. Then extended his arms out to either side. "A butterfly coming out of a cocoon."

Beth laughed at the theatrical display. "You're wrong, Vicar. I think I'm still in the caterpillar stage."

"Nevertheless, sometimes others can see things."

"Perhaps, though I often wonder if I'm looking through the window pane or just seeing my own reflection."

Beth and the portly minister stared at their empty teacups. The occasional clang of dishes from an adjoining room interrupted the silence. A few women had remained to tidy up. As one of the ladies opened the door to leave, a large dog of questionable ancestry bounded into the room. Spotting her mistress in the corner, she trotted over to Beth's side.

"Sit."

"How did she know you were here?"

"I told her to stay in the car. She saw that church was over and came looking for me, I suppose."

"Quite a smart animal."

Smiling, Beth looked down at her faithful companion. "Manna has that sixth sense, I guess. I'll wager the ladies don't like her encroaching on their territory."

"Don't worry about them. If they're not complaining about your dog, they'd be complaining about my sermons being too long." He reached down, stroking the dog's head. "But I'm curious, Beth. Where did you find your friend?"

"Well, it is quite a story, if you have time."

"Yes, I do. But if you don't mind, it's rather stuffy in here. Think I'll take off this jacket and my dog collar." Standing, the Rev. Sloan placed his coat and collar on a nearby table, and then settled back down.

"I was hiking up in the Welsh hills south of Conwy last year. One of my favorite places and unknown to tourists. The locals say the path followed one made by Druids thousands of years ago. After hiking most of the day, I discovered off the trail an enormous standing stone with pagan symbols. I sat down by the stone to rest, but fell asleep. The next thing I knew this big dog was licking my face. It was close to sunset and to top things off, a heavy fog had settled on the mountain. I couldn't see a foot ahead of me. No way to get down without a torch."

"You must have been scared up there by yourself."

"Not really. I've often camped out alone, but mostly in the Lake District."

"Oh, yes, the Lake District. Last year Mary and I visited Dove Cottage. Wordsworth's home is about as rustic as I would care for, but the guide gave an excellent tour, even explaining the phrase, burning the candle at both ends. That I can relate to," the vicar added, wiping his brow with his handkerchief. "Sorry, Beth, go on with your story."

Looking down at Manna, Beth smiled. "She walked a short distance away from the stone, then looked around as if to say, come on! Just enough moonlight filtered through the clouds on her white fur to lead the way. When I reached the safety of the village, I inquired about the dog. No one recognized her so I brought her home."

"And what about her name?"

"The next morning I was reading in Exodus about the Israelites in the desert. The Lord sent manna when they had nothing to eat. The white manna was a gift from God. If she hadn't appeared, I might have wandered in the wrong direction and fallen off the nearby cliffs."

"Well, that's some story. Do you know what manna really means?"

"It means bread, doesn't it? The bread that God gave the Israelites."

"In a way that's correct. The actual translation of the word, manna, is 'what is it?' That's also what my dear wife asks when I attempt to cook anything. So what does your mother think of the dog?"

"She thinks I should call her Ghost."

The two chuckled. Leaning closer, the vicar fixed Beth with a thoughtful gaze. "At least consider the possibility of ordination. I've watched your involvement with the church. You do so well with all ages--the children in Sunday school, the nursing home, hospital visits--why you even get along with the ladies."

"Well, Vicar, most of them. They still say I'm too young to be of help with the altar guild. If they thought I had any idea of becoming a deacon, they would put me in the stocks until next winter."

"I'm not talking about your becoming a deacon. I'm talking about your becoming a priest."

"A priest? My mother would never hear of it. It would be the death of her. Have you heard her latest diatribe? She sent a letter to the Archbishop of Canterbury saying any woman who said she wanted to be a priest should be locked up in a convent and never let out."

"I'm sure His Grace got a good laugh from that correspondence. But what about you, Beth? Haven't you ever considered it?"

Beth looked out the nearby window in silence, knowing the answer to the question.

"Yes, I have thought about it. There have been times when I felt like I've had what those evangelicals refer to as 'the call.' I hate that term. Sounds so trite to these Anglican ears."

The vicar laughed. Mrs. Jones, standing near the door with another lady, peered over her spectacles, squinting snidely.

"Vicar, we'll be going now. Do you require any further assistance?"

"No, thank you. I'll see you in the morning for the Mums and Toddlers program. Thank you, ladies."

"Very well then, Vicar. We'll leave the door open."

"Go on, Beth. Tell me about those times."

"Nothing specific. Just pieces and snatches. When reading certain scripture. In prayer. Even when I'm out hiking. In dreams. One dream. It keeps recurring."

The vicar leaned forward. "Tell me about that."

"I'm walking up the cathedral aisle, dressed in red and gold vestments, the last in the procession." Beth hesitated looking around to be sure no one could hear.

"Go on."

"Later in the service I'm standing in the pulpit giving the sermon. The main biblical text is 'There are varieties of gifts, but the same spirit."

"And do you remember any other words?"

"Oh, yes. And it's the same each time. Concerning the gifts God has given us. How we ignore some. How often times we misuse our gifts. And the other words from the

Bible are about Jesus speaking to his disciples after his resurrection. 'As the Father has sent me, even so I send you."

The vicar shrugged his shoulders. "I have no experience interpreting dreams, but this seems pretty clear. The color of the vestments and the scripture is for Pentecost Sunday. How many times have you had this dream?"

"About five or six times over the past few years." Beth whispered, "You're the first person I've told."

Stroking his chin, the vicar looked away, staring at the floor. After a few moments he gazed at Beth.

"A scripture comes to mind. 'For our gospel came to you not only in word, but also in power and in the Holy Spirit and with full conviction.' I suggest your keeping a journal. Write down your experiences and dreams. Might help you process." Rev. Sloan continued, "And other times?"

"The most powerful. A few weeks ago at a weekday service at the cathedral. The minister consecrating the bread and wine. In an instant I was transported up to the altar." Beth touched her right hand to her chest. "I was he. I was consecrating the bread and wine. Not in my pew kneeling, but up there. The instant I held the bread up and heard the breaking of it, I was back in my place." Beth lowered her hand to the table, clasping her fingers together. She stared at her hands.

Silence filled the almost empty room.

"Beth, we need to spend more time talking about all this."

"But Vicar, my life is so ordered now. Kevin and I will bc going off to Oxford, if I'm accepted. After graduation, we'll marry, unless Lady Gately can hire some gangsters from Liverpool to knock me off."

The vicar chuckled. "Now, Beth."

"She told Kevin she does like me, but I don't have the proper breeding and connections for a diplomat's wife. He hasn't started university yet and she already has him deciding the fate of the world for the next millennium."

The vicar nodded. "Well, you know, with his father in the House of Lords and he the oldest son, there's a likelihood he could find himself in such a position."

"Yes, I know. I suppose I don't like to think of such a possibility."

"What do you plan to study at Oxford?"

"General studies, playing my violin in an orchestra and some theology. Of course you know how I enjoy reading fiction." Beth sighed. "But the books I like aren't on the required reading list."

"O, yes, Bala Foresight. On your recommendation I purchased one of her books. The problem, though, was every time I had time to read, Mary was reading it." He smiled. "She has a real talent. The characters come to life, and the action scenes are quite vivid."

"Vicar, I'm curious about what she looks like. Did you see the last issue of The Sun?"

"You mean you read such trash?" he teased.

"Sometimes at the market when I'm in a queue. They're always trying to track down Bala Foresight. She's incognito, you know. The last article stated she'd been burned in a car wreck, scarring her face, and lives in a castle in the Scottish highlands. You should have seen the picture. Like Phantom of the Opera."

"I think she looks like the Queen Mum. Never goes out without her hat and gloves. I'll wager she's someone no one would suspect of writing such books. A proper English grandmother, if you ask me."

"I finished her latest. I'm convinced she's someone in London high society. How else could she describe in such detail the characters involved in that story?"

"The one Mary and I read had a hospital setting and one of the patients was a war veteran. The flashback took me right to the battleground. Amazing. She wrote like a man. I couldn't put it down." The vicar slapped the table.

The sudden noise woke the sleeping dog. Jumping to her feet, Manna started barking.

"Quiet down, Manna."

With head down she returned to her place.

"Now, Beth, about the possibility of ordination. I'm not trying to convince you of anything. But I want you to be open to possibilities in your life. Did you know I was an innkeeper before I became a priest?"

"You were?"

"I'm convinced it was the preparatory training I needed. The business of hospitality. You know, that's what The Church is about. We need to welcome all sorts and conditions of women and men. We only need to look at the hospitality of our Lord. He welcomed the lowliest of the low. What we need around this church are a few lepers to shake things up. We already have our Pharisees and Sadducees."

Glancing at his watch the vicar exclaimed, "My goodness! I best be on my way. Mary is waiting dinner and I have the Churchwardens meeting this afternoon. I wish we could spend more time talking. Remember, Beth, you have your whole life ahead of you. Don't be too quick to close some of those doors that may open for you. At least go in and see what the room looks like."

The two stood, walking in silence out the door with Manna in trail. Beth waited as the vicar locked the door.

"Thanks, Vicar. See you next Sunday, if not before."

As Rev. Sloan turned toward his car, Beth and Manna headed toward Grovesnor Park to meet Kevin.

Chapter Three

"Therefore encourage one another and
build one another up, just as you are doing."
(Thessalonians 5:11)

The sunny weather brought out a variety of people, from newborns to pensioners to joggers in shorts, even "Queen Mum" types properly dressed and carrying suitable purses. Men with their noses a little high strolled the walks, tapping their black umbrellas in rhythmic cadence. Ancient oaks swayed in the slight breeze carrying the sound of children hard at play.

Manna romped about with an occasional look back at her mistress. Beth noticed how the dog's size took some by surprise, but the wagging tail signaled safety.

Lost in thought, Beth ambled along, reflecting on the conversation with the vicar. True, she had entertained fleeting ideas of a lifetime commitment to the church; however, she always dismissed them as impractical.

Not an option, Beth thought. I'm going to marry Kevin, travel the world. And the London parties! Meeting all the high society and royalty! Not bad for a girl whose parents worked on the estate."

Stopping for a moment she surveyed her surroundings. Taking a deep breath Beth inhaled the fragrance of a nearby rose garden. All of a sudden a Frisbee whizzed past her head. Manna ran after it, almost knocking her down, then returned with the Frisbee in her mouth.

"Now where did you get that?"

"That your dog, ma'am?" shouted a young lad running across an open area.

"Sorry she took your Frisbee. Would you like to play with her? She does tricks."

"Sure! What kind of tricks?"

"Timothy, stop bothering the lady and come over here."

The young mother walking up the path was pushing a baby pram. Her stooping shoulders, tired eyes and rough hands suggested an age beyond her years.

"Sorry if he's bothering you. Come on, Timothy. Time to go."

"But, Mother, the dog does tricks. Can't we stay?"

"No bother at all ma'am, if you have time. She loves to perform, especially for such an appreciative audience."

Manna sat up, rolled over and played dead. Then Beth had Timothy ask the dog questions. By a signal in her eyes, Beth had trained the dog to shake her head yes or no. Next Beth took the Frisbee and threw it high and long. Manna ran and caught it in her mouth before it hit the ground. Within minutes several of the Grosvenor Park visitors had gathered to watch the performance.

She handed the Frisbee to Timothy. "Here, give it a try." She stood back and watched.

Glancing up the path toward the park entrance, she saw Kevin approaching. Tilting her head she smiled, admiring her handsome well-built boyfriend. *He walks with his patrician nose a bit high as though he were already Lord of the manor.*

Beth waved. "Over here."

His deep-set chestnut eyes lit up when he saw Beth. Walking over, he put his arm around her waist, giving her a kiss. She reached up and swept his dark brown wavy hair off his forehead. He laughed.

"I know. Time for another haircut." He held her hand.

"Sorry to be late, but it appears you haven't been too lonely without me."

"Great. You're here. Look at this trick, Kevin. I didn't know she could do this."

"Any chance you could train that dog for the fox hunt?"

"Oh, Kevin," Beth said, shaking her head.

Timothy threw the Frisbee again. It flew over an elderly lady walking with a cane. Manna saw her in time. Darting around, much to the lady's surprise, the dog charged ahead. Manna shot into the air and snared the disk in her mouth. She strutted back, returning the treasure to the young lad. The bystanders applauded.

"Come, Timothy. Your father will be wondering where his dinner is," his mother said. She turned to Beth, "Thank you, young lady. Been a real treat for my boy."

"Oh, you're welcome. It's been a treat for us too. And Timothy taught Manna a new trick."

The boy stood a little taller with his chin tilted up and a controlled smile on his face. "My pleasure, ma'am."

Pushing the baby carriage, the young mother wheeled off toward the entrance to the park with Timothy running ahead, throwing his Frisbee in the air.

"I tried to get away earlier. I thought the Hillbrooks would never leave. Their daughter is the biggest bore I've ever met. But Mother made it clear I was not to leave until they did. I wish my parents would stop inviting all those London snobs for weekends at the estate."

"Your mother trying to fix you up again? One of these days you might just fall madly in love with one of those jet setters and drop me like a hot potato."

"No way. You're my girl. Someday I'll put that ring on your finger. We'll have a bunch of wild brats and leave them with our parents. Holidays on the continent. Paris, Switzerland, the Riviera. But we'll have to wait till I'm out of Oxford. I promised the old duffer. I mean his Lordship."

Beth and Kevin held hands as they strolled down a shaded path toward the entrance of the city park. "Say, Beth, any news from Oxford?"

"No, but I should hear this week. Everything looks pretty promising. How was your bus ride into town?"

"I didn't take the bus. Mother didn't want me mingling with the commoners. She made some excuse to the Hillbrooks and asked if they would mind dropping me off on their way to London. And if that wasn't enough, at breakfast this morning Lady Hillbrook started talking about a party at Windsor in a couple of weeks. My dear mother graciously volunteered me to be Penelope's escort. My mouth was full of crumpets. By the time I swallowed, they had arranged all the details."

Beth burst out laughing.

"Will you get Prince William's autograph for me?"

"Come on, now. You know I don't want to go. It'll ruin the entire weekend."

"That's about the time I'll be going to visit Grandmother in Llandudno. What does your father think about all this?"

"Oh, he consents to whatever she wants. I talked with him right after breakfast. Told him I didn't want to attend this function. But he said I should go along with what Mother wants and be patient. Easy for him to say. He's off to London more than he's home. He doesn't have to put up with her scheming like I do. She'll be a lot less in my business when we're off to Oxford."

Kevin squeezed Beth's hand. "Sorry, Beth, guess I'll have to go to that boring party with Penelope."

They walked toward the entrance with Manna following behind. A shadow clouded Beth's thoughts. This wasn't the first time Lady Gately had interfered in their lives. Nor would it be the last. In the distance a church bell chimed one o'clock.

As they reached the entrance to the park, Beth gazed at the massive sandstone Church of St. John the Baptist.

"Look, Kevin, the stones almost glisten in the bright sunlight."

"I think St. John's is gloomy even in the sunshine. Don't know why you don't attend the cathedral."

"I do, on occasion."

"How was church this morning, my luv? Did you have to teach another class?"

"No."

"I'm sure that was a relief."

"You know, I actually did rather enjoy teaching that class a few weeks ago. In fact, I wouldn't mind doing it again."

Reaching his arm around Beth, giving her a hug, he suggested, "I've got just the place for lunch. Ever been to Stamford Bridge Inn?"

"No."

"This is a perfect day to go. We can eat outside with a view of the Cheshire hills. You'll love the gardens, too."

"Sounds great."

Beth handed Kevin car keys as they approached her navy Renault. Manna took her place in the back seat when Beth opened the door. As they traveled along the streets of Chester, Beth noticed people staring at the large white furry head protruding from the small window.

"All churched out, Beth? You spend a lot of time in those cold old places."

"I had a good chat with the vicar after the service."

"What did you two talk about?"

"Oh, nothing you'd be interested in. Churchy stuff."

Beth looked out the window as the car sped along. But she saw nothing, her thoughts focused on the recent conversation. How would Kevin react at her mention of the ordination? *Why can't I stop thinking about it?* She knew she'd have an easy road ahead with Kevin. Looking over at him, she smiled.

He caught her eye. "Penny for your thoughts."

"It'll cost you more than that."

"No, really. An interesting smile on your face."

"Just thinking about our future."

"That's my girl," he said patting her shoulder. "Now on to the immediate future. I'm starving."

Arriving at the inn took longer than expected because of Sunday traffic. The old, well-kept inn of white stucco with black shutters and window boxes alive with geraniums was ready evidence of the owner's pride. Several patrons sat at tables in front, enjoying a pint after lunch.

The owner greeted Beth and Kevin at the door. "Care to sit inside or out?" He pointed a finger at Kevin. "Say, you've been here before. Just last week with another lad. I see you have a much more attractive companion for this visit."

Kevin smiled. "Beth, where would you care to sit?"

"It's lovely outside. The back overlooking the countryside?"

Kevin and Beth followed the man through the unique dining area graced with timbered ceiling and large windows of cut glass filtering the warm sun of late spring. The dark wood paneling lent a comfortable feeling to the room.

Beth grabbed Kevin's hand. "What a delightful place. And quite romantic with all the candles. Perhaps we can come back for dinner sometime."

"Anything for my princess."

Two large hedgerows framed a manicured flower garden that bubbled with almost every conceivable color. In the distance the rolling hills of Chester formed a backdrop against a deep blue sky. Several wooden tables and chairs were placed about the yard.

"Choose any place you like. My wife will be out with menus and specials for the day. The soup is country vegetable."

Beth chose a table farthest from the inn. An attractive woman in her early thirties came out with menus and two glasses of water.

"Glad you're eating out here. It's too nice a day to be indoors. From around here or just passing through?"

"We're both from Hawthorne."

"Oh, that's a nice place. Over visiting there on the Gately Estate last week. The rhododendrons were beautiful. Nice of his Lordship to let us common folk in."

Beth kicked Kevin under the table.

"Yes, rather, I must say," Kevin replied.

Looking up from her menu, Beth asked, "And did you investigate the castle ruins? On a clear day you can see the ocean."

"No, but the husband and children did. Had a grand time, climbing all over that old castle. I'll give you time to look the menu over."

The woman walked slowly back into the inn.

"My goodness, Kevin. This is quite a menu. What sounds good to you?"

"Last time I had a great Stamford Burger."

"Better than McDonalds?"

"Just a wee bit." Kevin perused the entrees. "The Chicken Tikka Masala sounds good. I had some good Indian food my last visit in London. Never had it before and took to it. What about you?"

"I think the Lasagna Verde. Look at those desserts. Hot puddings of the day, spotted dick, sticky toffee. I'll have one of each and skip lunch."

The affable woman returned. "Is that your big white dog out in the car?"

Nodding to Beth, Kevin replied, "Yes, it's hers. There's almost no room for me in there."

"Be glad to have her back here. I've got a good size bone bout ready to toss out."

Getting up from the table Beth turned toward the woman, "That would be great. I'll have the lasagna."

She smiled at Kevin, "I'll decide on dessert later."

Beth walked toward the side of the building, then returned in only seconds with Manna bounding around the corner. She nearly knocked the innkeeper's wife over with a greeting.

"Manna, sit," Kevin scolded.

"Where did you get such a fine animal?" she asked.

"I guess you might say she found me," Beth replied, approaching the table.

"Better get your orders in. I'll be right back with her bone."

Beth watched the dog explore the myriad scents within the garden, testimony to previous canine visitors. She gave a harmless growl and her tail went straight up whenever an odor assailed her nostrils.

Beth returned her attention to Kevin. "Guess your father is glad parliament is over for a while. Glad to be home for a change?"

"Yes and no. He thrives on the conflicts and discussions in the House of Lords. But he's getting tired of the animal lovers versus the foxhunters. He's got more fox hunting friends, needless to say, but he can appreciate the animal lovers, too. I think the Americans call it "fence sitting."

The owner appeared with the promised bone. "My wife sent this out for your dog."

Beth called Manna over. "Sit up. Shake hands."

The owner smiled as he shook Manna's paw.

"Good dog," Beth said.

"Why your dog has more class than some of my customers."

Tail wagging, Manna gently took the bone from the man's hand and settled down near the table to enjoy her unexpected snack.

"Your food is almost ready," offered the owner.

As soon as he was out of sight, Kevin took Beth's hand.

"I love you."

"And I love you, Kevin."

The two sat in silence, enjoying the spring afternoon. Beth attempted to free her mind from the disquieting notion that all was not well. What was wrong with her? Why did she harbor an uneasiness that seemed to bear an unwelcome weight on her soul? The jigsaw puzzle of her life missed a few of its pieces.

Soon the host returned with a large tray filled with food. He was about to speak when the purring sound of airplane engines interrupted.

The two men spoke in unison. "A C 130."

They lapsed into a discussion of aviation. Beth had little knowledge of airplanes and her interest in the conversation waned. Her thoughts drifted as she visualized life at the Gately Estate.

Servants would be at her beck and call. Shopping trips to London. Harrods. The parties. And how wonderful for her family. No longer employees, but members of the Gately family.

Following the meal, Beth took Manna to the car while Kevin went inside to pay. The innkeeper and his wife were behind the bar visiting with some customers.

"The food was delicious. I'm sure we'll be back whenever we're over this way."

"Thank you, sir. Glad you enjoyed it."

"Credit card all right?"

"Of course."

While waiting for the approval, the owner motioned for his wife to come over. He pointed to the card. They stared at Kevin.

"My goodness," she exclaimed, "I didn't realize. You are the son of Lord and Lady Gately. I'm so embarrassed talking to you about my trip to your estate. Why I've seen your picture in the paper, too. It's an honor to meet you, sir."

"Why, it's an honor to meet you both. And I'll be certain to recommend your inn."

Chapter Four

"They who wait for the Lord shall renew their strength.
They shall mount up with wings like eagles."
(Isaiah 40:31)

Taking the wheel of Beth's car, Kevin eased onto the main road. After a few miles he turned onto a back road.

"Why are you turning? I thought we were going home."

"Just need to check something on my plane. You're not in any hurry, are you?"

"No, not really."

Kevin pulled in a parking space next to the main office of a small airfield and got out.

"I'll be right back. You might want to let Manna out for a quick run before we take off."

As soon as Beth opened the backdoor, Manna ran off exploring the smells of the airport grounds. Beth watched a small airplane glide effortlessly to the earth. Shortly Kevin returned.

"Ready for your first airplane ride?"

"Me? No way," Beth replied shaking her head.

"Come on now. You'll love it. Put Manna in the car and we'll be on our way. It's a perfect day for flying. No wind and not a cloud in the sky. You couldn't ask for more perfect conditions."

"You go ahead. I'll stay here and watch."

"Beth, the real watching is from up there," he pointed skyward, "not down here."

"If I get scared, will you put the plane back down?"

"Of course," he replied with a chuckle.

Kevin took Beth's hand as they walked toward the gray metal hanger that housed the Gately's plane. Sliding the doors back on either side displayed the Cessna 150 of blue and silver. Beth took a deep breath.

"I'm still not sure about this."

"Come on, give it a try."

Beth climbed in, fastening her seat belt. She watched as Kevin started checking knobs, switches and objects that looked like confused clocks. Suddenly the engine started. The propeller turned so fast she could no longer see the blades. Beth's stomach turned to butterflies. Her hands clung to each other like two lovers refusing to part. Breaking out in a cold sweat, she yelled at Kevin, "I'm scared. You better let me out."

"You'll be fine as soon as we get up."

"I think I'm going to be sick."

"Take a deep breath."

Edging forward, the plane bumped along the gravel ground that separated the hanger from the smooth pavement of the runway. Reaching the end, Kevin parked the brake and ran the engine in a final test prior to take off. Satisfied with what he saw and heard, he released the brake. The small craft catapulted down the runway.

"Here we go!" shouted Kevin.

Beth closed her eyes as she felt the moving prison gather speed. The noise of the engine muffled. Beth opened her eyes. She looked at Kevin who was smiling at her.

"Are you all right?"

"I think so."

Finally, she looked outside. They were in the air!

Rolling green hills of northern England stretched from horizon to horizon. Country roads appeared as friendly snakes twisting and turning. The village church towers stood out as sentries for the surrounding buildings.

"It's all so beautiful. But how do you know we're not going to crash?"

"No need to worry. Now let's visit Chester."

Kevin guided the metal bird toward the medieval town. The view of the River Dee and the old wall surrounding the city amazed Beth. The green of Grosvenor's Park beckoned to her left, while on her right she could see the reddish walls and tower of Chester Cathedral. Victorian half-timbered structures stood defiantly in the midst of the city.

"The people look like ants, Kevin."

"I'll swing around toward Wales and we'll go up the coast."

The plane flew north along the Dee Estuary until reaching the Irish Sea. Then a turn to the west to follow the coastline passing Point of Ayr and Prestatyn. Soon Beth caught sight of Conwy castle guarding the coast of north Wales. The top of the old suspension bridge reflected a ray of sunlight, reminding Beth of a scene in a childhood book.

Within minutes they reached the North Shore of Llandudno. Directly below the old Victorian pier jutted out like a giant finger to the north, while the majestic crescent of hotels and sandy beach lay in contrast to the blue green sea.

"Kevin, I can see Granny's house right there," Beth pointed. "And the tram up the Great Orme. And there's St. Tudno's Church. This is the most fabulous experience of my life."

Kevin smiled with a look of satisfaction. "And I thought you didn't want to come."

Kevin flew back inland so Beth could view the Snowdonia Mountains and the spectacular Nant Ffrancon Pass. The grazing sheep scattered when the plane came too close.

Beth didn't realize when the wheels touched the ground because the landing was so smooth.

"It was glorious. Like I was flying. Flying on eagle's wings!"

"You were."

"No. I mean me flying. So effortless. And seeing all that from a different perspective. It's a whole new world from up there. Must be like God looking down on us."

"Now you're going a bit too far," Kevin said as they returned to the car.

Beth talked on and on about her first airplane ride, glancing at Kevin, who drove along in silence with a satisfied look on his face.

"I wish Granny had been out taking her stroll along the beach. We could have swooped down low and waved. Let's go straight home. I want to tell Mum and Da all about it."

"Fine with me."

Manna acted glad to be home. With her back window down she hit the ground before the car came to a full stop. Beth was thankful the dog only practiced this trick at home. Running toward the path that led to the nearby woods, she was out of sight before Kevin and Beth got out of the car.

The front porch of the farmhouse held a much-used church pew with two simple rockers keeping it company. Hanging baskets swayed in the gentle afternoon breeze awaiting the advent of warmer weather. Within a month forget-me-nots and creeping buttercups would decorate the plain front of the home.

A side yard of overturned soil with neat furrows disclosed new seedlings peeking out here and there. Mr. Davies had won numerous prizes for his vegetables. His laburnum arch rivaled the one in Bodnant Gardens. Often a visitor would venture into the yard with camera focused. White lace curtains danced in the opened windows.

Beth opened the front door and shouted, "We're home."

"It's about time," came her mother's voice from the kitchen. "Lady Gately called twice to inquire if I knew where Kevin was. She's in a dither."

Kevin and Beth looked at each other with knowing smiles. Upon entering the kitchen they found Claire Davies sitting at the table, engaged with dinner preparations. She sat forward on an old straight back chair with her feet barely touching the floor. A tight bun held all but a few rebellious strands of gray hair and her round face glistened slightly from her efforts. Large brown eyes looked up at the new arrivals. Piles of potatoes, carrots and onions surrounded a small wooden cutting board. The workingwoman's rough hands moved with practical confidence as she deftly peeled the skin from another potato.

"Where have you two been?" she asked. "I've been almost at the end of my tether with worry."

"Kevin took me for a ride in his airplane."

Mrs. Davies suddenly stood up, the sharp tool dropping to the floor with a thud.

"You went where?" Looking up at the young man's distraught face more than a foot above her own, she glared at him. "How could you do such a thing like that? Taking my Beth up in a dangerous thing like that. Why I've got a good mind to call your father."

"I'm so sorry, Mrs. Davies," Kevin replied sheepishly, trying not to laugh. "I didn't mean any harm. It was such a perfect day for going up. No wind, no clouds. Next time I'll ask your permission, ma'am."

"Ump. What do you mean next time?"

Silence filled the room. Beth watched her mother turn and look out the kitchen window. She knew it was awkward at times for her parents, because of their employment at the Gately Estate.

Taking a deep breath, she turned back around. "Sorry, it just took me by surprise. Kevin, will you be having a cup of tea? And there's trifle in the fridge."

"No thank you, ma'am."

"I'll go up and change," broke in Beth. "I'll walk with you back home. Mum, where's Da?"

"He's up at the estate, checkin' on something. Should be home on a Sunday afternoon."

Turning to leave, Beth responded, "Maybe we'll see him when we walk over."

"If you do, tell him he's got chores to do around here, too."

Barking from outside the kitchen door signaled Manna's return. Kevin seized the opportunity.

"I'll go out and keep Manna company while you change."

"Thank you," Beth said and smiled at him.

Manna stood in the back with a stick in her mouth. The yard sloped down several hundred yards to an old rock fence. The field beyond had just been mowed and the scent of fresh cut grass wafted through the air.

Kevin threw the stick and stared off in the distance.

As was customary among many of the privileged class, Kevin had attended boarding school most of his life, except for occasional holidays at home. He never took much interest in the local villagers.

He still remembered with clarity that crisp fall day when leaves painted autumn pictures and his walk on one of the local footpaths.

Lost in thought, he came around an abrupt turn and bumped head on into Elizabeth Anne Davies. Both were shocked as they stood staring at one another. At the time, Kevin was a young lad beyond his years in social graces, never ill at ease among his peers or the nobility. But this unexpected encounter left him speechless. He gazed into the green eyes and admired the flushed face of the lovely young girl.

"Excuse me, sir."

The girl quickly vanished around the next curve of the path. Kevin wanted to go after her, ask her name, phone number. Surely he would see her again.

Returning home, Kevin changed to more suitable clothes for dinner with his parents. It seemed odd that he still recalled details of the evening. As usual the table was set with proper cloth and fine linen napkins. The delicate chandelier sparkled from the glow of the candles on the table. Fresh flowers supplied by the local florist blended perfectly with the ornate table setting.

"Order, perfect cleanliness, and good taste are as essential for the table as in dress," he remembered his mother saying many times.

Throughout dinner Kevin couldn't stop thinking of the girl on his afternoon walk. Lady Gately noticed Kevin's preoccupation with matters other than the usual boring dinner conversation. Rearranging his food on his plate, he ate little.

"Kevin, are you all right? You've barely eaten a thing."

"I'm fine, Mother."

"I hope you're not getting ill. You remember we have the trip to Paris on Wednesday before you return to school."

Looking off into the distance, he replied, "Fine, just fine."

Kevin would never forget his father coming up to his room after dinner that night.

"Anything bothering you, son?"

"No, Father. Not really."

"I think I know that look. It's a girl, isn't it?"

"How did you know?"

"I just do. What's her name?"

"I don't know."

"Don't know?"

"That's right. I literally bumped into her over in the park this afternoon. I've got to see her again. Any chance you can get me out of that trip to Paris? I hate the opera and those boring French restaurants Mother drags us to."

"Not this time, Kevin. Your mother is quite keen about this trip. Been planning it for some time. In fact we're meeting the Spencers over there."

"Oh no. She's always trying to fix me up with Penelope. I'm not surprised she didn't tell me about her plans."

Kevin spent the next few days looking for the girl, but with no luck. The Paris trip was more boring than anticipated. On his return he had little time to pack and leave for school.

Christmas holiday came. With nothing to do one day, Kevin walked to the village for lunch at the local pub. He chose the back room in the corner so he could watch people come and go. The low timbered ceiling, dark wooden floor and back fireplace gave a cozy feeling to the room in the dead of winter. Half listening to conversation at nearby tables helped to pass the time, although the subjects were limited to weather, crops and livestock. The couple in the opposite corner was obviously American. His Polo shirt and her heavy make up were definite clues. The shepherd pie and ale he ordered were welcome relief after the formal fare at Gately Estate.

Not noticing the three young people coming in, Kevin stood to leave. He leaned over to pick up his coat in a nearby chair, turned and bumped into someone. Before him stood the girl he had seen on the path.

"I've found you again."

"I didn't know I was lost," Beth replied chuckling.

"I'm sorry. My name is Kevin."

"Mine is Beth."

Kevin enjoyed re-living that day. The joy of the moment was dampened only by the reaction of his parents to his discovery. The love of his life was the daughter of the Davies', long time employees of the Gately Estate. He remembered his mother's words.

"Dear, go off and have your little flings. Get all that out of your system. That's what proper young men do all the time. Just be discreet."

At least Lord Gately was a little more encouraging later that evening. "Better not to mention Elizabeth too much to your mother. Give it some time. Things have a way of working out for the best."

A slam of the back door returned Kevin to the present. Manna was sitting at his feet looking up. He hadn't noticed the stick she had placed on his foot.

"Ready to go?" Beth's green eyes captured his attention.

He nodded.

The late afternoon sun shone softly on the young couple as they walked hand in hand toward the Gately Estate, a world away from the simple Davies dwelling. A world he hoped would someday accept Beth.

Chapter Five

"A man's steps are of the Lord; how then can a man understand his own way?"
(Proverbs 20:24)

On Thursday of the same week the Davies' phone rang just as Beth came in from Manna's afternoon romp.

"Beth, Kevin here. Sorry to ring you up so last minute. Just returned from errands in Chester to find my bags packed and waiting by the front door. Father has been called back to London and my mother insists we go with him. She says I need new tails for that party. Should be back in a few days."

"Don't worry, Kevin. Sorry you won't be going to the pub tonight. I'm taking my violin to play with the group from Wrexham. Remember me telling you about them? I heard them at Market Day in Mold a few weeks ago. John, the leader, called this morning and said their fiddle player was sick. Asked if I could sit in on some tunes. Been practicing ever since."

"Wish I could go. Much rather be there with you than having dinner in one of those stuffy London restaurants. We may have to put up with Mother for a while longer, but just wait till we're at Oxford. She won't be able to rule my life from there."

"Oh! I almost forgot. I've been so excited about to-night. I got my acceptance notice from Oxford in the post this morning. Didn't expect it so soon."

"That's super! I knew it. Your scores were so high. What a great time we'll have. Beth, afraid I must ring off. Talbot just notified me that Mother and Father are ready to go."

"Does that old stuffed shirt still call you Master Kevin?"

"Oh, yes. I think he knows how much it bothers me. I complained once to Mother, but she said it was the appropriate title until I achieved manhood, whatever that means. I'll miss you. I'll call from London when we get settled in. Good luck tonight. Love you, dear."

"Love you, Kevin."

Staring at the phone, Beth thought of Lady Gately. Her appearance was always impeccable with never a hair out of place. Her back never bent, just like her personality. But one could distinguish when she was displeased with something said or done. Her left eyebrow would arch just a bit. Beth remembered a friend's observation. "Seeing Lady Judith Gately in public is like observing the Queen Mum posing for the royal photographers."

Beth hurried back upstairs to continue practicing. Music was scattered everywhere – on the unmade bed, the dresser, and on the floor. She looked around in dismay. Remembering that she had a rehearsal on Saturday with the Chester Chamber Music Society, she put the Bach Brandenburg Concerto Number Three on her music stand. Opening the music to the marked measures, she repeated the two lines over and over, increasing the speed after each repetition.

"I've had enough of you, Mr. Bach!" she said in dis-gust, throwing the music on the floor. "I'll play something fun and easy."

Picking up an Irish reel she hadn't played in some time, Beth started off at a fast tempo until she arrived at the second part. Her bowing went every which way. It was the same bow problem as the Bach. She could play every note, every tune in the room, but only by reading the music. She sighed in disgust.

Devil's Dream and *Flowers of Edinburgh* were no problem. She placed the music to *Lord Lyndoch* on her music stand and played the dotted rhythm tune over several times. Then she turned away from the music and played a few measures. The abrupt stop of music and stomp of Beth's foot awakened Manna, who was curled up sleeping over in the corner.

"I'll never get this right!" Taking a deep breath, Beth turned slowly toward the music stand and continued her practice.

The village streets were crowded for a weekday evening. As Beth approached Sheep's Head Pub, she could hear noise from inside the tavern. As usual, Ol' Tom's laughter could be heard above all the rest. His chortle put a smile on her face. He had moved to the village from South Wales where he was a worker in the coalmines. Never said much about his past except to say, "The only time I'll ever pick up a piece of coal is to keep me buns warm." No matter how long he stayed at the pub every night, the next morning Tom would be at the bus stop at 7:00a.m. for the ride into Chester for his construction job.

"You'll never find me underground or working inside as long as I live. I'll go inside to drink, eat and sleep, and that's it. And in that order."

Opening the door to the pub, Beth was surrounded by a cloud of smoke. She blinked and stopped a moment to get accustomed to the shallow lighting. The smell of smoke, strong ale and pub food mingled together.

"Hey, Beth," Dave, the bartender shouted. "Glad you could make it. The Wrexham lads have been asking for you."

Beth passed through a door into a hallway leading to the back room, usually closed off except for special occasions. As she entered she saw several of her friends sitting at a front table.

"Don't expect too much. This is my first time to play with a band."

"Don't worry about us, Beth. We'll drink several pints to dull our hearing," retorted Robert, a good friend.

The band from Wrexham had already set up in the corner of the room. They were busy tuning instruments and warming up. John, the leader, noticed Beth. Setting his bodhran aside he greeted her with a friendly smile. He looked much different from the first time she saw him. His long wavy hair was pulled back from his boyish face. A clean white shirt was in contrast to the old plaid shirt he had worn at the faire. His jeans were new, but he still wore the soft leather lace up high boots that would fit quite well in a Shakespeare play. His clear blue eyes were dancing and full of life. A deep tan and rough skin were a testimony to a life spent outdoors.

"Great, lass. You're here. We'll go through a few tunes before the first set."

"I just know a few. Haven't had the chance to play with a real Celtic band before, but I'll give it a try."

"You name the tune and we'll follow along. Take it slow at first."

Beth opened her case, attached the shoulder rest and gave her bow a swift back and forth with the well-worn cake of rosin. She tuned and stood to the side awaiting instructions.

"Come, Beth. Stand here in the middle. You play the tune all the way through, then each of us will 'improv', then you finish."

"*Devil's Dream,* okay?"

"Jolly good."

As Beth played the lively Irish jig, she could hear the rhythmic strumming of the guitar chords behind her. The concertina played a soft counter melody as John thumped the bodhran with exact precision. Relieved when her part was done, she stood back and listened. Their musical notes danced around the main theme. One musician changed to flute and joined the guitar and drum playing the theme in double time.

"Okay, Beth. Almost time for you to come back in. Just watch me."

Beth picked up the fast tempo and her fingers flew over the fingerboard. Her bow moved like lightning. She heard the notes, but couldn't believe she was actually playing.

Keep going, she said to herself. *No time to stop.*

The music came to an end.

"Gosh!" She grinned. "That was fun. Can we do it again?"

"Beth, you did great. We don't have much time. What's another you'd like to play?" They went through the other songs Beth had memorized.

"We may just hire you as our fulltime fiddle player," John said. He grabbed Beth around the waist and gave her a hug. "And you're much better looking."

Beth felt uncomfortable at his boldness. She pulled away with a slight smile, remembering her mother's words. *Now you watch out for those roving musicians. I don't trust them for a minute. You have one of the town boys walk you home, since Kevin won't be there.*

The evening passed quickly. Several more friends came in to hear her. She often played at church and school, but this was different. The Wanderers Celtic Band had quite a following in the region and the pub was packed. Some customers stood outside open windows to listen. When Beth wasn't playing, she stood close to John, so he could give her pointers about the music. To her amazement she was able to pick up other tunes and play along. John called out chords and Beth joined in with harmonies.

Too soon it was time for the pub to close. With her talent and experience on the violin, she had already been offered an opportunity to play with a large orchestra in the area. She had always loved to play music, but this was such a different experience for her. What would it be like to lead a different life? To be one of those "free spirits" that travel about the country playing music for the love of it, not knowing where your next meal would come from. Sounded very romantic, but not too practical.

As Beth was putting away her violin, John came over and put his hand on her shoulder.

"Care if I walk you home before we start back to Wrexham? It'll take a while for the boys to load up."

She turned, seeing her father in the back of the room. Beth waved, "I'll be right there."

"Brought your chaperone, I see."

"Thanks, John. This has been such fun."

"You're good on fiddle, Beth. We all have day jobs, but hope to make it big some day. Any chance of your coming down to Wrexham to practice with us?"

"No. I'll be leaving for Llandudno for most of the summer and then to Oxford in the fall. But thanks for the invite."

Dave, the bartender walked up to John and handed him an envelope. "That was great. Any chance you can come on a weekend? This was the biggest weekday night we've ever had."

"Sure. Give me a call. We've got jobs the next two weekends, but we're free after that. John opened the envelope and handed Beth thirty pounds.

"Oh, I can't take that. Why, it would be a sin to get paid for having so much fun."

"Then I must sin a hell of a lot," chuckled John.

"Give it to the fiddle player," Beth suggested. "One of the boys said he was sick and had a new baby to boot. Besides, if he hadn't been sick, I wouldn't have had the chance to play."

"Okay. But think about what I said. You've got talent and we could make it big someday," John replied, his eyes still dancing to the music. He turned and walked away, muttering, "Perhaps another day I'll have a chance with that lass."

"Da, I'm glad you're here. Did you hear me play? It was such fun!"

"Your mother sent me down. Going to stay in the back and let you decide about getting home. For sure you've got your grandfather's fiddle blood flowing through your veins. I was afraid all those violin lessons would ruin you, but they haven't. Proud to call my daughter a fiddle player."

"Thanks, Da."

Beth grabbed her father's arm. "Now let's be on our way. You can bet Mum is waiting up for us."

The ringing of the telephone woke Beth the next morning. Sunshine filled her bedroom. Manna was not in her usual place at the foot of the bed.

"Beth, the tele is for you," Mrs. Davies shouted from the foot of the stairs. "It's Kevin. He's calling from London."

"I'll be right down, Mum."

Beth pushed her hair out of her eyes and walked slowly down the stairs to the phone.

"Hello?"

"Beth, is that you? You don't sound yourself. Are you all right?"

"Just woke up. Haven't even had a proper cup of tea. The connection isn't too good. I'm having trouble hearing you."

"That's because I'm in a phone booth. How did it go last night?"

"Had a great time. Played much better than I thought I could." She yawned. "You'll be glad to hear that Mum sent Da to the pub to walk me home."

Kevin laughed in her ear. "Be sure and tell your mother I appreciate her concern."

"Not on your life. Say, when are you coming home?"

"That's the reason I'm calling. Father has business in Zurich. Mother arranged for us to go with him. I told her I didn't want to go, but she said she just couldn't manage without me." Kevin mimicked his mother's voice with a whining tone. 'They are always speaking some other language like French, German or Italian. Don't know why they don't use the King's English. Kevin, you can converse with those foreigners. Your father will be so busy. I'll be a prisoner in my hotel room. I just can't go without you. You just must go. Just this time, dear."

Beth couldn't help giggling.

"Beth, I was hoping I would be back home in a few days, but it doesn't look that way. When do you leave for Llandudno?"

"I wasn't going till next Wednesday, but since you won't be back, I'll leave on Monday and spend a night or two at Holywell, if there's room at the Pilgrims' Rest. I haven't visited with the nuns in some time."

"I'm sure my accommodations will be far superior to yours, my dear Beth."

"Now don't be so haughty. At least my traveling companion only requires dog food once a day."

"You've got me there, Sweetheart. I'll call after we get to Zurich. I've got your grandmother's number. I won't bother to call at Holywell. Wouldn't want to interrupt the prayers. Beth, I'm really sorry about all this. Can't wait till the summer is over and we're off to Oxford."

"Yes, Kevin. I'll be counting the days. Now behave yourself."

"You think I have a choice? Not with this chaperone of mine."

"Take care of yourself."

"I love you, Beth."

"I love you, Kevin."

Beth heard the click and listened to the dial tone. Putting the receiver down she stared at the phone, whispering, "I wonder if Lady Gately will ever stop her meddling. Maybe Kevin and I will run away and elope. That would show her."

Chapter Six

"The Holy Spirit will teach you in that
very hour what you ought to say."
(Luke 12:12)

After breakfast of kippers, toast and coffee Beth called St. Winefride's to inquire about a room.

"Of course I remember you, Beth. We'd love to have you come for a visit."

"Thank you, Sister Clare. I'll have my dog with me."

Splendid. I have just the room for the two of you. Opens up to our back area with grass and fenced yard. We have two dogs of our very own. The nun chuckled, "We have to hide them every time Mother Superior comes for a visit."

After the Saturday morning rehearsal in Chester, Beth and Manna were on their way. When they arrived, the parking in front of St. Winefride's was filled with two coaches. A large group filed out from afternoon tea. Beth got settled in her sparse room with single bed, desk and chair.

Her close school friend, Edwina, first introduced her to St. Winefride's Holy Well when she joined her family on a seaside picnic near Holywell and a visit with the nuns. The religious community provided food and rooms for visitors to the site, sometimes called the Lourdes of Wales, because of the miraculous well.

As soon as the day visitors had left, Beth walked to the shrine. Standing at the iron gate viewing the large pool, she recalled the pictures on her grandmother's wall. One 1880's photograph illustrated wooden cubicles where pilgrims would change. Another displayed a sign of separate bathing times for men and women.

Beth smiled. "Times have changed. That's for sure."

Walking into the covered outside chapel she was startled by the life size statue of St. Winefride. Votive candles flickered on the saint's eyes giving the sculpture a living persona. A large polygonal basin, with steps leading down on opposite sides, provided a way for pilgrims to go into the moving spring to have their prayers granted.

Beth knelt, scooping up the cool water in her hand watching it return from whence it came. While making the sign of the cross she whispered, "In the name of the Father, and of the Son and the Holy Spirit. Amen."

After supper Beth helped the nuns clear the tables and wash dishes. Although this religious order did not practice complete silence, there was no idle conversation, a refreshing experience for Beth. The importance of hospitality in Welsh society fit these women who had chosen to be nuns.

That evening Beth heard a gentle knock on her door. She opened it. There stood Sister Clare, her round colorless face void of expression.

"Beth, would you please come with me to the chapel?"

Beth followed the stocky nun past the deserted dining area and into the dimly lit room. Sitting in silence, Beth wondered why she was there. Finally Sister Clare spoke.

"I want you to pray for me."

"But, Sister, you know I'm protestant, Church of England."

"Yes."

"But I've never prayed out loud. I mean without the prayer book. I could say the Lord's Prayer, but I'm not too sure about the Hail Mary."

Sister Clare responded with a hearty laugh. "Oh, my dear. God doesn't need fancy words. He needs words from your heart. Holy Spirit will give you the words. But first let me tell you about my need." The nun sighed and continued. "I've been here for a number of years, away from the motherhouse. I was assigned for only two years, but when Mother Superior became ill and had to return home, I was assigned her position. I slump into deep depression for days on end. I thirst for the silence and strict discipline of the convent. I'm afraid my depression might affect the others. I can't discuss any of this with them. It's just not appropriate."

"Have you talked to your priest?"

"Yes, on several occasions. In confession, in private appointments. He says God has put me here for a reason. I must bear my cross with great thankfulness. Then he assigns me the same dreary psalm and an extra rosary."

Reaching for a Bible on a nearby chair, Beth opened it at random, hoping for guidance or inspiration. She called it "Bible roulette." Often a passage would be exactly what she needed at the time. But not this time. "Thus far is the judgment on Moab."

Closing the book, she shut her eyes and prayed for help. She couldn't believe what happened next. She started praying. Beth was aware of her voice saying words, but she couldn't decipher the words. Her mouth was moving, but her thought process was in a way non-existent. The only word she understood was "amen."

"Beth, thank you. Your prayer spoke to my heart."

The cool air from an open window caused Beth to shiver. Putting her hands in her pockets she felt an envelope Edwina had given her the day before she left. She opened it. A drawing of a 16th century nun dressed in earthen tones adorned the front of a holy card. On the back of the card was a Prayer of St. Teresa of Avila. Softly Beth spoke the words:

"Christ has no body now on earth but yours, no hands but yours, no feet but yours. Yours are the eyes through which must look out Christ's compassion on the world.

Yours are the feet with which He is to go about doing good. Yours are the hands with which He is to bless men now."

She handed the card to Sister Clare and returned to her room for the night.

The morning breeze played with the muslin curtains as visitors enjoyed their breakfast in the dining room. Beth sat in a corner, entertained by the throng of pilgrims and tourists. Sister Clare had a peaceful smile on her face as she went about her duties. As Beth finished her coffee, the nun came over to the table.

"Thank you, Beth. God bless you in your ministry."

The nun walked away before Beth could respond. My ministry? She thought, I have no ministry.

After helping Sister Mary Ruth with breakfast dishes, Beth made a cheese sandwich, grabbed her backpack from her car and headed for a nearby park with Manna. Walking a short distance, she settled down under a large tree off the path. Manna ran off to inspect her new surroundings, occasionally returning to her mistress. Beth often felt the need to be away from humans and be nourished by nature. The stillness relaxed her so much that she fell asleep. A vivid dream materialized.

Beth was a little girl of about seven years, several hundred years earlier. Wearing a ragged dress and no shoes, she stood in the back of an impressive, ornate church with high vaulted windows. Men and women dressed in fine, rich clothing entered the structure to attend a service. She was invisible to them. Attired in elaborate dress and adorned with jewels, an older woman walked in, carrying a petite white dog in her arms. The animal stared at Beth and barked. Jumping out of the owner's arms, she ran to Beth, wagging her tail. The dog's mistress snatched it up, gave her a spank, and then handed the dog to a servant girl.

The smell of incense permeated the air. Complete silence engulfed the scene. Walking behind a golden crucifix a large choir processed toward the altar. Following them came priests, their robes of rich embroidered silk dazzling in the bright morning sun. The clergy faces were strange, painted like one of her grandmother's old dolls. There was no expression, a blank stare, as though not alive. Beth jerked as the shock went through her dreaming body.

As often happens in dreams, she was suddenly transported to another place. Her dress matched the flowers of a Monet painting. Her bare feet relished the warmth of the earth in contrast to the cold stone floor of the church she had just visited. Standing on the brow of a hill, she observed a stunning view of springtime countryside. Sweet fragrances filled the air. From a grove of massive oak trees in the valley below, Beth could hear voices singing the exquisite music.

Her body drifted over the ground leading downward to the woods. Beth walked toward the music. The ruins of a small church stood in a sizeable clearing. A diversity of humanity greeted her eyes. All races and colors of skin from different centuries. Peasants, the wealthy, beggars, merchants, soldiers, nuns, monks, the sick and lame, lepers and the disfigured of the world. Scattered about were an assortment of animals, tame and wild, at peace in this surprising environment. The scene was enhanced by thousands of Adonis Blue butterflies filling the air. A stone altar stood toward the back of the partial structure. To the side a gentle-faced man in a ragged brown tunic was speaking. Not being able to hear his words, Beth tried to move closer, but her feet wouldn't move. All of a sudden she felt something pushing her, nudging her.

Manna's barking woke her from her dream. The white furry head was cocked as if to say, "Are you all right?"

"How could you wake me up in the middle of such a dream? Oh go off and chase one of those dumb squirrels," scolded Beth.

For some time Beth sat, thinking about the dream. Reaching for her backpack, she pulled out a notebook that a friend had given her some time ago. She stared at the first page of blankness. Her vicar had suggested that she start writing in a spiritual journal, but she had resisted the idea. Perhaps now was the time to start. Surprised by remembering every detail, she wrote quickly, wishing she could paint the realistic scenes of her dream.

Later that afternoon, Beth decided to visit the well one more time before leaving for her grandmother's in Llandudno. The well was already closed to visitors for the day, but Sister Clare gave her permission to go in. As she came around the stone enclosure of the outdoor pool area, she was startled to see a woman on the far side. Dressed as though from another time, a beige scarf covered most of her hair. A long skirt of dusky hues flowed about as she danced and twirled around the pool. Lifting her outstretched palms heavenward, she sang an ancient tune. The language sounded familiar, resembling the ancient Gaelic that Beth had heard at the Eisteddfod. Standing still, Beth watched with bewilderment. Suddenly the woman stopped, realizing a stranger had entered. She put her head down, as if embarrassed, and ran over to join a conservatively dressed older couple standing just inside the well enclosure.

"Sorry. I didn't mean to interrupt. Go on. You dance and sing beautifully."

The woman smiled, walking over to Beth.

"Won't you join us, dear? We've come to pray to St. Winefride."

Beth responded, "Where are you from?"

Her soft voice almost sang as she spoke. "I live up in the hills alone. I'm a hermit. I come to pray when others are not here."

Looking intently into Beth's eyes, she continued, "You have the gift of healing. Please, come pray with us."

The woman turned, walking toward the couple. Beth hesitated for a moment and then followed.

"My husband has a heart condition. The doctors say he has only two months to live."

The man knelt at the statue of St. Winefride. The three women put their hands on his back. Just like the night before, Beth started praying out loud, but couldn't understand the words. She felt warmth radiating through her body into her hands. This time she wasn't uneasy. On the contrary, it was quite peaceful. The four reflected in silence for some time, with the sound of the soothing spring water lapping against the ancient stones of the well.

Beth left in silence, wondering about the result of her prayers for the man.

Chapter Seven

"For we are his workmanship, created in
Christ Jesus for good works."
(Ephesians 2:10)

Driving on to Prestatyn, Beth stopped by the beach for Manna to stretch her legs. She watched her frolic in the waves as she filled her lungs with rejuvenating air. Gazing out to the water as the sun commenced its descent, Beth reminisced about her childhood adventures in Llandudno.

She pictured the ornate Victorian pier with its rides and games of chance and could almost taste her first bite of candyfloss. Often in the mornings her parents sat on their deck chairs overlooking the bay while she played in the water and made sand castles. The hikes and picnics up the Great Orme were her preferred excursion, as were, of course, Easter services at St. Tudno's on top of the mountain.

But her choice haunt was the Alice in Wonderland Centre. Her favorite author, Lewis Carroll, brought characters to life in his vivid portrayals. Smiling, Beth remembered the first time she ventured through the "Rabbit Hole," a scary place for a child.

Several Llandudno establishments claimed Mr. Carroll as their distinguished guest. The parents of Alice Liddell, the inspiration for his books, owned a holiday home on the West Shore.

Manna almost knocked Beth over as she came running up, covered with salt water and sand. After washing the dog at a nearby faucet, Beth attached a leash and the two walked along the seashore until they were both dry.

As the car continued along the road, Beth kept glancing to the North. Finally it came into view. The Great Orme, the massive stone mountain almost surrounded by the Irish Sea. In less than fifteen minutes, she drove down the familiar streets that had changed little since her childhood.

Beth spent most of her summer days in the seacoast town. This summer she would work at her grandmother's Bed and Breakfast. The peninsula town followed the wide and gently curved bay. A phalanx of Victorian hotels lined the broad promenade. Regulated construction during the 19th century resulted in a garden town on the sea, a model resort for the upper middle class. Now most of the homes were converted to B and B's.

Beth's early spiritual life was nurtured by a man who seldom attended church – her grandfather. Times together were etched in her memory. He possessed a natural depth of theology and Welsh wisdom. His untimely death brought her much sorrow. Over the years her grief gradually healed, especially when she walked on their mountain, The Great Orme.

The profusion of many cultures of the area fascinated Beth. The Druids, Celts, Romans and Saxons all left their marks. An Iron Age fort, a Bronze Age cairn, the Roman well, the cromlech and St. Tudno's church echoed on the earth. Beth never tired of exploring the massive Welsh mountain.

Instead of going directly to her grandmother's, Beth parked next to the waterfront. Leaving Manna in the car, she got out and stretched, breathing in familiar salty air. The sun now hid behind the cliffs. Sea gulls soared, calling to one another while riding the wind currents. Remembering the song, *Wind Beneath My Wings*, Beth sang a few lines softly. Thinking of Kevin, she wondered if the clergy would allow them to have that song at their wedding. It could be called popular religious. *But it is biblical.* Beth smiled at the thought. Lady Judith would have a fit.

Getting back in the car she drove the two blocks to her grandmother's. The three-story house stood just off the coast street on the corner where the road divided. The end rooms facing the two streets provided views of both the ocean and the rugged steep side of the Great Orme. The house was alive with the presence of her great-grandparents and others who had passed over the threshold. Parking on the side street in front of the private entrance, she heard the familiar squeak of the old wooden gate. There stood her feisty grandmother with her hands on her hips. Beth and Manna got out of the car.

"Now just where have you been, child? I've been at the end of my tether with worry. A girl shouldn't be out late at night."

Beth held back a smile as she grabbed her violin case. "Sorry, Grandmum. Should have called. Stayed a little too long at St. Winefride's."

"I see you brought your white monster with you. She's twice the size the last I laid eyes on her."

"She's had two good runs today. Be ready for bed early."

"Speaking of bed, you'll need to stay in the attic. Your room downstairs is full of boxes. Got all those things from your Uncle Bedwyn in America. He said open the ones marked family and store the rest. Can't make myself open a single one."

Beth went over and gave her grandmother a long hug. "I'll be glad to help you with that anytime, Grandmum."

Mrs. Hughes looked away to hide her misting eyes. "I miss that rascal of a son."

The familiar smell of lamb stew greeted Beth as she opened the back door. "Smells like you cooked my favorite. Jolly good to be back in my other home."

"Suppose that animal of yours can have some, too. I made plenty."

After supper the two women settled in the parlor for a cup of tea, a ritual in the Hughes home. Beth stared at a familiar picture hanging over the fireplace, an old portrait of a young girl with a porcelain face. No one knew the origin of the picture. Piercing blue green eyes seemed to be alive. Dark brown ringlets cascaded from a lace bonnet.

The summer of Beth's twelfth year when she visited her grandparents, she recalled her grandmother's words, "You look enough like that girl to be her twin sister. No doubt that she's an ancestor of ours." Beth promised some day she would find out about this girl who she sensed resembled her more than the oil and canvas.

"Before your Uncle Bedwyn left for America, he was working on our family history. Said he might have a lead on her. She's staring down at us right now. Not sure how I feel about her. Some days I like her, some days I don't."

"So you see it, too, Grandmum. I thought I was the only one."

"Even visitors see it. What ever it is. One man last summer offered several hundred pounds for her. I could have used the money, but she's like family. Could be the answer down in one of those boxes. A strange thing it is," she said shaking her head. "Yesterday a note from Bedwyn saying not to worry. I wouldn't be hearing from him for a while."

"Oh Grandmum! Let's have a look."

"Someday, child. Someday." Mrs. Hughes tightened her lips. "But it's bed time for these old bones."

That night Beth concluded her prayers with a special thank you for her Llandudno family – the only one remaining and all who had gone before.

Awakening early the next morning Beth tried to remember the muddle of dreams. The fragments made no sense. Places she had never been. People she had never seen, except for one, the girl in the portrait. She stood in a fog on the brow of a hill looking at distant mountains. Turning towards Beth, she spoke, "Live your life. You have freedom. I didn't. Listen to your soul."

As she wrote the words in her journal, she recalled the advice of the vicar at St. John's in Chester. "Be open to possibilities in your life."

The next several days were filled with preparations for the expected guests. One evening after supper Mrs. Hughes suggested, "Beth, why don't you and Manna take tomorrow morning off?"

"Thanks, Grandmum. Love to. A hike up the Orme."

A clear bright day greeted the girl and dog as they walked up the road to the trail sign. Turning the corner just down from the King's Head Pub, Beth was surprised to see the tramway station already open. Two men were loading the car with supplies to take up to the Summit Complex.

"How about a free ride for you and your dog, Luv?" called out one of the workers. "For sure there's no passengers this early. Better to ride up and walk down."

"Well, as a matter of fact, I'd love to. Can I help you with any of the loading?"

"No, thanks. 'Bout all done here."

Settling in the front seat for the best view, Beth and Manna prepared to enjoy the ride. The sudden jolt of the moving car jump-started her memory as well.

A little girl again, sitting in her grandfather's lap in this same seat, she remembered the fear and excitement. Insisting her grandfather keep his arms securely around her, the train lumbered up the steep side of the Great Orme. Beth became more frightened as the houses diminish in size. Reaching the halfway station, she pleaded with her grandfather to get off the train. Laughing and winking at the conductor, Beth's massive, gentle grandfather carried her off to the comfort of the earth.

Walking a short distance down the mountain past a few homes, they saw the large stones. Some were upright, supporting a large flat capstone. Beth smiled as she heard her childish voice, "Is that someone's playhouse?"

"No, my dear. It's called a cromlech. They say that over 4,000 years ago that's how the folk buried their dead."

"Are there any bones in there? Can we go in?"

"No bones, but we can go as far as the fence."

The two generations stood hand-in-hand in silence staring at the structure for some time. Beth spoke first.

"I think the tombstones at church are much prettier, especially the ones with angels."

She remembered the delightful smile on his face.

"Why are you smiling, Grandfather?"

"Suppose I'm thinking of years from now. You'll be a lovely young lady, walking on this very earth and hiking our mountain."

"And you'll be here with me, won't you, Grandfather?"

"Yes, Elizabeth. I'll be here. You may not see me, but I'll be here, walking and smiling beside you."

Rowan Hughes knelt on the ground, surrounding the little girl with his muscular arms.

As tears emerged from Beth's eyes, she reached for a tissue. Manna got up and put her head in Beth's lap. Stroking the dog's head while looking off to nowhere, Beth responded, "It's all right. These are thankful and sad tears mixed together."

"Half way!" shouted the conductor. "Off here or to the top?"

"Off here, if you don't mind. Want to go over to the cromlech."

"Ah, Lass! Visiting your relatives, are ye?"

"Yes. Suppose I am, in a way," she said, getting off the rail car. "Thanks for the ride."

The tram lurched forward as the brakeman reengaged the cog. "You two can ride my train anytime," shouted the workman. "But you may need to pay, if my boss is on board."

As the tram disappeared in the distance, Beth wondered how many thousands of visitors had ridden to the top, then back down.

"This mountain is so alive!" she said to Manna. "A pity most have missed really seeing it. Come, girl, it's off to visit our ancestors."

Angling across a grassy field toward a grove of ash trees, Beth happened across a recognizable landmark. A small bubbling stream coursed down the hillside. Sunlight, peeking through the leaves, danced on the water's surface like so many diamonds. Making her way to the trees, Beth plopped down under a familiar one.

As she closed her eyes, Beth returned to her childhood again. It had been a warm day. Taking off her socks and shoes she remembered wading in the water. Grandfather rested under this same tree with his eyes closed. She busied herself by picking up nearby blades of grass and watching them amble down the mountain in the water. Finally tiring of the play, Beth joined her grandfather under the tree.

"Are you asleep, Grandfather?"

"No."

Why are your eyes closed?"

"I'm talking to Him that made me. I can listen better with my eyes closed."

"You mean you're talking to God?"

"Yes. And listening. Too often we do all the talking. How can you listen at the same time you're talking, or praying, or whatever you call it. Like that stream over there. The water goes down to the sea. Then up to the clouds. Back to the earth. Continuous. That's how we need to be with God. Always flowing, always going somewhere, but we don't need to know exactly where."

"Can I get back in the water? I want it to be like it was before."

"Can't be."

"Why not?"

"There's an old saying. 'You can't step into the same river twice."

"Yes, I can. Just watch me."

Beth remembered standing in the middle of the stream with her arms defiantly crossed, a smug look on her face. Her grandfather's jovial laugh caused her to giggle.

"See. I've done it!"

"Not quite, Elizabeth. You see, we are constantly changing. You're not the same girl you were a few minutes ago. And is that the same water?"

That day they hiked up to St. Tudno's church and witnessed a wedding in progress. How she wished her grandfather, the wisest man in all the world, were still alive. Shortly before he died, he gave her a small book of Welsh sayings. The ones she remembered the most-"Patience is the mother of all wisdom," and "Determination is a good horse." How proud he would be of her now. The first Davies to go to university, and Oxford at that.

Thinking again of her grandfather's words, she heard, "You've a good mind, Elizabeth. Use it for good. The only thing for sure in this life is death. Death of this life, but birth into another. People all over the world have these different names for God. But if I had to come up with one word, it would be home. Cause it's where we came from and where we're going."

After vowing to write down everything she could remember about her grandfather, Beth took off her shoes and socks, wading in the stream once more.

Chapter Eight

"Ask for the ancient paths, where the good way is;
and walk in it, and find rest for your souls."
(Jeremiah 6:16)

The summer passed quickly for Beth and her grandmother, with the B and B filled to capacity almost every night. Kevin spent most of his time traveling about the continent with his parents.

Beth came into contact with visitors from foreign countries, as well as the U.K., which broadened her view of the world. She often took guests on walks about the city and hikes up The Orme.

The Americans amused her the most. She recalled the first visitors she met from Texas when she registered them into the B and B. Mr. Perkins wore blue jeans, plaid shirt and cowboy boots. A polyester pantsuit and white tennis shoes was the choice of Mrs. Perkins.

"Ya'll got a room?"

"Would you like to book a room for the night, sir?"

"We don't need no books, we want a place to lay our heads. Been up all night long from New York City. Got the train straight to here. And I ain't drivin' on your crazy roads in those little cars."

"We have a room available on the third floor, but we don't have a lift."

"A lift? Don't you use the stairs? I see 'em right thar."

She would never forget another conversation that evening. Mr. Perkins came downstairs that night carrying a pencil with no eraser.

"Ms. Perkins can't do her crosswords without an eraser."

"Yes, sir. I'll get you a rubber."

Beth didn't understand why his face got so red. He returned to his room without even a thank you. Later, when telling a girlfriend about the incident, she discovered the difference in meaning for the Americans.

On one of the last days of August, Beth packed her belongings and drove away from her tearful grandmother. Before leaving Llandudno, she parked at the promenade above the seashore. She and Manna got out of the car and walked a short way. She stopped, stared at the water gripping the sand and sighed. "Manna, I feel as unsettled as the water below. It's as though I'm leaving my childhood behind." She looked up at her mountain, knowing that the ancient paths would be there when she returned.

Beth had only a fortnight back home in Hawthorne before her departure to Oxford. Her father secured her old bicycle on top of the car with an assortment of ropes.

"Elizabeth, could be a sticky wicket if there's heavy rain. Back windows can't go up all the way. For sure, it won't come off."

"Looks to me like our daughter is a traveling gypsy with all her worldly possessions," chimed in Mum. "Why don't you go up to the estate and bid Lady Judith Gately a fond farewell?"

"Now, Mum, behave yourself."

The last item she packed was her violin. As Beth and her parents said their last goodbyes, Manna jumped into her usual place in the front seat. Beth broke into tears.

"I swear, daughter, you love that dog more than you love your own parents," her mum declared.

"Come, Manna."

The dog obeyed. Kneeling, Beth hugged her friend. Mr. Davies put his hand on his daughter's shoulder, "Now I promise I'll take good care of her. She'll go up to the estate every morning with me and have the run of the place."

"I'll see that she gets fed proper," Mum added. "You know I do care for that mess of trouble, whatever I say."

"I know. But I'll miss her."

Beth's mother's eyes started filling with tears. "Now get on with you girl. You've got some learning to do."

Beth and her father laughed as they walked to the car. She knew he'd keep a firm grip on Manna until her small car was out of sight.

As Beth approached the city of Oxford in the late afternoon, golden hues gave an ethereal glow to the medieval city. The sun shone on the numerous spires reaching heavenward. Beth had visited Oxford several times, but this day the city looked different. She would be living in the oldest university in all of England among the saints of the church. The Oxford martyrs, C.S. Lewis, a favorite author, and countless others. This "steeped in tradition" place would be her home for the next few years. A history remote from the Great Orme of Llandudno, but much more concrete.

Beth turned off the main road into Oxford, glad to have arrived early before Michaelmas term begins. Nought Week should be interesting. She remembered what the vicar's nephew cautioned: "Sign up for anything that interests you, but don't pay any money till you've had a few visits. I joined so much the first term that I had little time for study."

As soon as she parked in a temporary spot in front of Keble College, one of the porters greeted her, and gave directions to her room.

Noticing the bicycle on top, he mentioned, "Looks to me like you brought along a perfect Oxford bicycle."

"Are you jesting at my means of transportation?"

"No. Not at all. Most of you 'freshers' bring their brand new bikes, and wonder why they get stolen the first week. Got your chain and padlock too. Now about your car."

"That's no problem. I've got a place to park it up at Littlemore."

Some students came by and helped Beth unload her belongings. Completing the arrival procedures, she retreated to her room after declining to go to a pub with her new acquaintances. Beth finished the lunch her mother had packed, and then ventured out for a walk at University Parks. As the sun set, the lights of Keble College Chapel beckoned her back to her residence. Tomorrow would be a new day and a new life.

The next morning her pigeonhole contained a note from her supervisor, arranging a meeting for the afternoon. The MCR calendar was filled with all sorts of events, both social and functional. A short note from Kevin, posted from London, reminded Beth he would be arriving late the next day. Some information encouraged "freshers" to associate with the other new students to get settled in, but Beth had always been more of a loner. She'd wait for Kevin's arrival before planning her social calendar.

Hurrying out a side door, she headed down St. Giles in search of breakfast. The Lamb and Flag Pub didn't open till 11:00. Beth pressed her nose against the front window looking in, imagining C.S. Lewis and JRR Tolkien enjoying one of their frequent visits. At the same time she wondered what St. John thought about his symbol adorning a pub.

The aroma of fresh baked bread lured Beth down a side street where she discovered a baker just opening his door. The warm pastry melted in her mouth as she walked along the cobblestone streets of the college town. Coming into the center of town she turned toward her planned destination, Magdalen College.

Entering the chapel for prayer, she stayed only a short time in the abysmal surroundings. Out again in the sunshine Beth continued toward the River Cherwell and Magdalen's deer park. A heavily wooded path known as

Addison's Walk made her feel at home for the first time since she left Hawthorne.

I have a feeling this is where I'll spend a good deal of my time. Only wish Manna where here with me.

After walking for some time, Beth glanced at her watch. Surprised by the time she hurried back into town for some necessary errands, the main one being the purchase of her Oxford University gown and mortarboard. No one would be admitted to the evening dinner unless wearing the required attire. She was both nervous and looking forward to the occasion of dinner in the Great Hall of Keble College, watching the college fellows and tutors process in to sit at the elevated *High Table,* the grace prayed in Latin.

The afternoon meeting with her tutor, Alastair Fulham, was more enjoyable than expected. Musty books lined three sides of the room. His desk appeared in disarray with papers, files, unopened letters, and two cups of cold tea. A soiled napkin held breadcrumbs. A pot of English ivy sat on the sill of a small opened window, begging for a drink.

Beth had trouble taking her eyes off the display of pictures on a shelf behind his desk. One in particular caught her eye, an old photo of a young man with sensitive face looking off to the side. She couldn't take her eyes off him.

"Miss Davies, you have an interest in one of the pictures?"

He stood and pointed. "That is Gerald Manley Hopkins, my favorite poet. Died at forty-five and never saw a single poem published. But his spirit lives in his words."

Alastair Fulham bowed his head for a moment and sat down.

At first Beth was put off by his formal appearance, dressed in tie and academic gown accompanied by a stuffy intellectual accent. He reminded her of a picture she once saw of a youthful C.S. Lewis. After visiting with Beth about her background and interests, Mr. Fulham opened a file. He glanced at her records, and then looked up.

"Did your vicar tell you we were classmates at Cambridge?"

"No, sir."

"I received a note from Gareth last week about you."

Beth smiled, shaking her head.

"These extra courses should stand you in good stead here at Oxford, Miss Davies." With a slight smile, he continued. "You have an interest in the church?"

"I'm not sure how to answer, sir."

"Are you considering ordination to the priesthood?"

Beth looked down at the floor without speaking. She could feel her heart beating faster. It seemed an eternity before Mr. Fulham spoke.

"Miss Davies, let me assure you I have no opinion one way or the other. I'm here to guide you. Appears to me the church gets so involved in practicalities, rules and regulations, they have precious little time for religion."

He handed Beth a folder with course selections. "Introduction to Philosophy and Biblical Hebrew with your basic courses might be advisable."

Beth thought for a moment of her Jewish friend back in Hawthorne and the celebrations in her home. The smattering of Yiddish she learned would be of no help here.

"Look over these possibilities. Keep informed of orientation programs and lectures available. I believe there is one that includes the demands of discernment and the church of today."

He stood, extending his hand. "A pleasure to meet you. I pray our time together will be most beneficial. We will meet again on Thursday afternoon, and outline your Michaelmas term."

Thanking him, Beth hurried off to finish errands before Kevin's arrival later that evening. Christ Church would be his residential hall while at Oxford, the 500-year-old college steeped in the traditions of law and politics.

After the formal dinner that night, Beth checked her pigeonhole and found a note.

"Arrived later than expected. Must attend a function this evening. Meet at Blackwell's for coffee at 9:00. Kevin"

She walked out into the hallway glancing at a signboard. A notice for a Café Scientifique meeting caught her eye. "Blackwell's Book Store – This Evening – Dr. Diana Pearson – Subject: Ecology and Our Environment"

"Going to the lecture?" a voice asked.

Beth turned to see the girl who had sat across from her at dinner. She was several years older than Beth, plain looking, slender with thick glasses and brown hair pulled back in a bun.

"I'm Jane Hensley."

"Elizabeth Davies. Nice to meet you."

"I've heard her several times. Want to go with me?"

"Not sure," Beth replied. "I saw her on the tele this summer. It was a panel discussion with men and women from different religions. I remember one quote she said.

"What was it?"

"God is a circle whose center is everywhere and circumference nowhere."

"That certainly gives you something to think about." Jane looked at her watch. "Just enough time to put my things away."

"Jane, I think I would like to go with you. I'm to meet a friend there at 9:00."

"Good. See you back here in five minutes."

All ages, students and visitors crowded the bookstore café. Beth and Jane found a table for two in the back corner. Just as the discussion came to a conclusion Beth saw Kevin standing by the entrance. She waved, "Over here. I've a table."

Kevin strolled over. "What's going on here? I've never seen it this crowded."

"A great lecture about ecology. I was able to ask about the Irish Sea pollution. Good discussions. Sorry you missed it."

"Well, I'm not," he smirked. "The Whigs should leave well enough alone. This Tory could have asked a few questions, but they wouldn't have appreciated it."

"Now, Kevin," Beth patted his back, "we must take care of our world. It's our future and those who come after us." Beth turned to introduce her new friend, but she had disappeared. "You must have scared off Jane."

"Jane?"

"A friend from my college. Met her after dinner. We came here together. Blackwell's has these lectures every first Tuesday."

"Remind me not to come here on Tuesdays."

"Don't be so narrow minded."

Kevin pursed his lips. "Beth, it's best you choose your friends with care. I don't want to see you out in the streets of London parading for animal rights or some such nonsense." He kissed her on the cheek. "Now let's sit and chat. I'll be right back with some tea.

Kevin returned shortly with cups and two ample servings of fudge cake. "Sorry I'm so late tonight, but it was good to visit with some fellows I've known for some time."

"Who?"

"Classmates from school and sons of my father's friends. You'll meet them in good time."

Kevin's eyes glistened with excitement as he talked about his social and political plans at Oxford. Beth listened, interjecting interested comments now and then, but concentrated more on how many times he flipped his hair out of his eyes. It must have been at least ten during the course of the evening.

"Closing time in ten minutes," a loud speaker announced.

As they walked to Keble College, they got out their calendars for the coming week. Kevin shook his head. "A shame our colleges are so far apart. Opposite ends of the city."

After kissing Kevin goodbye, Beth walked into her new residence and then remembered something she forgot to mention to him. Smiling she went to a phone, called his college and left a message. "You need a haircut."

During the next several weeks, Beth and Kevin saw little of each other. Most of their opportunities were spent in the library or an occasional stroll along the picturesque rivers of Oxford.

One morning after class Beth sat in a crowded tearoom, enjoying her coffee. Two women about her age asked if they might share her table. The three students enjoyed conversing about a wide range of subjects, including theology. They invited Beth to a meeting the next evening focusing on the ordination of women. Beth was curious, but made an excuse of a prior commitment. As the girls were leaving, one of them wrote down the location and time, handing the paper to Beth.

The next day Beth thought about the chance meeting with the two women. That evening after supper, she decided to go for a short walk before studying. Because of a soft rain, Beth put her jacket hood over her head and hands in her pockets. She felt the piece of paper from the day before. Staring at it she nodded her head, turned and started walking in the opposite direction.

From the door of the crowded room, Beth could see her new friends on the front row. She chose an inconspicuous chair in the back. The first speaker began with the words of George Herbert. "I will complain, yet praise; I will bewail, approve; And all my sour-sweet days, I will lament, and love."

What she heard that night spoke to Beth in a refreshing way. The path to ordination for women in the Church of England had been a difficult process. Discrimination in assignments and duties for ordained women was common. Beth continued attending various meetings, but avoided social contacts. She kept telling herself she had no serious interest in becoming a member of the clergy of The Church of England.

Several weeks later, she received a phone call from her vicar, Gareth Sloan.

"Just on my way to London. Any chance we could meet for tea?'

"Yes. How about Convocation Coffee House on High Street at 1:30?"

"Perfect," he said. "See you then."

Seeing her priest brought back memories of Hawthorne and Chester. Beth had been so busy since arriving in Oxford, she hadn't thought much about home. She flooded her vicar with questions about everyone and everything back in Chester and Hawthorne.

"Now, Beth, tell me about you. How do you like Oxford?"

"I like it much more that expected. I had reservations about the teaching methods, but Mr. Fulham is perfect for me. Helpful and affirming. Oh yes, and thanks for warning him about me."

"I hope you didn't mind."

"No, but it was a surprise," said Beth. "Fortunate to be assigned to him instead of one of those anti-women tutors. And while we're on the subject, how is the Bishop of Chester?"

"Why, the other day the bishop and I talked concerning the need for more vibrant young leadership in the church. I told him of a young person attending Oxford who had outstanding possibilities." Rubbing his chin as if in deep thought, the vicar continued, "But for the life of me I can't remember if I mentioned that young person was a woman."

The twinkling eyes and sly grin told Beth the truth.

"Now, Beth, tell me. How is your spiritual life here at Oxford?"

"It seems a little underground at times."

"Underground? That's a peculiar term. Tell me more."

"All the theological and philosophical studies occupy my thoughts most of the time. Once in a while there's a spiritual glimmer, but not like it used to be. I go for walks quite often. I do more praying outside than in church, that's for sure."

"Um. Sounds like things are progressing nicely."

"What do you mean by that?'

"What you're experiencing is quite normal. Remember to keep balance in your life. Rather like describing your spiritual life. You know how a river might be flowing along and then disappear?"

"Yes. I've read about that, but never seen it."

"That's how our spiritual life might occur. At times it's hidden, like going underground. It's still there. Perhaps purified before exposure back out in the world, but it's there. Just remember to tap into it when you need it. Go to your spiritual well, as it were."

"I like that concept. I might use it in one of my papers. Although it might not be stuffy and intellectual enough," Beth responded with a smile.

"One more thing before I leave." The vicar held up an index finger. "I've seen too many young folk receive a substantial religious education, go out into the world, be assigned a parish, and forget the real reason why they decided to become a priest in the first place. Getting all wrapped up in the trappings, the prestige, the ladder climbing, and I don't mean Jacob's ladder."

Beth nodded. Later she watched Gareth Sloan's car disappear into the traffic of High Street on his way to London. Walking in the same direction, she decided to spend the remainder of the afternoon in the Botanic Gardens instead of the library.

Chapter Nine

"Oh send out thy light and thy truth; let them lead me, let them bring me to thy holy hill and to thy dwelling."

(Psalm 43:3)

Beth remembered her second year at Oxford as the one when she met her best friend. Fall leaves fluttered down, coming to rest on the River Thames. On her early morning jaunt, Beth walked along the river path outside of Oxford. As she crossed over at Ifley Lock on her way back to Keble College, Beth noticed a woman about her age walking at the same pace a few yards ahead. The morning sun bounced off her red hair. She wore scruffy boots, an ankle length tan skirt and faded flowered blouse with the shirttail hanging out. Dressed for comfort and not for style, Beth thought.

She spent the remainder of the morning in the library preparing for an afternoon lecture. The research and reading for Systematic Theology contrasted a great deal with the dreary class experience.

The professor, a stuffy, Church of England clergy, Reverend Doctor Horton, took particular delight in his status and left little doubt in the minds of his audience regarding the 'proper' role of women in the church.

"After all," he once said, "if God had wanted a woman to have priestly authority, He would have made her a man. Seems simple enough."

He reminded Beth of her own bishop. She thought how well the two of them would get along. Two peas in a pod.

"Are there any questions or comments?" inquired Dr. Horton, surveying the class with narrowing eyes, almost daring anyone to speak.

"Yes," came a woman's voice from the back of the room.

He glared at the student over the top of his glasses. "Yes, Ms. Seymour?"

"I can understand and appreciate the historical significance of your lecture. The quotation from St. Augustine, "Our past goes before us," is quite applicable, especially in our present situation. Would you agree that at times there might be confusion with God and the church versus the institution of the church?"

He clenched his teeth, staring at the outspoken student. Taking a deep breath, he responded in a condescending tone, "Brigid Seymour, I believe. You consider yourself an authority on this matter?" Clearing his throat, he continued, "I do believe you possess more Irish than English flowing through your veins. Perhaps restraint rather than boldness would serve you well."

"Sir?"

"Ah! Ms. Davies, I believe."

"Only this morning I was reading of the division that occurred in the seventeenth century between academic theology and practical training. It seems in some ways we have not recovered."

Several students in front of Beth turned, looking at her in disbelief.

"What do you mean, recovered?"

"Theology can't be studied in a vacuum. Every statement has moral, spiritual, and sociological nuances. Jesus often taught in paradox. He used empirical situations to teach spiritual concepts."

The professor took out his pocket watch, studying the time. "My heavens, class dismissed."

The class dispersed quickly. Beth felt relieved to be out in the crisp fall Oxford air.

"Ms. Davies?"

Beth turned and saw a pretty face framed with the crimson hair she had followed into town that morning.

"I'm Brigid Seymour. Thank you for speaking in class. I don't know what came over me."

"Or me," replied Beth with a smile. "Have time for coffee?"

"Love to."

The White Horse on Broad Street offered the perfect place. A few patrons sat at the bar with their pints. The girls settled at a table in the back of the pub with their coffee, falling into effortless conversation. Beth shared her story of Hawthorne and Kevin.

"So, Brigid, our professor was correct in assuming your lineage?"

"By all means. My father met my mother when on vacation at Kilarney. He fell in love with her and Ireland. My parents sent me to Oxford to receive a proper English education."

"And then you'll return to Ireland?"

"Eventually I plan to return and teach. But I would love to work in London for at least a year or two, perhaps in the publishing business. I'm a writer of sorts."

"Have you started investigating job possibilities?"

"I went into the city once to answer an advert. But that didn't turn out too well." Brigid stared at her cup.

"What happened?"

"The interviewer seemed ill at ease during the entire process. I answered all the questions, my resume fit the position, and the timing was perfect. She walked me to the door, shook my hand and thanked me for my interest. I remember her exact words.

'Nothing against you, my dear. It's difficult for me. My husband was killed by the IRA last year."

"Oh, Brigid. What a tragedy."

"I never heard anything from the company. Too bad my parents didn't name me Mary or Elizabeth. I'd fit in much better over here."

"But to be named for St. Brigid. What an honor and what a woman."

"You know of St. Brigid?"

"Oh, yes. A woman of the fifth century traveling about the countryside in her chariot, preaching the gospel and caring for those she met along the way." Beth laughed, "And her driver was a priest! Perhaps Dr. Horton would have interest in such a position."

"You know, Beth, St. Patrick baptized St. Brigid. Her father objected to a religious life for his daughter. He took her to the King of Leinster, planning to sell her into slavery. As Brigid waited outside the castle, a leper came to beg for alms. She gave him her father's sword. The king was so impressed by her generosity, he declared Brigid would serve God."

"Interesting story," said Beth.

"In fact, King Leinster gave her land at Kildare where she built a monastery beneath an ancient holy tree.

"You Irish have a wealth of Celtic stories and legends. Much more than the Brits."

"Our island kept us isolated from European influence until the Reformation. So much destroyed. A devastating time for Ireland."

"And for England as well. We tend to avoid the dreadful in church history."

"Not much has changed over the centuries in some ways. Now we delight in tearing down people rather than buildings."

Beth enjoyed visiting with her new friend, taking little notice of others arriving for drinks and dinner. A young waitress came in for her evening shift. The sudden change of music in the background stopped their conversation.

"*Looking for Love in all the Wrong Places*," blared over the speaker. They smiled at one another.

After paying the bill Brigid and Beth went out on the busy street. Dinnertime filled the best of the local pubs to capacity.

"Where do you live, Brigid? I forgot to mention that I followed you into the town this morning along the river."

A slight smile emerged on Brigid's face. "I'm actually staying with the Roman Catholic nuns at the Cardinal Neuman residence. I help with duties in exchange for a room and food. I'll take you there one day."

"I'd love to. I've been curious about it. And you will come home to Hawthorne with me and we can visit the nuns at St. Winefride's Well."

"Are you Roman Catholic, too?"

"No, but I always say there are multiplicities of pathways leading to the same place. We get so focused on our way of doing things. I often remind myself of the rogues Jesus chose. Their resumes certainly would have been in question, especially in the Church of England."

"And Roman Catholic, as well."

The girls walked along the bank of the River Thames. Beth realized she cared more for conversation than supper.

"Have another story about St. Brigid?"

"Do you know the one about the bishop's blessing?"

"No," Beth shook her head.

"After establishing her place at Kildare, other women joined her. Brigid asked a traveling bishop to pray for God's blessing on them as they took their vows as nuns. When the bishop lifted his hand in blessing, he saw tongues of fire descending on Brigid's head. The Holy Spirit caused him to speak over her the words of consecration of a bishop."

"I'm sure we won't hear about that in Systematic Theology," Beth mused.

Brigid giggled, "Whatever the truth of this story, Brigid traveled widely, holding some form of authority within the Church. She preached to rich and poor alike, and was even allowed to speak at Church synods."

"Well! What an uppity woman! So, Brigid. How do you feel about women priests?"

With a frown and shaking her head, Brigid replied, "I just can't see it. It's not the way I was brought up."

The girls walked along in silence. Finally Beth spoke.

"What would you say if I told you I was considering the possibility of ordination?"

Brigid sat down on a nearby bench in silence staring at the water. Beth sat beside her wishing she hadn't spoken. Would this end their new friendship? Finally Brigid spoke.

"You don't seem like the type. The few I've met have been outspoken and pushy. You're so refreshing and open. You've got a Celtic way about you."

Looking intently into Beth's eyes, Brigid took her hand. "I've known you only for a few hours, but I feel we are kindred spirits. If your decision comes truly from God, then do it. And may all the saints be with you."

"Thank you, my new friend," said Beth.

The two walked on in silence until they reached their parting at Ifley Lock. Beth walked back into Oxford along the quiet river just as the sun was setting. Somehow the city appeared much more welcoming than the first evening she spent in the university city a little over a year ago.

The next few days were quite busy for Beth. Dinner with Kevin and his friends one night, and course work in the library. Beth saw little of Brigid except in passing. She wondered if the talk of ordination had resulted in the loss of their friendship. On Friday of that week, Brigid waited for Beth after class.

"Have any plans for Sunday?"

"No," answered Beth. "Kevin is going with friends to an out of town soccer game."

"I know a grand place we can go walking up in the hills. There are some ancient ruins I discovered a few weeks ago."

The girls left early Sunday morning accompanied by ideal weather. Its invigorating fall freshness encouraged the companions to walk quite a distance.

Settling down for lunch on a grassy knoll, first Beth brought out her cheese sandwich, two apples, and a jug of water.

Brigid unpacked a faded flower tablecloth, laying it carefully on a level area. Next came two plates, utensils, cloth napkins, and small glasses. Beth watched as she brought forth small finger sandwiches, assorted crackers, cheese cubes, and crisps.

"And now the best part," Brigid smiled, producing a bottle of red wine."

"Well," Beth said, impressed. "You certainly know how to pack a picnic lunch."

"Life is meant to be lived. If we don't celebrate every chance we have, we miss so much. We spend too much time in the past and in the future. Look about us. How can we not celebrate the beauty of God's creation and gifts? I struggle to stay attuned to the Celtic ways here in England. Everything is so regimented and precise."

"You're right. You're absolutely right and the wine is a grand idea."

"Well, why not? The first miracle Jesus performed was at the wedding feast in Canaan. The Celts celebrate not only life and death, but also every moment in-between--being aware of God in every breath, the present moment."

Brigid poured the wine. Lifting their glasses to toast, Brigid exclaimed, "To my *Anam Cara*."

"My what?"

"*Anam Cara*. Means soul friend. *Anam* is the Gaelic word for soul and *cara* means friend. The early Celtic church used the words to describe a distinctive spiritual friendship. It goes far beyond what you might call a social acquaintance. The superficial and practical side we see in most people fall away and you can be who you really are."

"Is it something like the relationship one has with a spiritual director?"

"Yes, in some ways. In the early church it was often someone you confessed to, revealing your true self. But today I understand *anam cara* as more of an equal friendship that frees the soul."

"That's lovely," said Beth. "Freeing the soul. Yes, we are given freedom and creativity to experience life, but so often we tie ourselves up by listening to the expectations of our society."

"What are you smiling about?" Brigid's voice sounded amused.

"Oh, it's so ridiculous. I was thinking of an American novel when two boys decide to be blood brothers. You know, like the Indians. They cut their fingers and mingled their blood."

"Not a chance!" laughed Brigid.

While they packed their belongings for departure, the wind increased in velocity. Innocent white clouds that had dotted the horizon all day darkened and massed together.

"Looks like we're in for a storm, Brigid. Better start back down. Don't think we can make it to the car. When we were coming up, I spotted a hut on the other side of those trees," Beth said, pointing to the east. "Not much out of the way. Let's give it a try."

A few drops hit their faces as they started down the hill. The rain increased. Beth ran ahead. Reaching a tree line, Brigid called out, "Beth, let's wait here under these trees."

"No. Come on. It's not much farther," Beth shouted over the thunder. "We don't know how long this storm will last."

Ahead in a clearing was the small cottage with smoke coming out of the chimney. She stood beside Brigid, shivering. "Let's go," Beth said with confidence.

They ran quickly across the open space to the dwelling. The weather-beaten door swung open from the force of their knock. They stepped inside out of the weather, shaking the rain off their water soaked jackets.

"Thought you might come this way," said a deep voice from across the room. "Saw you two going up. Knew you would get caught in the storm. The fire's ready for you to dry off."

On the far side of the room knelt a man tending the fire, his back to the girls. Beth surveyed the rest of the room. A sheep dog lay by the fire, eyeing the girls with keen interest. She looked at Brigid, who shrugged and tried to smile.

Beth spoke first. "Thank you, sir. That's very kind of you. We'll be on our way shortly."

The stranger stood, his head almost reaching the ceiling. He turned slowly to greet his visitors. An abundant beard that reached just below his collar surrounded a pleasant smile. He extended his hand as he introduced himself.

"I'm Brendan."

"I'm Beth, and this is Brigid. We're just up from Oxford on a hike."

Beth studied the stranger, trying not to be too obvious. His scraggly clothes and old worn boots gave him the appearance of a drifter.

"I have only one chair to offer," he said, nodding to an old chair by a table in a corner.

"We'll sit by the fire, if you don't mind," Beth said formally.

"Please, call me Brendan. Here," he motioned, "get close to the fire." He walked over to the chair and sat down. The multicolored dog got up, and then settled back down at his master's feet. Beth and Brigid sat on the floor in front of the hearth, took off their wet shoes and socks, warming their feet by the fire.

"That's a lovely animal you have, Brendan," said Brigid.

"Yes. Shane's this man's best friend, that's for sure."

"Do I hear a little of an Irish brogue?" asked Brigid.

"For sure, lass. I'll wager we come from the same emerald isle."

The two smiled at one another, as Beth looked on suspiciously.

"Any idea how long this storm will last?" Beth inquired.

"I think it'll be over before night. I'll walk you two back down."

"That won't be necessary. We can find our way," Beth said.

"It's a little tricky getting down from this place. If you take the wrong path you end up at a hundred foot drop. If you could sprout wings, you'd have no trouble."

Brigid laughed at the idea, but Beth was not in the least amused.

Brendan and Brigid started talking about Ireland. Beth ignored their conversation as she surveyed the room.

Half-used candles rested on a roughly made shelf. A black kettle hung over the open fire. Some paper and a few books lay on a corner of the table against the far wall. *At least he can read and write, but I still don't trust him.*

Two small windows with hanging shreds of rotten material were on either side of the door. A small open cupboard held a few cans of beans, canned meat, a jar of marmalade, a tin of crackers and a tin of biscuits. Stacked on top were some plates, glasses and mugs. A crude iron bed with a sleeping bag on top stood in the other corner. Hanging on a nail by the door was a rain jacket with black Wellington boots underneath, ready for this kind of day.

"Think the water is ready. How would you girls like a cup of tea to warm you?"

"That sounds delightful, doesn't it, Beth?"

"Fine." She wished they had gone back the way they had come, completely soaked, instead of being here with this stranger.

"All I've got is Earl Gray. And believe it or not, I've got three mugs and a few biscuits. A proper English tea for two lovely ladies."

Brendan carefully put down a cloth on the floor in front of the fire. Bringing the teapot with tealeaves inside, he slowly poured the steaming water into the pot. Then he arranged some biscuits on one of the plates, setting it in the center. Next came three mugs and a small chipped bowl with sugar. Beth watched every move without a word, somewhat amused. The hot tea warmed Beth, changing her mood considerably. Perhaps this man wasn't so bad, after all. But she was curious about him, so she decided to find out more.

"So, Brendan. Do you live here?"

"Oh, no," he laughed. "Come up quite a bit. Mostly on weekends. A friend owns the property and seldom uses it. A quiet place. You girls are my first visitors."

"But you seem to have extra provisions, like these three mugs."

"Most of the contents were left by an old sheep farmer who lived here many years ago. He's the one who sold it to my friend's father."

"And what do you do during the week?"

"I work part time at Oxford."

"You mean the university?"

"Yes."

The three sipped on their tea while munching the biscuits. Beth thought smugly to herself. Brendan must work as a janitor or some similar job.

"Are you girls students at the University?"

"Yes, we are." Brigid perked up. "I'm more in general studies and Beth can speak for herself."

"I would say Beth would do quite well in criminology. She's quite observant and good at asking questions," he said smiling. "So, do you think you've figured me out?"

"Not completely, but I think I'm on the right track. Can I ask some more questions?"

"Only if I get an equal number. And that means I've got four before you ask me any more."

"This should be interesting," responded Brigid. "I'll probably find out more about both of you."

"So, Brigid, you haven't known Beth very long?"

"No. We met in one of our classes, mainly because we both spoke out in Systematic Theology. Became close friends in one afternoon. Kindred spirits, you might say."

"Interesting," he replied, rubbing his beard with narrowing eyes. "Very interesting. A negative into a positive."

The girls looked at each other and giggled.

"Hey. You're supposed to ask me the questions. I won't babble on like some people I know," Beth said, smiling at Brigid. "And that counts as your first question."

"Okay. Who is the most important person in your life?"

Beth thought for a moment. Then with a pleased smile on her face, she answered, "The Trinity. God, the Father, God the Son, and God the Holy Spirit."

"All right. If you could be any place in the world at this very moment, where would you want to be?"

"Good question, Brendan," Brigid encouraged.

"Hey. Whose side are you on? I thought we were an *Anam Cara* to one another."

"*Anam Cara* is it? That opens up other possibilities. All right, Beth. Anyplace in the world."

"Heaven."

"Heaven? I said any place in the world."

"Yes. But you didn't limit it to physical or spiritual."

"Good one, Beth," Brigid smiled.

Brendan stared at the fire for some time. While warming the three mugs with more tea, he asked the third question.

"Beth, you appear to have an interest in what we call Celtic Spirituality. How would you explain the Celtic mind in ancient times and how it applies to the world in which we live today?"

That one took Beth by surprise! "That's an entire paper, or even a book. But I'll give it a try." Beth paused to collect her thoughts. "The Celtic mind embraced all that is. The human world, nature and divinity. The Celtic cross signified this concept by the never-ending circle. They followed the words of St. Paul, 'pray without ceasing.' Prayers for every occasion of simple living. Upon waking, making the bed, tending the fire, growing crops, fishing. Countless prayers from the heart. Love of nature and the beauty of creation. Their life was a life filled with creativity, no matter how grand or simple the occasion. And hospitality was natural for them. Welcoming strangers and living life to its fullest. Celebrating birth and death and all that's in-between."

"And now?"

"Now our world has become addicted to the external. Sad to say that not only our society, but the church as well is guilty. Many are aware of this emptiness in their lives, but are searching for answers elsewhere. To befriend our souls is to have a relationship with God. We tie ourselves down with human expectations. The young live in a death-denying culture. Celtic spirituality frees us to love and live with what is seen and unseen."

"Bravo! Bravo!" exclaimed Brendan, clapping his hands.

"Question four?" responded Beth, quite pleased with herself.

Brendan got up slowly, opening the door. The rain had stopped. A faint glow of sunlight and blue sky promised a clear night.

"Better pack up. We've enough time to get down before nightfall."

Not a word was spoken on the way down as the girls followed Brendan.

One afternoon a few weeks later, Beth was in her room at the college immersed in the most recent Bala Foresight book instead of her studies.

"Beth, phone call," shouted a voice from the hall.

"Coming," Beth said. She walked out of her room, still holding the novel and picked up the receiver.

"Beth, Brigid here. There's a lecture tonight. Visiting professor. Specialty is the Book of Kells. Remember us talking about it just last week? Can you go?"

"Love to. Usual time?"

"Yes. Same hall as the lecture last week. Meet you just outside at half past. I hear he'll fill up the place."

Beth and Brigid sat on the front row busily talking to one another. Beth took no notice of the arrival of the guest lecturer approaching the stage.

“Good evening,” came a strong resonant voice from the speaker’s stand.

Conversations filling the hall ceased as everyone gave their attention to the front of the room. The girls stared in disbelief. Looking at Brigid and Beth, with a smile, Brendan added, “And a special welcome to two of my closest friends here at Oxford.”

Chapter Ten

"In my Father's house are many rooms."
(John 14:2)

Times with Kevin at Oxford blended together like a partly cloudy sunrise with merging colors and changing light, appearing unreal at times, as though an artist attempted to reenact life on a gigantic canvas. Visits to lavish country estates as guests, the simplicity of studying together, noisy meals at local pubs, walks in the countryside and excursions to nearby villages. Beth enjoyed flying with Kevin's friend, Winston, who had a plane at a nearby airport. However, the trips to London were the clearest of all other memories, in particular, the unexpected trip.

"Beth, Kevin here. Did I wake you?"

"Yes. Up late last night reading. Why on earth are you calling this early on an off day?"

"Pack an overnight bag and put in your nicest dress."

"Where are we going?" Beth asked.

"No questions. I'll be by in thirty minutes."

As soon as the car turned onto the M40, Beth knew the destination.

"London. That's it. No wonder you said bring a fancy dress. Where in London?"

"You'll have to wait for one surprise."

Busy London roads were crowded with Saturday morning shoppers and tourists. An overabundance of black cabs dotted the streets. Stopping at a red light, Beth watched with amusement at the punk clothes and wild hairdos emerging from an underground station.

"Are we going to one of those funky rock clubs with your friends again, Kevin? That's what I call a jolly good time. We're staying with them, aren't we?"

"No. This trip to London will be like no other."

Staring at Kevin, Beth tried to read him. He looked straight ahead with an assured smile on his face.

"Are we going to one of the parks first?"

Kevin made no reply. Driving along Bayswater Road on the north side of Hyde Park gave her a clue. A right turn on Park Lane, then left on Piccadilly. She could stand it no longer.

"I knew it. We'll have a whole day at the parks of London. How delightful!"

"Well, not exactly all day. Would you settle for half a day?"

Resting her hand on Kevin's shoulder she gazed at him, thinking how much she enjoyed his companionship. Kevin turned to the left and came to an abrupt stop. Looking out the window she couldn't believe it. The Ritz Hotel.

"What on earth are we doing here? Meeting some friends?"

"No. Staying here. Separate rooms, of course," he said in a teasing way.

As Beth started to open the car door, it flung open. A doorman, wearing a scarlet uniform trimmed with black velvet, extended his hand.

"Welcome to The Ritz. I trust your stay with us will be most enjoyable."

"Why thank you. I hope your day will be a smashing one too."

"Thank you, ma'am." He returned to his regal pose, his head held a little higher and an ever so slight smile on his face.

Kevin stood nearby waiting to take her hand. Noticing a young man had their bags in tow, she held Kevin's hand tightly without saying a word. Elizabeth Davies walked through the doors of The Ritz Hotel of London and into another world.

Trips to London for the Davies family on holiday had been a rarity over the years. The family accommodations were the least expensive and the balance of their meals was food brought from home. She remembered walking by The Ritz one day, trying to see into the lobby. To a young girl from a modest family, the clientele would fit into a movie titled, "The Wealthy and Fabulous." She often daydreamed about leading such a life.

The ornate décor took her breath away. She surveyed the shiny spotless marble floor, antique furniture, original oil paintings and lush arrangements of flowers and plants. She squeezed Kevin's hand extra hard.

"You all right, luv?"

"Yes. This is a bit overwhelming, she whispered. "This place must cost a bundle."

"Not to worry. The folks are paying for it. But I guess I better tell you the whole story. They're staying here, too."

Beth let go of Kevin's hand.

"It'll be all right. Mother rang up late last night. Said they would be here for the week and invited us to come down for the weekend."

"Us?"

"Yes, us. Mother checked ahead and reserved two extra rooms, in case I would agree."

"That's quite nice of them," Beth said, attempting to sound sincere and trying to convince herself.

"We're to meet them for lunch, so we've got the rest of the morning to ourselves."

When they arrived at the reception area, a well-dressed, spectacled gentleman greeted them with a friendly smile from behind a massive dark wooden desk.

"Kevin Gately. I believe you are expecting us," Kevin said with an air of authority.

"Yes, we have been expecting you, Mr. Gately. No need to sign. Lady Gately has taken care of the arrangements. Our porters will show you to your rooms. I believe they are on separate floors," he whispered, peering over his glasses while observing the dress of the young couple.

Beth had to look down at the floor to keep from laughing. She'd wager his mother had her in the basement and Kevin on the top floor.

The receptionist snapped his fingers. Two porters picked up their bags and followed Beth and Kevin to the lift.

"Madam, I believe you will be on the fourth floor. The gentleman will be on the seventh," one of the porters said. Even the interior of the lift created an ambience of wealth with red velvet walls and gold trim.

"Beth, you get settled. I'll be down in about ten minutes. We'll have the rest of the morning at the parks."

Without a word Beth followed her porter off the lift. She hesitated, looking back and smiled at Kevin as the door closed.

Beth's attendant swung open the door to her room, stepped back while giving an ever so slight nod and motioned with his hand. Crossing the threshold, Beth entered a small hallway between three rooms: a sitting room, a bedroom and a bathroom. The rococo style of Louis XVI with lashings of genuine marble and 24 carat gold leaf dazzled her eye. The subtle coughing of the man holding Beth's bag caught her attention.

"Oh! So sorry. A bit overwhelmed by all this."

"Yes, Madam. Where would you like your bag? And would you like for me to call a girl to assist with the unpacking?" he asked in a condescending manner.

"Thank you, but that won't be necessary," Beth responded while walking over to the tall window at the end of the long rectangular sitting room. Overlooking Green Park and west London, the window offered a spectacular view. She stood surveying the scene until she heard the sound of the door closing behind her.

After examining the three sets of lavish curtains encasing the window, she turned around and looked wide-eyed about the room almost shouting, "Gosh! I'm staying at The Ritz!"

The tall mirror at the opposite end of the room reflected her simple clothes. "I must be the worst dressed guest you've ever seen."

On one side of the sitting room was a marble fireplace complete with an original copper coalscuttle. Finding a remote on a small table, Beth looked around for the TV, but found none. Pushing the power button she heard a man's voice coming from behind the French paneling. Pulling on a discreet small knob, the paneling opened to reveal a TV hidden in the wall.

Sitting down carefully on one of the elaborate chairs, she surveyed her new surroundings. The furniture was quite similar to a grand estate of The National Trust, but without the familiar sign, "Please do not sit here." By the window a lovely writing desk held an abundance of the hotel stationary.

"Must write Mum and Da from here. That will give them a good shock."

The carpet carried The Ritz color scheme of blue, peach, pink and yellow in subtle tones matching the luxurious rich fabrics and textures of the room. A curved doorway led to a walk-in wardrobe about the size of Beth's room in Hawthorne. The safe ready to receive valuable possessions brought a slight smile. Reaching her hand inside and resting it on the velvet interior she asked, "And just how many millions of pounds have you taken care of?"

The gilded paneling continued into the bedroom with yet another marbled fireplace and more sumptuous furniture. The large bed was adorned with a variety of pillows. Beth pulled back the spread to expose the starched Irish linen. A bottle of Ritz champagne was placed on a side table along with a supply of the latest upscale London property guides and other magazines to suit the taste of the typical guest. As

Beth peeked into the bathroom, she heard a knock at the door.

"Beth? It's Kevin. Ready to go?"

They walked into Green Park. Beth felt invigorated by the air and nature's colors. Noticing the numerous dogs enjoying the idyllic day with their owners, she said, "Manna should have come with us."

"Fine for here, but not quite appropriate for The Ritz."

"Now, Kevin, don't be so stuffy. I'm sure there're some dog lovers staying there."

"Probably are, but perhaps with a pedigree to match their masters."

"It's quite fascinating to observe another side of life. All the staff seems quite nice, except for that snooty man who showed me to my room. And that room! Never seen anything like it."

"Well, just enjoy and get use to it. That's the way we'll be living after we're married."

Joining hands, the young couple walked across the grass, stopping under a tree to kiss.

"Just think, Beth. Charles II walked under this same tree. I wonder if he met a merry maid here to steal a kiss."

"I haven't read that in the history books, but I do know about the numerous duels that took place here. The earth is mingled with their blood," she said in a mysterious tone.

"Ah, my lass, you have such a romantic way about you. Seriously, though, I am glad we have this time together. Haven't seen enough of you lately. Our schedules seldom match up. When I've had any free time, it seems you're off to a rehearsal or church. I've really missed seeing you."

"I've missed you, too, Kevin." Beth tilted her head. "I wonder if we'll tire of one another in our old age."

"You may tire of me, but I'll never tire of you." Walking across Green Park toward Buckingham Palace,

Kevin continued, "I suppose our expectations are partly what we've been exposed to."

"What do you mean?"

"What we see in others. I mean other couples. What we like and don't like about them. For instance, take your own parents. They seem so content, comfortable with one another. Rather like a matched set – salt and pepper."

"Boring, if you ask me." Beth reflected for a moment. "But there is a love between them that goes without words."

"On the other hand" said Kevin, "my parents seem to lead separate lives, except for social occasions. I see no love between them, although I suppose at one time.... Well, here we are. Shall it be Buckingham Palace or St. James Park?"

"Need you ask?"

Beth and Kevin hurried across the busy street to another oasis of green in the city of London. They walked around the lake watching the birds, especially the awkward pelicans.

After returning to the hotel, they sat over to the side of the lobby waiting for the Gately's arrival. The variety of men and women passing by fascinated Beth. Exquisite clothes and jewels caught her eye. Looking down at her dress, she said, "Kevin, I'm afraid this is the best dress I had in Oxford. Doesn't quite fit around here."

"It's fine, dear. We don't have anything fancy planned." Putting his arm around her, he gave her a reassuring hug. "Why I would love you even if you had nothing on."

Blushing, she looked up and saw Lord and Lady Gately exiting the lift. Crossing the lobby, they stopped to have a brief conversation with a couple checking in. The elderly man walked with the aid of a cane. His wife, considerably younger, carried a collection of shopping bags from trendy boutiques in Paris.

"Well, hello you two. So glad you could join us," said Lady Gately, as she gave Kevin a hug. Nodding to the couple at the registration desk, "We met the Count and his wife in Monte Carlo last year. Obviously she's what those Americans call an airhead, but they seem quite content with their situation, so who am I to judge? Well, let's have some lunch here so we can discuss the rest of the day."

Beth's heart sank, thinking of what lay in store.

"That would be lovely," she responded.

The maitre'd greeted Kevin's parents by name, sitting them in a prime location overlooking a lavish garden area. After ordering, Lord Gately spoke to Kevin about a business meeting he had planned for the afternoon.

"I hope you don't mind coming along, Kevin. It's time you got a little more involved in some of the family business, and this would be an excellent opportunity. Besides I think Judith has an afternoon planned with just the girls in mind," Simon Gately added, smiling at Beth.

"Oh, yes, Elizabeth. I have a dress waiting for me at Harrods. And afternoon tea there is simply a must. Not to worry. We have reservations. And I have a little surprise for you, too, my dear."

Kevin took Beth's hand under the table, giving it a comforting touch. Looking at him, she reassured him with a slight smile, as if to say, "I'll behave myself and survive this ordeal."

Too soon lunch ended. Standing by Judith Gately in front of the hotel, Beth watched as Kevin drove off in a taxi with his father. Immediately a limousine drove up in front of the hotel. A sharply dressed chauffer exited.

"So good to see you again, Lady Gately."

Following Lady Gately into the limousine, Beth settled comfortably into soft leather seats, viewing the outside world from a different perspective.

"Kevin has told me a great deal about your plans."

"My plans?"

"I mean the plans you and Kevin are making for the future. It appears that you two are set on getting married after your university years. So, dear, I've decided to help you."

Staring straight ahead, Beth sat in silence, not knowing what to say, wishing Kevin were there. She wondered if he knew about this planned shopping trip.

"So, Beth, we'll stop by Harrods first and then on to some other stores if there's time. Also I have a close friend who recommended a special lady who will assist you with the social graces. I can't remember her exact title, but it's rather like having your own private finishing school. It's the proper training for all the young ladies. But that we'll do another day."

"That's very kind of you. But really, it's not necessary."

Now, Beth. You know I've never had a daughter, so please indulge me a little. I would so enjoy getting you a little something."

Beth couldn't think of anything to say, so she sat quietly, looking out the window. Soon they were driving along Brompton in the Knightsbridge area of Central London. Stopping the limousine in front of Harrods, the chauffer waited until the uniformed doormen had escorted Lady Gately, followed by Beth, out of the limo. Beth had walked through Harrods many times just to look. But this was the first time to arrive in such a grand manner.

"We will stop by the food section first. I have a few gifts to purchase." Judith Gately pulled a list from her purse and handed it to an attentive sales lady who followed her obediently while she gave instructions. "This box of chocolates to each of the first three on the list, this champagne to the Bishop of Chester along with an assortment of cheeses and biscuits, and this food hamper to the Count and his wife. They are staying at The Ritz, of course."

The sales lady responded after each order, "Very good, madam."

Beth glanced at the price of the hamper. 150 pounds! The food halls reverberated with shoppers milling around glass cases and shelves stocked with everything from gooseberry and lime glaze with elderflowers to Scottish smoked salmon.

Next the women walked through the adjacent toiletry area filled with heavenly scents of potpourri and soaps spilling from copper buckets. Music from a flutist in the corner filtered above the voices.

"Selections from this area, Elizabeth? Be glad to purchase anything that strikes your fancy."

"No, thank you, Lady Gately. So kind of you to ask."

Judith Gately responded with a false smile and slight nod. "Then let us proceed to the designer shops." An older saleslady was obviously expecting them.

"Lady Gately. How good to see you again. Your dress is ready for you in your usual fitting room. I've taken the liberty of displaying a few more possibilities for your approval. So this must be your young lady. I've got everything ready, except the shoes. What size do you wear, my dear?"

"Usually an 8 narrow."

Beth followed her back to a quite large dressing room with a dress rack full of clothes. On a smaller rack was a selection of several black dresses. Handbags, scarves, gloves and jewelry were meticulously arranged on a table in the corner.

"Lady Gately insisted that we start with a basic black dress. You look through and decide on the ones you want to try first. I'll be back in a few minutes. This Christian Dior might be a good one to start with. Want to be sure Lady Gately has everything she needs."

Beth stood motionless, except for her eyes that kept looking about the room. Staring at the dresses, she walked over and started sorting through them. Reluctantly, she tried on the one the clerk had suggested. Perfect. The smooth expensive material felt scrumptious against her skin. Walking over to the multiple mirrors, she inspected her image.

Excellent fit," announced the saleslady walking in the dressing room carrying four shoeboxes. Here, try these. All the latest. Just in from Italy. These Ferragamo shoes would look perfect with that dress…these pearls and this small black Channel bag. Excellent. Now we're ready to show Lady Gately."

Beth had never felt more out of control. What could she do? Kevin could straighten everything out later.

"Don't you want to try on more of the dresses? A young lady can't have too many black dresses."

"I really do like this one. How much?"

"That's not your concern, dear," the woman said in a rather condescending tone.

Because of her height, Beth had seldom worn shoes with very high heels. She practiced walking around the dressing room. "All right, I suppose I'm ready."

The saleslady walked before her. Lady Gately sat over in the corner, enjoying a cup of tea.

"My goodness, Elizabeth. That looks marvelous. Oh, Ms. Tittle, you have such exquisite taste. Do you like it, Elizabeth?"

"Yes, Lady Gately. It's quite lovely."

"And the accessories are ideal. Now go and select some more. Ms. Tittle, we'll need an outfit for church in the morning and afternoon tea."

"Yes, Lady Gately. I have several possibilities. And I selected some casual ensembles, as you instructed."

Beth followed Ms. Tittle back to the dressing room. After selecting a Donna Karan taupe suit and a soft flowing navy dress, Ms. Tittle left in search of additional shoes. Being curious about the prices, Beth sorted through the clothes looking for price tags, but there were none. I guess if you have to ask the price, she mused, then you can't afford it. When we get back to the hotel, I'll have Kevin send everything back. Going over to the black dress she whispered, "But I really wouldn't mind keeping you."

Beth put on a gray matronly suit and stood in front of the mirror. Ms. Tittle returned with a young woman walking behind her balancing twelve boxes of shoes.

"That will be all," she said with an air of authority. "Now let's see how this suit fits." Ms. Tittle adjusted the jacket shoulders, then stood back and inspected the hem. "Perfect, but it's not quite you, is it, dear."

Beth pulled her hair back tightly and turned around. "Makes me look like the Duchess of Windsor, if you ask me."

Ms. Tittle tried to keep back her smile. "Yes, it certainly does. Let's try one of these tailored dresses. Do you know which service you'll be attending in the morning?"

"Not a clue."

The ordeal went on for some time. Finally Lady Gately and Ms. Tittle were satisfied. The last outfit consisted of dress slacks, a tailored blouse, Armani leather flats and a Louis Vuitton bag.

"Now, Beth. Leave that on. Change your purse contents into your new bag. Ms. Tittle will have everything delivered to our hotel before we return."

"Aren't we going back now? Kevin and his father may be at the hotel."

"Lord Gately has a busy afternoon planned for Kevin, too. We'll be back in plenty of time to change before cocktails and dinner. We have a special evening planned for the two of you."

Glancing at her watch, Lady Gately exclaimed proudly, "Perfect. Just in time for tea."

Beth followed lady Gately into the grand Art Nouveau Georgian Restaurant at Harrods where afternoon tea was considered a special occasion. The original Art Deco Skylight and intricate plasterwork spoke of the 1911 opening of this elegant dining salon.

To Beth's surprise she felt at ease as she entered the restaurant beside her future mother-in-law. Holding her head up a bit and wearing her new expensive ensemble gave her an air of assurance in this foreign environment. The maitre'd led them to their reserved table.

"I prefer the Harrods Afternoon tea. It's milder than the others. And the egg and cucumber mini sandwiches are the best," Lady Gately suggested. "I'll be glad to order for you, Elizabeth."

Beth was determined to make at least one decision for the afternoon. As soon as the lady arrived to take their order, she spoke first. "I would like the scones with clotted cream and preserves."

"The tea, Madam?"

"The Assam."

"My goodness, Elizabeth! I hope all those sweets won't spoil your dinner. Are you aware that the Assam tea has liquor?"

"Why yes. I remember the exact description. Brightly colored liquor with a distinctly malty, creamy taste from North East India. Sounds delicious!"

During tea, Judith Gately babbled on about some of their friends in London, describing several of the parties they had attended. Beth listened with her face, but not with her ears. Every morsel of food melted in her mouth. She imagined having afternoon tea like this the rest of her life. Then she would eventually grow to a tremendous size and Kevin would lock her in the Tower of London until she lost fifty pounds.

After tea, they headed back to the limousine.

"On to the Salon, driver," commanded Lady Gately.

"The Salon?" questioned Beth.

"Yes, dear. You will love Maurice."

Beth sat in a stylish salon with her hair freshly washed, staring in the mirror. Lady Gately sat nearby having her nails manicured.

"A pity. A real pity." Maurice flitted about Beth on either side running his fingers through her hair. "You have such a pretty face. Your face would look simply marvelous with your haircut short and straight. You know that is the latest rage from Paris."

Holding her naturally curly hair up in clumps against the side of her face, he tried to give the appearance of short hair. "Yes, straighten the hair. That would work and I can send the solution home with you. What do you think, Lady Gately? The latest style for this lovely young girl?"

"Maurice, you're such an artist. Do whatever you think best. We'll be going out for dinner tonight."

Grabbing his scissors with flair, he grabbed a section of Beth's hair.

"No!" she protested.

He jumped back, dropping his scissors. Lady Gately stared at her in shock.

"Elizabeth! Whatever is wrong? Maurice is considered to be the greatest hairdresser in all of London."

Maurice held his head high and looked about the salon, hoping everyone had heard Lady Gately's comment. He slowly approached Beth. A young woman picked up his scissors that had fallen on the floor and handed him another pair. Beth took a deep breath, trying to regain her composure.

"I'm so sorry, Maurice. I didn't mean to startle you. It is obvious you are quite an artist. But for the present, I prefer to keep my hair in this manner. As a student at Oxford, I have very little time. Perhaps you could trim it a bit and give me some suggestions."

Why, yes, Miss Elizabeth," he responded cordially. "So you're going out tonight? Perhaps we could put it up for the evening. Then tomorrow you could wear it pulled back with one of our quite fashionable tailored hair clips."

"That sounds delightful, Maurice."

Taking hold of Beth's hands, Maurice examined her nails, shaking his head in dismay.

"I'm simply astounded at the condition of your nails, Miss Elizabeth. Why they look like the nails of a common laborer!"

This time Beth thought it best not to make any comment. Maurice and Lady Gately wouldn't be interested in hearing about her father's vegetable garden, how she enjoyed working by his side, getting her hands dirty with the moist rich soil of his garden.

Maurice nodded to a woman in a white jacket. She quickly arrived with a stool and the necessary equipment for a manicure. Elizabeth Davies stared in the mirror as though she were watching someone else in a movie.

After arriving back at the hotel, the receptionist informed them that Lord Gately and Kevin had been delayed, but would return in time to change and meet for cocktails at six. When Beth returned to her room she found her new clothes from Harrods. The garments hung in her closet and the shoes were neatly placed on a closet shelf. A velvet box contained some of the jewelry from the store. Opening the top drawer she discovered other accessories. Another drawer contained an assortment of under garments and hosiery. Her unpacked suitcase lay in the corner, undisturbed. Next to it sat a large black designer suitcase. Immediately she called Kevin's room.

"Kevin! I can't believe what your mother did. I feel like a six-year-old getting ready for the first day of school!"

"Now, calm down. Tell me all about it."

Beth relayed every detail of the afternoon, occasionally interrupted by Kevin's amusing comments. By the time she finished, Beth laughed along with him.

"Now the bottom line is, do you like the clothes?"

"Of course. You might say it's all absolutely fabulous."

"Now, Beth, don't tell me Mother bought you clothes like your favorite British sitcom, "Absolutely Fabulous."

"No, Silly. Nothing that stylish," she responded sarcastically. "I can't keep any of it. It's all too expensive, but I couldn't argue with your mother. I decided to let you handle her."

"Look, Beth. Mother told me she might take you shopping, but as usual, she's gone overboard. Apparently she wants you to have those things, or she wouldn't have bought them for you. And hang the expense. Mother couldn't spend all her money if she went shopping like that every day. As for me handling Mother, you'll never guess where Father and I spent the afternoon.

"You two had some sort of business meeting, didn't you?"

"Yes, but first we went to a quite stylish men's clothier. Father insisted I try several suits. Had me keep on one with a vest and ugly tie. Then we drove to Pall Mall. That's why he had to dress me up. Can't walk into The Oxford and Cambridge Club unless you're suitably attired. That leather-chaired sanctum of stale cigars and port!"

"Now, Kevin, you'll probably just love the place in fifty years."

"The supposed business meeting was with some of his friends from the House of Lords. They babbled on and on in their cultured murmurs. One of them mentioned some militant females threatened to come into the club. Another replied, 'By George, if one came into the backgammon room, she'd be stoned!' I thought we would never leave. Some business meeting."

"Sounds utterly delightful!"

"I did talk Father into a more modish type suit to wear this evening."

"Do you know where we're going?"

"Not a clue. Didn't ask. I think others are joining us. Some bishop and his wife."

"Hope it's one of those liberal bishops who supports the ordination of women."

"Wouldn't count on it, my love."

"I'll try to mind my manners. But, Kevin, sometimes I just have to say something."

"I know. You don't have to remind me," he said in amusement. "Want me to mention a few?"

"Don't think we've got that much time. Will you come by my room? I really don't want to go down to the lobby alone."

"Certainly. I was planning on it. Just before six. Now relax, take a bath and look forward to a magnificent London evening. I love you, Beth."

"Love you, too, Kevin."

Beth couldn't help thinking how attractive they must have looked, waiting in the lobby for the others to arrive. Kevin glanced over toward the entrance of The Ritz Hotel. Two portly Church of England bishops entered, accompanied by their attractive well-dressed wives.

"Not them again! Don't know why my mother keeps inviting those two along. Haven't figured it out. I do know they're in with the Bishop of Chester. They're on all the number one invitation lists. Asked Mother once, and all she said was, 'Certain people have certain connections and it's not polite to ask.' At least their wives have a little life in them. I swear if either of them stood still for any length of time, he'd turn into a statue like that one over there."

Noticing their girth, Beth replied, "Well, I hope it wouldn't be a nude statue."

"Beth, let me warn you. I am talking ultra conservative. We'll try to sit by their wives. I think you might enjoy them. One is involved in some sort of garden club and actually gets her hands dirty once in a while. The other one has a good sense of humor and tells silly little jokes.

Judith Gately had arranged the seating ahead of time with ornately written place cards resting on the round table. Kevin had been placed between the clergy wives with Beth across the table stuck between their husbands. Lord and Lady Gately sat directly across from one another. Subdued classical music on the grand piano in the corner added to the elegant sophisticated surroundings.

Reading the elaborate menu gave Beth quite an uneasy, confused feeling. She knew what she didn't want. No oysters glazed with champagne. No oscietra caviar and blinis. Looking at Kevin, he took the cue and offered to order for her.

Lavish golden curving drapes framed large windows reaching from the floor to the expansive ceiling. Mirrored walls reflected the sparkling chandeliers and also gave opportunity for observing other dinner guests.

Beth studied other women to observe their ensembles and mannerism. She realized that someday, she'd be the one arranging the dinner parties, shopping at Harrods, planning trips all over the world. In no time, she'd feel at home in a place like this, just as in her kitchen back in Hawthorne. For a moment Beth felt a tinge of loneliness in the crowded room.

The bishop on her left spoke first after ordering.

"So, my dear, Lady Gately tells me you're a student at Oxford. Quite commendable, I must say. And what classes are you attending at present, and do you have a favorite?"

"Theology would be the subject of most interest."

"My goodness! A pretty young girl like you. Oxford and Cambridge should start having special classes titled Fortnum & Mason's, Harrods, and all those specialty shops you women adore."

Beth retorted, "And for the men, a class on the tailors of Savile Row and Jermyn Street."

Glancing at Kevin and Lord Gately she observed that they were trying to hold back a smile.

"Well said," said one of the wives. "And are you pursuing a degree in theology?"

"At this point, I would venture to say it would be God pursuing me and not me pursuing anything but an interest."

"That's all well and good," countered the man on her left. "Good insight into the working of God can only enhance our lives. It will stand you in good stead as you mature. The opportunities for charity work will be much enhanced by your depth in spiritual intellect."

His wife reacted to her husband's haughty attitude. "I perceive there might be something more to your journey, Elizabeth."

"Yes, ma'am. You know we are constantly making choices in life. Often a metanoia."

"Metanoia?"

"Yes. A walking in one direction and then doing a complete about face. A turning, as it were. In Christian terms, a change of heart, an orientation of a life centered around Christ."

"Go on, my dear," encouraged the other wife.

"I feel we perceive life too much from the outside. The influences by the society in which we live. We often tend to close a door before examining all the possibilities."

"What do you mean?" asked the bishop on her left.

"Rather like a room with several doors. It's prudent to open each one and examine the possibilities. Then make a choice."

Lord Gately enthusiastically agreed. "Right on, Beth. Right on."

Realizing her words caused some to be uncomfortable, she lightened up. "Recently when assigned an English paper on poetry, I sat in a dark, dusty, dreary library. An opened window let in some fresh air." Beth continued in an almost dramatic way. "Did I sit and write about the poet's words describing a perfect spring day? Or did I go out to relish the day. Take off my shoes and enjoy the emerald grass oozing between my toes?"

Lady Gately gave a little gasp.

"Touching the velvet petals of a new born flower. Allowing the fresh scents to reverberate through my lungs." Beth paused for a moment. "Or do I stay in the dark, musty room lined with the wisdom of the ages and complete my assignment?"

"And what did you do?" asked one of the wives.

Smiling, Beth responded, "I returned to the library that evening."

No need for Beth to question which of the women opposite her was the gardener. Her face was beaming. She was the next to speak.

"And how far do you plan to go with your theological education?"

Beth spoke slowly and deliberately, not the usual flippant way most say the familiar phrase. "God only knows."

Kevin stared at Beth. No one spoke for several uncomfortable moments. The waiter arrived with the first course. Beth waited for the blessing, but nothing was said.

Watching the others discretely, she selected the correct eating utensil for each of the five courses.

Tedious conversation about weather and traffic continued for some time until one of the clergy mentioned the excitement in Parliament concerning fox hunting. Heated debates monopolized the newspapers and television.

"I don't know what all the fuss is about," commented the bishop on Beth's right. Gives the fox a jolly good run and besides he often gets away, don't you know."

"Fun for the hounds and fine exercise for the horses," the other clergyman added. "And hunt balls are jolly affairs. Don't you agree, dear?" he said nodding to his wife. "And besides fox hunts are a part of our heritage, our tradition. Merry old England, I must say."

The gardening wife smiled at Beth and asked, "Do you have an opinion, Elizabeth?"

"I did a research paper on fox hunts a few years ago. The history, ethnicity, social consequences and conflicts."

"Good! But do you have an opinion?" asked Lord Gately.

"Let me say that I concluded my report with an opinion expressed by Oscar Wilde. 'Chasing a small russet dog-like creature to exhaustion constitutes the unspeakable in full pursuit of the uneatable."

Lord Gately roared with laughter. Several of the respectable clientele at nearby tables stared in disbelief while Lady Gately's crimson face displayed her disapproval.

"Well said, Elizabeth." Lord Gately nodded and smiled. "Mind if I use that next time I speak in the House of Lords?"

"Not a bit, sir."

Lady Gately maneuvered the remaining dinner conversation to quite boring subjects that no one would remember the next day. Finally the dinner concluded with flaming Crepes "Suzette" prepared at the table.

Entering the reception area of The Ritz, the two clergy couples courteously thanked their hosts and left immediately, mentioning early church services the next morning.

Smiling at Beth and Kevin, Lord Gately spoke. "You young folk have the rest of the evening. Sorry it's too late to take in a play. Perhaps a drink in the bar to end the evening," winking at Kevin. "Judith and I are going to our room."

"Let's join Kevin and Elizabeth. An after dinner drink sounds delightful."

Taking her arm firmly, Lord Gately responded, "Fine. We'll have our drink upstairs. See you in the morning. Ten sharp. The St. Paul service is at eleven."

Watching his parents walking toward the lift, Kevin commented, "Well! He sometimes wins the battles. I'm glad he won this one. I really do love my mother, but at times it's most difficult to like her."

The young couple hurried to their rooms, changed into comfortable clothes and enjoyed the remainder of the evening strolling around the streets of London, hand in hand, much to Beth's delight.

Chapter Eleven

"Lord, even the demons are subject to us in your name!"
(Luke 10:17)

Another excursion to London in the spring of Beth's final year at Oxford had a profound effect on her. Some friends invited her to go to an all day church meeting on a Saturday. The gathering of people interested in the ministry of healing filled the usually empty church of St. Augustine, located in a poor section of London. Some of the participants traveled from as far away as Scotland and Ireland to attend. Others, like Beth, came because they were curious.

During the morning tea break in the refectory, Beth was surprised to see her minister, The Rev. Sloan, from Chester.

"Vicar! I had no idea you would be here."

"Why Beth Davies! I'm surprised to see you here, too. Sorry I was out of town when you were in Chester a few weeks ago. Let's get away from the crowd and go outside."

The aged churchyard with weather-beaten tombstones offered respite from the noise inside. They walked along a path between the headstones and found a wooden bench under a tree to sit on.

"How's that young man of yours?" he asked.

"Fine, I suppose."

Beth knew he was studying her. She glanced down at dandelions in the grass.

"You don't sound too sure. Everything all right?"

"We're both so busy at Oxford. We spend little time together. Sometimes I feel I hardly know him."

The vicar nodded. "Yes, university life does tend to change people." His gaze followed a butterfly winging from flower to flower. "New ideas and perspectives. A transition for both of you."

"I miss Hawthorne and of course, Manna. But I do love Oxford. The lectures, reading, new friends, and the orchestra. We're playing all six Brandenburg Concertos this year."

"And Mr. Fulham, your tutor?"

"We get on quite well. Asked me the other day if I had a spiritual director. I suppose I think of you as my spiritual director, but we never called it that."

"Speaking of spiritual direction, how is the direction of your spiritual life coming along?"

Beth glanced at a Celtic cross standing watch over a nearby grave and pointed. "Rather like that cross. At times going around in circles. Once in a while venturing into the center."

A bell signaled a return to the nave for the remainder of the morning. "Sorry, Beth, perhaps we can talk after the service."

The day culminated with a healing service in the evening. After the conclusion, a few remained for additional prayer. Beth knelt in a pew midway back, but her thoughts were other than prayer. Many had gone on to the pub, but she had promised the vicar she would stay.

The descending sunlight through the stained glass window behind the high altar brought the figures of the marriage in Cana to life. Crimson, blue and gold colors continued down from the window and danced on the altar. A faint smell of incense covered the musty smell of ancient stones.

A minister from Liverpool and two ladies from the church were gathered around one young woman who knelt at the altar rail for healing prayer.

The sexton came in, extinguishing the candles on the altar and proceeded to the Lady Chapel to snuff out the remaining ones. Beth watched as the smoke wafted up the architectural features of three centuries. Turning off the main lights, the sexton locked the side doors and nodded to Rev. Sloan, who sat in the front pew.

Pulling her wrap about her shoulders, Beth shivered, as an eerie darkness enveloped the scene. The reserved Sacrament light to the left of the altar seemed to glow brighter in contrast to the dim shadows.

One of the women near the altar rail hurried down the steps to the vicar, whispering something in his ear. He stood, looked to the back of the church and motioned for Beth to come. Reluctantly she followed him.

The young woman lay on the floor beside the altar rail moving about in wild contortions. Kneeling at her head the vicar from Liverpool took out his holy oil. Gareth Sloan knelt at her feet while the two women sat on the altar rail cushions holding on to her agitating body.

Beth stood motionless, staring at the scene in disbelief. She wanted to turn and leave, but her feet were glued to the floor.

"Beth! We need your help," her vicar said. "Get down here and hold her other arm before she injures herself."

Kneeling on the floor Beth clutched the woman's cold clammy hand. Chills riveted through her body. The woman began uttering an unintelligible language. As the minister touched her forehead with holy oil, she let out a bloodcurdling scream. Her body twisted and turned. Beth held her hand with all her strength. The power in her one arm was almost more than she could bear.

"Beth, put your other hand under her back and keep praying."

Beth's own body ached with pain in the cramped position, one hand trying to control the strong, constantly moving arm and the other hand under the woman's back on the floor. When Beth took a deep breath to calm down, she smelled a nauseating odor.

The vicar from Liverpool took out a small bottle of holy water. As the first drop hit her body, the woman convulsed and started screaming profanities. Her icy cold body bore down on the floor. Beth tried to pull her hand out, but the force of the woman's body held it down. The pain was excruciating. The constant screaming of the creature obliterated the priestly prayers.

"Maranatha, maranatha." Beth kept repeating the one word prayer that ends the Book of Revelation. "Come, Lord Jesus." She could think of nothing else.

All of a sudden the woman's body relaxed. She turned on her side, facing away from Beth. The two priests looked at one another, nodded and rose to their feet. Beth remained on her knees staring at the limp body.

The ministers came over to Beth, helping her to stand up. She watched as the two women took their jackets and covered the women's body until only a tangled mass of brown hair was visible.

Beth heard one of the women say, "We'll stay with her. Go over and join the others. We'll take care to lock the church."

The Liverpool clergyman shook Gareth Sloan's hand. "Glad you were here. Haven't had much experience with this sort of situation."

"By God's grace, we managed," Vicar Sloan said.

"Sorry, Gareth, but I won't be able to join you this evening. I need to get back to Liverpool tonight. I'll ring you tomorrow afternoon."

"Right. Talk to you then."

As Beth and the vicar made their way down the steps into the main part of the church, she watched the Liverpool clergyman make his departure through a side door.

Beth turned to look back at the altar. The two women sat on the kneelers to the side of the woman wrapped in their jackets. The Sacrament light shone on the tranquil scene.

"Vicar, is she going to be all right? I don't understand what happened. I wanted to leave, but I couldn't."

"Let's go, Beth. We'll talk later. I could do with some fish 'n chips and a pint after this long day. The group has gone to *The Fox and the Grapes Pub.*"

The votive candles in the back corner illuminated the main aisle leading to the back of the church. Slowly the massive wooden door gave way to the vicar's push. The bright late afternoon sun blinded their eyes for a few moments. After walking a few steps Beth saw the entrance to a park, the sun still shinning on the tops of the highest trees.

"I feel like I've journeyed from one world to the next," she said. "It's good to see the light of the sun."

She looked back at the entrance of the church now in darkness. With a look of determination, Beth turned to the vicar, "On to the pub. Let's get back to the real world."

"Beth, the real world? Sometimes I wonder."

Standing in silence they waited for a chance to cross a busy street. The noise contrasted to the silence they had left. An abundance of buses and cars mingled in either direction, filling the road. Townspeople crowded together waiting for the light to change. Several women and men dressed in medieval costumes came walking toward them.

"Must have been another festival in London today," he grinned. "At least we didn't hear bagpipes in the middle of the service."

Faintly in the distance, came the sound of pipes. Gareth Sloan and Beth stared at each other in disbelief. Their uncontrollable laughter caused some people to stare at the priest and young woman. Still giggling, they crossed the street, dodging a BMW going too fast. They turned the corner to Lower Bridge Street. Laughter came pouring out the opened windows of the pub.

"Well, Vicar, sounds like our group has started the party without us."

"No, the usual locals. We have one of the large rooms upstairs. Probably the one with the old church pews for seats. The owner says it gives the place atmosphere. I say it gives me more than that."

"Where did they get the pews and how did they get them up the stairway?" Beth asked.

"They came from a church in Dorset. The priest moved out the pews, had new ones built and painted the walls white. The other vicar said it was a blessing from God, because within a year his parish rolls doubled." He pointed to the second floor. "I hear they used a block and tackle to hoist them up from the street and through that window."

The vicar opened the pub door. The smoke-filled timbered room was alive with animated conversation. The low beamed ceiling and Tiffany lamps gave a warm comfortable feeling to the bar area. The adjoining room was crowded with clientele eating generous pub meals. Groups of two or three stood around the bar area attempting to "out-story" one another. The owner, busy serving ale and other drinks, looked their way, recognizing the vicar.

"The usual, Vicar?" he yelled across the room.

"Aye, and a gin and bitter for the young lady."

Several turned and gave the vicar a wave.

Beth asked mischievously, "Do you come here often?"

"Elizabeth Davies, you've been watching too many old movies."

They picked up their drinks at the bar and made their way through the crowd and up the narrow stairs. A waitress stood at the top.

"Are you two the last of the group?"

"No, there may be two or three more," he said. "Please bring four more orders of fish 'n chips and we'll make out fine. All right for you, Beth?"

"Fine."

Several tables arranged about the room provided ample seating. The vicar's wife and another couple sat in a far corner.

Beth spied the cushioned vacant chair next to Mrs. Sloan, "Looks like someone has saved a special chair for you, my Grace."

"Now, that's what I call a good wife."

The two parted company as Beth approached a large table to join her friends from Oxford.

One of the young men stood. "Beth, I've saved a place for you, so you can hang your head out the window if the smoke gets too much."

"Thanks," Beth said. "You can't see a foot in front of you downstairs. You know, in America, some restaurants won't allow anyone to smoke. I call that progress."

"I call that invasion of a man's rights," spoke Paul, a strapping young man."

"And women's rights, too," chimed in one of the women. "Why it makes me want to have a smoke and I don't smoke."

The group laughed as they held up their glasses for a toast. "Here's to Her Royal Majesty and the rights of her loyal subjects!"

Turning to Beth, her friend Kate asked, "What took you two so long? I thought the service was over, so we came on."

Beth had managed to block the recent scene in the church from her mind for a short time. But now it all came back. Chills shot through her body. Remembering the screams, the contorted body and foul smell made her feel nauseated.

"Beth, you're as white as a sheet! Are you all right?"

"Open the window a little more," Beth said. "I need some fresh air."

Taking several deep breaths seemed to help. The group started talking about plans for the next weekend and the visit of Prince Charles to Oxford. Beth sat back and listened to the energetic conversation, glad to have the role of a bystander. Just as the waitress had finished serving the food orders, two girls came in the room.

"Look!" said Paul. "Here come Christine and Margaret. We have plenty of room. One of you girls can sit in my lap."

Beth turned to see her friend, Christine, but didn't recognize the girl with her.

"Thanks for the offer, Paul," said Christine, but we'll sit down here with Beth where it's safe."

The group laughed. Paul obviously enjoyed the attention.

"I suppose I'll need to get my guitar and sing that country-western song that so perfectly describes me," Paul said.

"And just what might that be?" Beth asked.

"*It's Hard to Be Humble, When You're Perfect In So Many Ways.*"

The students continued their congenial meal. Everyone seemed to have met Margaret, except Beth. She turned toward her. "Margaret, I don't think I got a chance to meet you today. I'm Beth."

"It's good to meet you, Beth."

Beth waited for further conversation from Margaret, but only received silence. She wondered if she were shy or perhaps stuck up. Margaret had delicate features, sorrowful eyes and curly brown hair that framed her gentle face. Something seemed vaguely familiar about her, but Beth was sure she had never seen her before.

"Margaret, do you live here in London?"

"Yes."

"Are you in school or working?"

"I'm employed at Harrods in the office, and going to school part time."

Beth glanced toward the entrance to the room and recognized one of the women from the church who had stayed with the young woman on the floor. She surveyed the room and then walked straight over to Margaret.

"Are you all right, my dear?"

Margaret smiled sweetly and looked up at the woman. "I'm better than I've been in my entire life."

The woman handed Margaret a slip of paper. "Call me if you need anything."

"Thank you, ma'am."

The woman turned and left the room.

Beth stared at Margaret for several moments. A look of disbelief came to her face.

This can't be the same person, she thought. That creature in the church was ugly, repulsive. Can't be, and yet…

"Margaret?"

"Yes, Beth."

"Are you…Were you?"

"Was I what?"

"Nothing."

Beth took several gulps of her drink. Her eyes narrowed as she studied Margaret's features and hair.

Gradually, a peaceful, knowing, smile emerged on Beth's face. Yes, I do know her.

Chapter Twelve

"I will lead the blind in a way that they know not."
(Isaiah 42:16)

Kevin had mentioned the night before graduation on several occasions with a hint of anticipation. Beth looked forward to the evening, but she didn't expect it to turn out the way it did.

"Wear that scrumptious black dress you wore in London. Can you put your hair up? Makes you look so sophisticated."

"Where are we going, Kevin? One of your fancy political parties?"

"No. I'll pick you up at 7:00, Elizabeth Ann Davies."

Placing the phone down, she thought, "He never calls me that. Wonder what he's up to."

Arriving at a fashionable restaurant in Oxford, the manager escorted the young couple to a private dining room. Roses and sweet scented candles adorned the linen-covered table. Over in the corner a violinist was playing *Fascination.* Holding back her smile, Beth tried not to notice his out of tune notes and wide vibrato. He finally stopped playing and left the room. A waiter entered with a bottle of Dom Perignon. After ceremoniously opening the bottle, he served the young couple and left.

"Kevin, aren't you going to smell the champagne?" You always do in those fancy restaurants."

"No, Beth. Not champagne, he replied with a chuckle. "Only wine. Red wines have a distinctive bouquet, a unique fragrance. Adds to the taste to follow. It's not unusual for wines to become corked."

"I thought most of them are corked," she said.

"No, corked means that the wine has turned to vinegar in the bottle. And as I always say, life's too short to drink a bad wine, or for that matter, a bad champagne. Here's to us and to our future." He raised his glass.

After the toast, Kevin stood, went over to Beth and got down on one knee.

"Did you drop something?" She bent over, looking on the floor, almost bumping his head.

"I knew I should have done this on the top of some mountain." He searched his pockets and pulled a ring box out of his vest pocket. He opened the box.

Beth gasped. "It's beautiful, exquisite!"

He slipped the three-karat diamond ring on her finger.

"Elizabeth Ann Davies, will you marry me?"

"Of course I will. Now what's for dinner? I'm starving."

They were doubled over in laughter when the waiter came in with appetizers.

Beth didn't recall the dinner, but she vividly remembered the conversation.

"Mother thinks it's best to wait a year. A June or July wedding."

"Oh, Kevin, I thought we would marry in the fall."

"There's not the time. Planning a wedding at St. Paul's for several hundred and of course all the parties before..."

"St. Paul's in London? Parties? Why not St. John's in Chester?"

"That would never do, not for a Gately wedding," he frowned. "Mother said for you not to worry about the details." Kevin studied Beth for a moment. "Sorry, dear. I promise, after we're married, we'll make all the decisions."

"We better." I can play her game, she thought, but it may not be until after we're married.

"Besides, Beth, I know you've planned to spend most of your summer in Llandudno with your grandmother."

"Yes, and I suppose it may be my last," she said sadly.

Kevin frowned. "See here. If your grandmother needs assistance, we can help. Why she could close the B & B and move to a home in Hawthorne."

"Oh! That's what keeps her going. Some people have been coming to Llandudno for over thirty years. Her guests are more like family to her."

The waiter arrived with their chateaubriand. Kevin waited for him to leave before he spoke. "We've had precious little time together here in Oxford. After the summer is over, Mother and Father have offered us a trip abroad."

"That's nice of them," Beth said, attempting to sound sincere.

"I told them to hold off on the planning until I talked with you. I know you'll want to visit some of those musty old churches."

"About church, Kevin."

"Ah! Yes, church. I can see you going about doing grand charity work. And with your degree in theology from Oxford. You really don't mind visiting those hospitals and convalescent homes, do you? For the life of me, I can't see why you do it."

"I do it for the life of them," she said slowly.

Silence filled the room prepared for a joyous occasion. Beth took a deep breath, said a quick prayer and spoke.

"Kevin, I want more involvement than charity work."

"What do you mean?"

"I'm considering ordination."

The clang of his fork dropping on his plate reverberated in the room. He stared at her in disbelief.

"I've tried to tell you, she said. "But every time I do, you change the subject. Start talking about our future, our lives together, our holidays abroad."

"I know, Beth. I thought it would eventually pass, especially with us getting married. I suppose you would have to wear a black dress to every party. But would you have to wear that white dog collar all the time, even to bed?"

"Kevin!" she said with impatience. "You're not taking me seriously!"

"I am. Humor is the only way I know to deal with it." Taking her hand, he smiled. "We love each other. That's what counts. We'll work this out someway."

After dinner, Kevin's roommate, Trevor, had asked them to meet him at one of the nearby pubs. Some friends surprised them with a party to celebrate their engagement. Trevor knew of Beth's close friendship with Brigid and had invited her, too.

Beth didn't feel like celebrating. She spotted Brigid at a corner table in the back of the crowded pub. After greeting some friends and showing her ring, she headed for Brigid and sat down.

"I'm so glad you're here."

"Beth, what's wrong?"

"I'm not sure. I should be ecstatic, but I'm not. Look at Kevin with his friends. I've never seen him so happy."

"But you're not happy."

"At dinner I finally got through to him about my possible vocation in the church."

"Splendid."

"But Lady Gately has plans for a big wedding at St. Paul's. And we can't marry until next year."

"Maybe that's for the best. It'll give you both some time."

"I should be the happiest girl in the world. I do love Kevin. The perfect husband, a bright future. But I feel restless, unsettled."

Chapter Thirteen

"Knowledge puffs up, but love builds up."
(I Cor. 8:1)

A few days after graduation, Beth settled back in Hawthorne for a fortnight before going to Llandudno for the summer. The phone rang one morning. Beth answered.

"Yes, Vicar? Are you sure?" She sighed. "I'll keep the appointment, but I'm not looking forward to it."

The cold walls of the lengthy Chester Cathedral hall spoke of silent figures who had walked on the gray stones centuries before. Beth shuddered as a chill passed through her body. Pulling her wrap around her, she walked toward the massive wooden entrance at the end of the hall. Light emerged from beneath.

The door creaked open with a pull of the latch and there stood Mrs. Richmond with the usual scowl on her face.

"The bishop is waiting for you. Do go right in."

Beth walked across the room and knocked.

"Enter," said a harsh voice.

Beth walked in. The door closed with a loud thud behind her. Bishop John Dakyn stood behind his immense desk. His pectoral cross caught the glimmer of the morning sun in contrast to his purple bishop's shirt. He wore his usual austere black suit with a padded jacket.

The bishop's smile and his cold gray eyes gave opposing impressions. Beth thought he had the eyes of a cat–no warmth or emotion. Relieved to find the room sunlit and warm, she entered with optimistic anticipation. Maybe this dreaded meeting won't be so bad after all, she thought.

He walked over, holding out his hand with palm downward, exposing his elaborate bishop's ring. He waited for a kiss on the ring and a genuflect. Beth took his hand and shook it.

"Take a seat, Miss Davies," he intoned, nodding to a chair across from his desk. Will you be spending the summer in Hawthorne?"

"No, sir, I'll be in Llandudno helping my grand-mother with her B and B."

"I hear the town is quite run down. Not much church activity there either."

Beth sat down and watched as the bishop walked over to one of the windows overlooking the cathedral grounds. He stood with his back to her.

"The Reverend Sloan discussed this appointment with me. I told him there was no need, but he insisted."

"I came because he is my spiritual director," she said. He advised me that it might be of interest to both of us."

The bishop cleared his throat. "I see."

He turned, his hands folded across his chest, tapping his fingers on his arm. Walking over to the plush leather chair, he stood, looking down at Beth. She averted his icy stare. An uncomfortable silence filled the air. He picked up a folder on his neat well-organized desk, flipping the cover back.

"I see you have done quite well on your studies at Oxford. I'm a Cambridge man myself. The theologians at my institution have more in-depth theological works published than your Oxford."

"That's quite commendable, sir."

While Bishop Dakyn looked at the papers in the folder, Beth glanced about the room. Her eyes rested on a striking icon of Mary and Jesus painted with intense detail and deep colors.

"What a lovely icon. It must give you inspiration for prayer and meditation."

"Yes, isn't it magnificent? A group of friends here at the cathedral gave it to me. It was clearly stated I'm to take it with me when I retire. Painted by a monk who lives in the monastery on Patmos, the very island where John wrote the book of Revelation. A close friend told me it's well worth a thousand pounds. I'm very proud of it."

"Yes, Bishop. It is a work of art and prayer."

"Well, Miss Davies, your work is quite commendable, but you and your spiritual director are aware I oppose the ordination of women. Perhaps you should direct your intellect to the noble profession of teaching. I could recommend any number of positions."

Beth took a deep breath and stood to face him. She looked into his cold narrowing eyes. "Bishop Dakyn, I regret we do not agree on this matter. I plan to continue my studies and ministry. I pray to follow the path God has chosen."

The bishop slapped the folder down on his desk. He looked at his watch.

"My goodness, I quite forgot. I have some preparation to do before my next appointment."

"Thank you for your valuable time, Bishop Dakyn. May God's peace and blessings be with you."

She turned and walked out, leaving the door open.

A few days later Beth attended a weekday service at Chester cathedral. A stranger came in and sat close by in the same pew. She noticed his well-worn sweater, scruffy shoes and snow-white wind blown hair. At the passing of the peace, she shook his hand, looking into the clearest blue eyes she had ever seen. After the service, Beth went over to him.

"Hello, my name is Elizabeth Davies. May I be of any assistance, sir?"

He smiled. "I'm visiting Chester. I just returned from a walk in the country in time for the service. I'm afraid I look quite a mess. Miss Davies, are you a member of the cathedral?"

"No, but I come to weekday services quite often. And personally, sir, I think you look just fine. There's tea in the common room, if you would care to join me. Sandwiches and cakes, too."

"That sounds delightful. And you could perhaps give me some information about the Chester area. I lived here as a boy, but have been away for some time. Impressive sermon given by the young minister today."

"Yes," she said. "I try to attend when he is on the schedule. I like the story of Peter and Cornelius and the way he applied it to our world today. God shows no partiality. That's a hard lesson I struggle with often."

"And I struggle along with you, Elizabeth."

"And your name, sir?"

"Edmond."

"Well, Edmond, let's have tea, shall we?"

They walked down the side aisle, meeting Bishop Dakyn and the archdeacon coming from the other direction.

"Bishop Dakyn," Beth said, "allow me to introduce you to one of our visitors."

"Not now, I'm late for lunch."

The bishop hurried on his way. As he started out the side door he turned and looked at Edmond. "Something familiar about that chap," he said to the archdeacon. Bishop Daykn shrugged his shoulders. "Probably reminds me of someone else." He turned, continuing on his way.

Beth noticed her new acquaintance was smiling as they walked into the dining area.

"Something amusing?"

"Yes, quite. But perhaps it's best that I explain later. Now, about the tea and sandwiches. I've worked up quite an appetite after my long hike. Perhaps I should go across the street to a tea room."

"There's plenty here. And besides, the tea room will be crowded with all the tourists and visitors on such a lovely day."

Walking into the room, Beth pointed to a corner table, "There's our place just waiting. You make yourself comfortable."

Beth returned with their lunch on a tray. She settled into a pleasant conversation and Edmond asked her several questions, mainly about herself and Chester.

"And how do you like your Bishop Dakyn, Elizabeth?"

"He's... an interesting man."

"That's a rather non-committal answer."

"And, Edmond, tell me about yourself. You said you had lived here as a child. What kind of life have you led since you left the Chester area?"

"My father was a clergyman, but our family spent most of our time in the London area. I attended Cambridge."

"I just finished my education at Oxford," she said.

"And your degree and plans for the future?"

Beth studied the man for a moment, trying to decide whether to tell him more about herself. "You might say I'm at an in-between place at the moment. Edmond, tell me about your area of interest."

"You might call it public relations," he said.

"And have you been living in the London area since you left Chester?"

"No, actually, I've just returned from South Africa."

"South Africa! Tell me about it. What part? What kind of work did you do?"

"Let us say, a certain situation got a little warm for me, so I decided it best to leave the country for a while. I was planning a trip to England, but not quite this soon."

Beth sat back in her chair and looked at him. For all she knew, he could be some sort of criminal.

Edmond said, "Now, Elizabeth, there's nothing for you to worry about. I have quite excellent credentials, I can assure you."

Standing up, Beth offered, "I'll get us another pot of tea and bring some dessert."

"Sounds splendid."

As Beth approached the table with the tea and cake, the archdeacon walked in a side door. "Edmond, why you old scoundrel. What are you doing here? We didn't expect you until later in the week."

Bishop Dakyn followed behind him. The bishop looked surprised. His face was as red as his shirt. Stammering, he attempted to talk. "My, my extreme apologies, Edmond. I, I didn't recognize you. Why it must be 20 years. You're looking extremely fit after your dreadful stay in that God forsaken country."

"Let us pray God hasn't forsaken South Africa. I would have stayed on, but the pressure from the authorities… I hope to return when things calm down a bit."

"By all means. Edmond, come to my office and we'll have tea and visit. I insist. I've planned a delightful dinner party for you on Friday evening next."

Beth stood motionless near the table with teapot in one hand and dessert in the other staring at the bishops.

Bishop Short got up and walked over to Beth. He took the teapot out of her hand and smiled. Whispering so the others couldn't hear, "Sorry, my dear. It's such a bore being a bishop all the time. Now let's go on with our delicious lunch."

She smiled and followed him over to the table.

"Sorry, fellows. I have a previous engagement. I'll ring you up tomorrow for an appointment."

The Bishop of Chester Cathedral glanced at Beth, turned and walked out the door without a word, followed by the archdeacon on his heels.

"Well, Bishop Short, you certainly had me fooled."

"Now, Elizabeth, call me Edmond. Yes, I knew John quite a number of years ago. One of our brightest stars at Cambridge. Had a real love for the church. Interesting the paths we choose to take in life. Then wonder how in the world we got there."

Chapter Fourteen

"Come, let us walk in the light of the Lord"
(Isaiah 2:5)

Beth awoke just before dawn the morning of her departure for Holywell and Llandudno. Looking out a window to the east she saw a faint glow, partially covered by clouds.

She turned on her bedside lamp and discovered a burned out bulb. Grabbing her Bible, Beth went over and sat on the window seat. After saying a few prayers by rote, she closed her eyes and tried to remember the names on a prayer list she had packed away the night before. "And, dear God," she sighed, "all those I can't remember."

Enough light penetrated through the clouds for Beth to look at the readings for the day. She looked up the chapter, read a few verses, then slammed the book shut. *Too many churchy rules and regulations. I'll play Bible roulette.*

Beth shut her eyes, opened the Bible again, and pointed to a line. She opened her eyes slowly and read, "Arise, shine, for your light has come, and the glory of the Lord has dawned upon you."

When she looked out the window Beth witnessed an intense sunrise. The rich crimson and golden hues shot out from behind random clouds, reminding her of a Gaugin painting.

Beth closed the Bible and looked out the window until the colors changed into the blue of a clear day. "Some prayers are said with the eyes."

Downstairs in the kitchen, Beth put the kettle on and started frying bacon. After a few minutes the kitchen door swung open.

"What's going on here?" said her mother. "You've never been up before me, except when a wee one wanting your milk."

"Thought I should cook you a proper English breakfast before I leave for the heathen land of Wales, my lady."

The women laughed and shared a hug. Beth's mum set the table as the aroma of the sizzling bacon permeated the kitchen.

"Don't know why you have to go early and visit the nuns at Holywell," her mother said. "Seems you get enough church without visiting those Catholics. Protestants and Catholics are like oil and water. They don't mix."

"They do if they focus on what's important."

"And what might that be, dear Beth?"

"Love."

Beth's mother put her hands on her hips. "Love, is it! Each killing the other for the love of Christ. Literally, for the love of Christ!"

"Mum, I met a girl from Belfast at Oxford. She said most of the Irish want peace. In her neighborhood, the Catholics and Protestants are friends. But someone's always stirring up trouble. The press doesn't print the good stuff."

"That could be true, Beth. I wish the fighting would stop."

"But there must be forgiveness on both sides," Beth said. I don't know how I would cope with the killing of someone I love. I don't walk in their shoes and I'm thankful for that."

"So! Have those Catholics and Protestants go to church together, have a party and get roaring drunk. That would settle the problem."

"Mother!"

"Well, they've tried about everything else."

Beth turned around, folding her arms. "I think the churches are too focused on their individual traditions, rules and regulations. That's what keeps us from being who God created us to be. Jesus spoke against it, too. He ministered to lepers, the poor, beggars, women, and even tax collectors."

Beth's mother slapped the table. "All right, Beth. I haven't had my first cup of tea and you're giving me a sermon. At least the vicar waits for a decent hour of the morning."

Beth laughed, and gave her mother a polite curtsy with a little girl smile. She turned off the stove, covered the bacon and put the bread in the oven to toast.

Her mum sat down at the table with a pot under the tea cozy and two cups. "Come have a seat, daughter."

Beth did as she was asked and poured the tea.

"I've never gone to St. Winefride's Well," Beth's mother said between sips. "My grandmother use to take my mother there. The family traveled in a wagon from Llandudno to stay with her brother at Holway. She saw a paralyzed woman get into the water and come out cured. It must have been quite a place."

"There are still quite a few visitors who come to the well and some bathe in the water," Beth said. "The Hospice run by the nuns is often full in the summers with travelers and groups on retreat."

"Beth, I forgot the story of St. Winefride. Something about her head being cut off?"

Beth frowned. "This is certainly pleasant breakfast conversation. Want strawberry jam with your toast this morning?"

"Oh, Beth! I'm right, aren't I?"

"Yes, the story took place in the Seventh Century. Winefride was a young girl, alone at home one day. Caradoc, the son of a neighboring prince, came by and tried to seduce her. She escaped and ran toward the church where her uncle, Saint Beuno, was a priest. Caradoc caught her in front of the church, drew his sword and cut off her head."

Beth picked up a knife off the table and swished it through the air. Her mother grabbed her throat and gasped. "Go on, Beth. Then what happened?"

"Saint Beuno prayed for his niece. She came back to life with only a white line encircling her neck. On the spot where her head had fallen, a fountain gushed forth. St. Winefride's Well has flowed freely ever since."

"That's quite a story. What happened to Caradoc?"

"He sank into the ground, never to be seen again."

"You don't really believe that, do you Beth?"

"I hadn't thought much about it. People still claim to be healed by the waters. I know, when I go, I feel a peaceful presence. A lot needs healing in this world besides aches and pains. The shrine is in good condition, one of the few to survive the Reformation, because it was medicinal."

The two women sat in silence for some time, quietly sipping their tea. Beth's mother took a deep breath. "The bread's burning!"

Chapter Fifteen

"He who has ears, let him hear."
(Luke 8:8)

The azure sky greeted Beth as she drove away that morning, burnt toast forgotten, with Manna sitting in the front seat. Her parents stood on the front lawn waving their goodbyes. She decided to drive the A55, the inland road, since she had seen the coast route numerous times from car and train windows. And besides, she thought, the inhabitants of cramped caravan parks along the seacoast road slowed the traffic in the summer.

Beth arrived at the parking space in front of St. Winefride's Rest in less than an hour. A dark roof covering the three story white building held the words, *Hospice*, in large white letters. Beth glanced at the attached two-story building and wondered how many guests would be staying overnight. As soon as she opened the door, Manna jumped out, running to a patch of green grass.

Sister Clare stood at the front door. "What a delight to see you again, Beth. I'm just on my way out to visit a sister, but that can wait. Come, let's have tea. I think we have some breakfast left."

"Super! I haven't had much to eat this morning." Beth thought of her early morning attempt to make breakfast.

She followed the nun into a simple dining room. Flowered plastic tablecloths covered long tables. Four elderly ladies sat at a small corner table, chatting and sipping tea. Beth accompanied the sister to a side room reserved for special guests. A teapot, cups and a plate of Welsh cakes were on the table. Sister Clare poured the tea while Beth lost no time devouring two of the pastries.

"Beth, would you have time to go with me to visit Sister Gertrude? It won't take long. Just a short distance."

"Yes, it'll give us a chance to talk. Do you have many guests this week?"

"Not many, but we'll be full this weekend and all next week. We often don't know how many to expect, especially for lunch and afternoon tea, but we always manage, thank the good Lord." The nun stood. "I need to take care of something and then we'll be on our way."

Beth and Sister Clare drove past St. Beuno's Convalescent Center, an unimposing, gray building. Beth noticed the security keyboard on the front door. Parking was limited on the dingy back street of Holywell. After driving a few blocks they found a space to park the dented brown Toyota belonging to the sisters. When they arrived at the front door, Sister Clare punched in a digital code.

Stench of urine mixed with disinfectant filled Beth's nostrils. They walked to the front desk where a matron sat working on papers. She raised her sour face and nodded at the nun. "She's been asking for you. Pretty restless the last couple of days. Go on, I'll sign you in."

They turned left down a wide hall. On either side, patients sat in wheelchairs, staring at nothing. One woman tried to grab the nun's hand as she walked by.

Sister Clare smiled at her. "I'll visit with you on my way out, dear."

"Don't forget, sister." She pointed with a shaky hand. "I need your prayers."

The nun whispered to Beth, "These poor souls. I'll be glad when Sister Gertrude can leave this place. I hope it won't be much longer for her."

Beth looked back and forth from room to room. Some were vacant. Most had two beds with still bodies lying under the covers. At the end of the hall was a half glass door, letting in the morning sunlight, the only sign of life in the otherwise bleak place.

Sister Clare stopped outside a room. "Beth, it's best for me to go in first. I'll let her know I've brought a friend along. Then you can come in for a visit."

The nun tapped on the door and went inside. Beth leaned against the wall to wait. Across the hall a woman sat in a wheelchair in the doorway of her room. She wore an institutional white gown that hung on her petite frame. Auburn hair with streaks of white framed an oval face. Her large brown eyes came to life when she smiled at Beth just as Sister Clare came out.

"Young lady, are you here to visit me? I pray the answer is yes. I never get any visitors."

"Go ahead, Beth, if you don't mind," said the nun.

The woman backed up the wheelchair. Beth followed her into a gloomy room furnished with bare essentials. One faded print tacked on the wall illustrated a little girl sitting in a field of wild flowers. The woman looked up at Beth.

"Dear, would you open the curtains so I can see?"

Beth went over, opened the discolored drapes and turned back toward the lady. The sun reflected off the cross Beth wore around her neck, reflecting on the woman's face. Beth saw the reflection.

"Is that…is that a cross?"

"Yes, ma'am."

"Are you from the church? Have you come to ask questions?"

"No, I've come with Sister Clare from St. Winefride's to visit one of her sisters across the hall. I can leave, if you want."

"No, please don't. I…it's just that…Oh, never mind. I'm so glad to have someone to talk to from the outside. Tell me about yourself, young lady."

"My name is Elizabeth Davies and I'm from Hawthorne, near Chester."

"Oh, I'm so sorry, Elizabeth. How rude of me. I didn't introduce myself. My name is Victoria Martin."

"How long have you been here?"

"Some days, I'm not sure…lose track of time here. They're late with my medicine this morning, so I'm more clear-headed. As soon as the sergeant comes in and gives me the pill, I'll be sleeping most of the day."

"You mean the pleasant nurse at the front desk?"

Victoria nodded, smiling. "She got her training at a concentration camp. Anyway, let's visit. She'll be here any moment."

"Do you have family, Mrs. Martin?"

"Please call me Victoria." She smiled. "Yes, I have a son. He works in London and Paris." Victoria looked out the window. "We've never been very close. And then after his father died and the mess afterwards... He says he's coming but then cancels at the last minute."

"Victoria, I don't want to pry, but if you want to talk, I'm a good listener."

"That's kind of you, dear. I could tell you my story. You could write it out, sell it as a novel and make a million pounds."

"If I do, I'll split it with you."

Victoria chuckled. "I haven't laughed in ever so long. Are you sure you want to hear my dreary tale?"

"Of course, if you feel like it." Beth patted her shoulder. "And please call me Beth."

"Then have a seat, Beth." Victoria said, nodding to a chair in the corner. Beth brought it over and sat down close to Victoria.

"Many years ago I was a proper young English girl who fell in love with a handsome solicitor. His father had established him in a reputable firm in London. We had an extravagant wedding at Westminster Abbey, a honeymoon around the world and settled down to the perfect life on an estate outside of London. Jonathan and I were blissfully happy. Our son, Gavin, was born a year later. I busied myself with social obligations, charities, and our local parish."

Victoria closed her eyes for a moment and took a deep breath. "Dear, would you please fetch me a damp cloth. It might help me focus."

Beth got up, went over to a washbasin, and found a washcloth on a shelf. She soaked the material, rung it out and returned to her chair.

"Thank you, dear." Victoria patted her face with the cloth, folded it and held it in her hands.

"My husband often had business trips to the continent and occasionally spent several nights a week in London. Late one night I received a call from a hospital in London." Victoria started twisting the washcloth. "Jonathan had a heart attack. I reached him just before he died. All he would say was, 'I'm sorry. I'm sorry."

Tears filled Victoria's eyes. She dropped the washcloth on the floor. Beth handed her a tissue and leaned forward, touching her shoulder.

"Victoria, if this is too much, perhaps we should talk about something else."

"No, I want to go on." She dried her eyes. "Our friends were so caring after the funeral. My son and I had never been closer. I thought perhaps this would be the one positive thing that would come out of my husband's death.

"A few weeks later we met with family and friends for the reading of the will. My husband had made a number of bad investments. His so-called business trips had been to the Riviera to gamble, where he lost a considerable amount of money. To top it off, my dearly beloved husband had been keeping a mistress in London for a number of years." Victoria clenched her mouth, shook her head and looked out the window.

"Nothing much left except the estate. Gavin had to sell almost everything to pay off his father's debts. He was devastated. Couldn't cope with his own feelings, much less mine.

"He bought a small cottage for me in the nearby village, so I could be close to friends and the church, the only world I had left. Little by little, acquaintances stopped calling. I hit rock bottom, as they say. My doctor called it depression and gave me pills. I started counseling sessions with the vicar. We met weekly and it helped to have someone to talk to.

"One evening I was feeling pretty low. I took a couple of sleeping pills and got ready for bed. And then the knock on the door."

Victoria hesitated. Tears flowed down her cheeks. Beth patted her shoulder and gave her another tissue. "That's alright. You don't have to go on. Besides, I should go see how Sister Clare is doing."

Beth got up and moved the chair back to the corner.

"No, don't go. I didn't mean to distress you."

"You didn't. But you're upset."

Victoria looked at the institutional clock on her wall. "She's late with my pill. I'm starting to remember everything more clearly now. I tried to tell them, but no one would believe me."

The matron came in the room. "Just what do you think you're doing in this room? Who gave you permission to come in here?"

Beth looked at Victoria's face and saw terror.

"She asked me to open the curtains for her. That's all. I'm here with Sister Clare to visit her friend."

"Then go visit and leave this patient alone. You are not on her list of suitable visitors. I have my orders."

Beth left the room without saying another word or looking at Victoria. She went across the hall to join the nuns. After being introduced and sharing a few pleasantries, she asked Sister Gertrude if she knew the woman across the hall.

"They keep her isolated. Doesn't have any visitors, except once a week. Comes by every Tuesday afternoon at 2:00." She smiled, nodding. "He's dressed in regular clothes, but I can tell he's Anglican clergy. Never stays long. I tried to talk to her once, but someone told me they had orders to leave her alone."

"Sister Gertrude, she was telling me an interesting story. I admit, I'm rather curious to hear the ending."

"Beth, I need to come back tomorrow after some errands for Sister Gertrude. The old grouch at the front desk is off duty on that day."

"Sister Clare! I'm surprised at you calling that lovely lady a name like that."

The nun grinned.

Beth went out in the hall and observed the head nurse returning to the front desk. She walked across to Victoria's room. Victoria was slumped over in her chair, half asleep.

"Victoria, wake up. It's me, Beth."

She opened her eyes, managing a faint smile. "Yes, Beth, my new friend. She gave me the pill. I can barely keep my eyes open."

"Listen carefully, Victoria. When she comes tomorrow morning, don't take the pill. Act like you've taken it. Act sleepy. I'll be back tomorrow, a little later in the day." She shook Victoria gently. "Do you understand?"

"Yes. Don't take the pill in the morning. Yes, Beth. I understand."

Victoria slumped over and fell asleep. Beth left and joined the nuns across the hall.

Before leaving, Beth spoke to Sister Gertrude. "If you have a chance, remind Victoria not to take the pill in the morning. I'm not sure if I got through to her or not."

They walked back down the hall and stopped by to visit the woman in the wheelchair. After they said the Lord's prayer together, Beth and Sister Clare approached the front door of the nursing home. Sister Clare punched in the numbers again.

"Sister, doesn't it seem strange that this nursing home has such a tight security system? And the head nurse certainly likes to run a tight ship."

"Yes, dear, it did at first. But they said it is because of the neighborhood. They had some break ins."

"I can't imagine anyone wanting to break into this place. Something's not quite right, especially with Victoria."

The sun shone down on Beth and Sister Clare when they emerged from St. Beuno's. Beth looked up, squinting.

"This is a welcome relief from that dreary building," she said.

Sister Clare smiled. "Yes it certainly is, dear." As Sister Clare pulled out of the parking space she said, "I asked Sister Gertrude the name of the lady you were visiting. Mary Jones."

Chapter Sixteen

"Guard the truth that has been entrusted to you by the Holy Spirit who dwells within us."

(2 Timothy 1:14)

After Beth got out of the nun's small car at St. Winefride's, she stretched. Cramped muscles reminded her that she and Manna had missed their usual early morning exercise. "Sister Clare, think Manna and I will go down to Basingwerk Abbey. I'll have lunch at the pub down the hill."

"Fine, Beth. If I'm not available when you return, take room number 13. It's ready for you anytime."

Beth and Manna crossed the parking area toward a path. Beth thought this day couldn't get much better. First she burned the toast, then she spent the morning listening to a crazy woman, and now was assigned room number 13.

Looking up as a gray cloud covered the sun, the first gentle drops of an early summer shower hit her face. She smiled at Manna, "Well, at least we like to walk in the rain."

The dog ran ahead down the gently descending path following the course of an old railway. *Greenfield Valley Heritage Park* linked Holywell with the ruins of Basingwerk Abbey. Beth took a deep breath and relished the peacefulness of her surroundings. She knew the nourishment nature could give her. Noticing a man in uniform picking up trash, she thought how his job might appeal to her-outside all day, no stress, no decisions to make.

Looking about, she saw Manna chasing a squirrel in a grove of trees to her right. The rodent scampered up a tree in time. As the path opened onto a meadow area, Beth glanced over at a young couple under the sheltering branches of a large oak tree, their picnic basket close beside.

In the past, Beth had enjoyed this walk in the sunlight, listening to the birds, but the rain silenced the skylarks that frequented the area. Coming to the end of the trail, she walked over to a reconstructed farm and remembered a school trip from Hawthorne. The hens in the barnyard looked up at the noonday visitor. No volunteers scurried about demonstrating countryside skills and crafts. A large sign read *Closed Today*.

Beth turned toward the abbey ruins for cover from the increasing rain. She entered the twelfth century when she walked through the thirty-foot stone archway into the remains of the nave. Vegetation engulfed the floor and the crying sky was now the roof. She hurried through the area, turning right through a doorway. The rain intensified. She stayed close to the wall of mossy medieval stones. Going through another doorway she found a room with a roof holding back most of the rain. Glancing out a window, Beth saw Manna running about. She shouted, "Manna! I'm in here."

A mass of wet fur ran in and stood next to her, shaking off the water. Beth laughed. "Thanks, girl, I needed to get a little more wet." She pulled out a guide to the abbey from her pocket and discovered she was in the chapter house. She sat down on a section of stone bench that had survived over the years, thinking of the monks occupying this very room, listening to the daily readings, disciplines and temporal affairs of the monastery.

Manna lay at her feet, soon asleep. Listening to the rain tapping on the wooden roof, Beth closed her eyes and folded her hands in prayer. She thought of the familiar phrase, communion of saints. How many holy men and women no one remembers have walked this earth? Our humanity, so closely linked, and yet so far apart?

Her meditation carried her back in time, into holy space, a peaceful place. She could see colored light with her eyes closed. Beth sensed her breathing slowing down and felt a comfortable presence of others. She wanted to open her eyes, but resisted the temptation. She had no idea how long she sat there.

Manna growled. Beth opened her eyes. A noise came from the cloister area. A large shadow covered the ground outside the doorway of the chapter house enclosure. A muscular man with scruffy beard and old clothes stood in the doorway. His height made him stoop as he passed through the opening.

"Sorry to bother you, Ma'am. Just like to come here for some quiet time."

He turned around and left. Shocked by his sudden appearance, Beth said nothing. She and Manna walked out into the opened cloister area. The stranger had disappeared. The rain had stopped.

"How long have we been here, Manna?" She glanced at her watch. "It's almost time for supper at St. Winefride's."

Taking one more look around, she left Basingwerk Abbey and the communion of saints.

Ringing bells woke Beth the next morning. Hurrying downstairs she arrived as the nuns were clearing away breakfast.

"Still some left?" she asked one of the sisters.

"Of course. Sit at the end of the large table. Just help yourself. I'll start clearing the other tables. The tea's still a bit warm."

Beth was glad to have something to eat, even if the toast was cold and the tea tepid. She and Sister Clare had stayed up late last night chatting. Today Beth would prefer a peaceful walk back down to the abbey ruins than a visit to St. Beuno's again. She gazed out a window, thinking of her afternoon the day before. A voice startled her.

"Are you ready to go?" asked Sister Clare, standing at the dining room door. "And your detective work?"

"Detective work? I think not. I'll just listen to that poor woman one more time and that will be that."

"Don't be too sure. I have a feeling there's more to it."

Beth was relieved to see a different nurse at the front desk when they entered the depressing institution.

"Good morning, Sister. And you brought a young friend. Our patients brighten up when young ones come."

"This is my friend, Elizabeth Davies from Hawthorne, Miss Wimple."

The nurse smiled and nodded.

How is Sister Gertrude this morning?" asked Sister Clare.

"She's doing quite well."

"And how are you today," the nun asked.

"Very busy. One of our staff is sick, so right now I'm leaving the front desk to take care of the patients upstairs. Need anything?"

"Not a thing, dear. You go on with your duties and we'll have a nice long visit with Sister Gertrude."

Beth and Sister Clare walked down the hall, passing a young girl with a mop and cleaning bucket. Beth felt a little uneasy. *I'm imagining things. Such a depressing place. Be glad when I'm out of here.*

"Well, Beth, did you like the nurse at the desk a little better today?"

"As different as night and day."

Looking toward the end of the hall Beth noticed an attractive woman sitting in a wheelchair. She wore a pretty frock with hair neatly combed and a hint of makeup. Finding Victoria's room empty, Beth went back out into the hall.

"Beth, it's me," said the woman.

"Sorry, I didn't recognize you. You look so…so different."

"Come, dear, help me back into the room. We'll have privacy there."

Beth pushed Victoria into her room and retrieved the chair from the corner.

"I did it. I hid the pill when she came in last night. I've got the morning pill right here in my tissue. And last night I was able to stand and even walk a few steps. Here, let me show you."

Bracing herself on the arms of her chair, Victoria winced as she stood. One foot moved forward, then the other, again and again. Beth stayed in front of her and backed up as Victoria came toward her. They almost reached the doorway.

"Better get the wheelchair, Beth. That's all I can do for now."

"That's splendid!" said Beth.

She helped Victoria sit down and then pushed her over to the window. The two women sat in silence for a few minutes watching a busy mother robin preparing her nest for a new family.

"I'm so glad you came. I want to tell you more. I lay awake all night remembering."

"We'll have more time today, Victoria. The head nurse said she would be upstairs for a while."

"Good. Nancy's a gentle soul. She's not strict with me like the others. Now, where did we leave off yesterday?"

"You told me about your husband's death, the loss of your home and your illness. And about the night you took an extra pill."

"Yes. The night that would change my life forever. He came that night."

"Who? Your son?"

"No, the vicar. Late in the evening. It was raining. He saw my light on and stopped by to see how I was doing. Helped himself to several jiggers of whiskey. Poured one for me each time."

Shaking her head Victoria sighed and continued. "So foolish of me to drink, especially after taking those pills. If only I could go back and change that evening." She looked out the window.

"Victoria, I wish we could change our past mistakes. But we can learn from them and go on with life," Beth responded.

Tears filled Victoria's eyes. "It was awful."

Beth handed her a tissue. "Perhaps it's better if you rest."

"No! I've got to tell someone. You'll believe me. I know you will."

"All right then, go on."

"I remember every detail. It started to rain. A knock on the front door. The vicar said he didn't have an umbrella and could he come in until the rain stopped. He made himself a drink and he sat on the divan next to me.

I talked about how my friends had deserted me after my husband's death. I cried and cried. He put his arms around me, I thought to comfort me. Then all of a sudden he was kissing me."

Beth gasped. "O no! What did you do?"

"I told him to leave immediately or I would call the constable. The next morning I found his umbrella on the side of the porch. I called a friend from church and told her what had happened. She wouldn't believe me. I went to see my doctor, a member of our parish and told him. He said I shouldn't mix the medication with alcohol and refused to discuss it any further."

"So what did you do?"

"A few days later I marched into the vicar's office."

"And what did he do?"

"He said he was aware I had been spreading vicious rumors. He admitted to coming by that night, but didn't come inside. Said I was overwrought with all I had gone through and obviously needed psychiatric help.

"What did you say?"

"I lost my temper! Told him I did not imagine what he did and expected an apology. That nasty man said I better not make trouble. Actually threatened me. I stormed out of his office and never saw him again."

“Victoria, that’s just awful. You’ve been through quite an ordeal, haven’t you, poor dear.”

“Oh, Beth. That’s not the end of it. That coward contacted my son. He and the doctor convinced Gavin and my daughter-in-law I was mentally ill and needed to be committed. I thought Gavin was taking me to a nice respite in the country. But here I am in this horrible place.”

A noise out in the hall interrupted the conversation. The cleaning girl came in and began to mop the floor. Victoria turned and stared at her. “Have I seen you before, young lady?”

“No, Ma’am. Just here to clean your floor.”

Turning to Beth, Victoria started to continue the conversation. She looked back at the girl. “But you look so familiar. Yes, I do know you. You’re Mary Williams’ daughter, from the village where I used to live.”

“Yes, ma’am. I am that.”

“Your mother worked at our estate. When you were very young, I remember you playing with Gavin in the nursery.”

“Yes ma’am. I told my mum you were here, but she said to leave well enough alone. Not to talk to you. And not to mention you when I went back home for a visit.”

“What did she mean by that?”

The girl started to mop the floor. “The gossip is when you were sent off, you died there. My mum said she felt sorry for you. She believed your side of the story, about the vicar and all. I had a chance to work at the vicarage with good pay after school, but she’d have none of it. ‘Don’t trust that man.’ That’s all she’d say.”

Beth and Victoria looked at one another.

“What are you doing in Holywell?” Victoria asked.

“I married a fellow from here. Got this job a few weeks ago. Good pay for around here. Was told by the old nurse that hired me not to talk to you. Every time I’d come in here, you’d be asleep.”

Finishing the floor, she looked up at Victoria when she picked up her bucket. "I'll stop by again when I get a chance."

"Thank you. I would appreciate a visit." Victoria watched as the figure from her past walked out the door.

"Can you believe it, Victoria? What a coincidence." Beth stood to leave. "I have to go on to Llandudno this afternoon. But there must be something I can do. I'll pray for you."

"I don't need prayers. I need your help!"

Looking down at Victoria's lap, Beth noticed the pill peeping out of the tissue. "Why don't I take that pill and have a druggist tell me what they're giving you."

"That's a good idea. You can't imagine how wonderful I feel without the medication. And to be able to walk again!"

"Victoria, I hope you don't mind my prying, but what was the vicar's name?"

Victoria rose out of her chair. She straightened her frail body and looked coldly out the window. "You would never believe it. You would never believe it."

Chapter Seventeen

"Is a lamp brought in to be put under a bushel,
or under a bed, and not on a stand?"
(Mark 4:21)

The nun's car purred along the rough Holywell street. A sudden red traffic light caused an abrupt stop.

"Have a nice visit with your new friend, Beth?"

"An interesting visit, to say the least. Do you know a druggist in town?"

"Oh, my dear, I hope you're not sick!"

"No, but I do need to ask a favor."

"We always get our prescriptions at the pharmacy close to St. Winifred's. It's on the way home. Pardon me for asking, but if you're not sick, why do you need a pharmacist?"

Beth took the pill out of a tissue.

"What is that for?"

"It's probably best you don't know, but do you mind stopping at the druggist?"

"Not a bit, dear."

A blaring horn behind them signaled the change of the light.

The pharmacy was a picture of days past. Displays of faded photos and antique medical paraphernalia lined the walls. The scene reminded Beth of her childhood and the free candy sticks on the counter of her village store. A balding man in a white jacket peered over his spectacles as the women entered. His face lit up when he recognized Sister Clare.

"Hope no one's sick at your place, sister."

"No. We're all quite well, except for our usual aches and pains. When winter comes again, you'll see more of us."

"How can I help you?"

"Mr. Morgan, this is my friend Elizabeth Davies from Hawthorne."

"Nice to meet you, Miss Davies."

Sister Clare nodded to Beth. Gently Beth unwrapped the pill and handed it to Mr. Morgan.

"Can you identify this medication?"

His eyes narrowed as he looked up at Beth and then to Sister Clare. Turning slowly he took a few steps to a side counter. He flipped through the pages of a thick dogged-eared book. Mr. Morgan stopped and pointed with an aged finger.

"Just as I thought. Dalmane, but wanted to make sure." He turned to Beth. "Having trouble sleeping, young lady? This will put you out for quite some time. Don't believe in anything this strong, but if you've got doctor's orders, I've got a small supply on hand."

"No, sir, it's not for me. Is it habit forming?"

"Can be. But I don't think it's usually given for any long period of time."

"What about side effects?"

"Well, you sleep. That's what it's for."

"And if a person were to take one at night and one in the morning?"

"Well, young lady, you just wouldn't do such a thing. They're too strong for that. Why you'd be sleeping all the time. Could ruin your body over a period of time.

Handing the pill to Beth, Mr. Morgan looked at her. "Tell your friend that prayer and not pills is a better way to get a good night's sleep."

With a smile the nun replied, "Why Mr. Morgan, what a wonderful thing to say."

"Excuse me," Beth said. She turned and walked out the door, leaving Mr. Morgan and Sister Clare at the counter.

She leaned against the building, oblivious to the passing pedestrians, staring at the pill in her hand. *Now what am I to do. Throw it away? Why did I ever talk to Victoria in the first place.*

Sister Clare came out. "Doesn't sound too good for Victoria, now does it."

"How did you know it was Victoria's pill?"

"As they say, I wasn't born yesterday. But I wouldn't mind being a few years younger. I have one quick errand and then you can help with lunch at St. Winefride's."

Beth welcomed the idea. *Anything to get my mind off Victoria. After lunch I'll be on my way to Llandudno.*

St. Winifred's dining room bustled with a large group of tourists who had stopped to visit the well. The Celtic Pilgrimage Institute was a frequent visitor to the site. St. Asapf, Wales' smallest cathedral, had been their morning stop.

Their tour guide stood. "Finish dessert. Almost time to visit the well and walk down to Basingwerk Abbey. The bus will pick us and we'll return here for afternoon tea."

Beth stood by the kitchen door waiting to clear the tables. The guide walked over to her.

"You're new around here," he said.

"Yes," Beth said.

"Clive Browning from Bristol."

"Elizabeth Davies from Hawthorne."

"You don't look like the nun type."

"And what does the nun type look like?"

"Sorry if I've offended you."

Beth smiled. She observed his wrinkled shirt, tie and tweed jacket with elbow patches. His dark hair hadn't seen a barber in quite some time. Strands touched the top of his horn rim glasses. He held the usual tour guide equipment, a black umbrella.

"And you don't look like the tour guide type I see in Chester."

"I'm a professor at Bristol University. The Reformation, my specialty. I lead about four tours a summer. Rather enjoy the Americans."

"Are they usually this old?"

"No, my last group was teenagers with two counselors. They snuck out to a pub late at night."

"Did you have to go looking for them?"

"I knew exactly where they were. They were checking it out on the historical tour that afternoon. At least with this group I get eight hours sleep a night."

He tilted his head and looked at Beth. "And now, tell me about your job description."

"Just out of Oxford and on my way to Llandudno to help my grandmother with her B and B for the summer."

"And after that?"

Beth looked out a nearby window. "I'm engaged."

"Ah, the perfect life," he said. "Settle down and have a bunch of kids."

Beth shrugged. "Perhaps."

"And your main interest at Oxford?"

"Theology."

He smiled and nodded his head. "I perceive a restless soul at work."

An older woman in an aqua blue jogging suit and Reebok tennis shoes walked up to them. "Mr. Browning, I believe our group is ready."

With a tap, tap, tap, of his umbrella, the group quickly filed out of the dining area.

Beth started to clear the tables. Sister Clare approached.

"Come with me to the chapel. We need to talk and that's the only quiet place around here. The others can finish the dishes."

Sister Clare led Beth down the hallway to the chapel door. They entered the dimly lit room. Chairs lined the wall on three sides. A realistic crucifix hung above a simple wooden altar. Fresh flowers in vases adorned either side, giving color to the room. A votive candle hung above a wooden tabernacle, signaling the presence of the Blessed Sacrament.

Beth felt a peace as soon as she sat down and looked at the burning candle. She tried to remember the scripture that had something to do with not hiding your light under a basket.

The two sat in silence for some time. Beth thought about the scripture, focusing on the flame.

"Beth! Beth!"

Sister Clare's voice startled her.

"What are you going to do about Victoria?"

"I thought we came here to pray."

"Amen," the nun said. "Beth, this woman needs help. I think there's a reason she's entered your life. We can go back this afternoon and perhaps find out more. And with this being Tuesday, we don't expect many over night guests."

"Tuesday, Sister? That's the day the mysterious priest comes to visit her. What time is it?"

"1:30. And the nice nurse will be on duty till 3.00. I'd be glad to help. In a way, it's kind of exciting. Like being a detective."

"Sister Clare! You're certainly not acting like a nun."

"Yes, I know," she smiled.

Precisely at two o'clock Beth and Sister Clare entered the nursing home. They brought two generous servings of chocolate cake. Miss Wimple sat at the front desk.

"Surprised to see you two back so soon."

"I forgot something for Sister Gertrude this morning. So careless of me." Beth glanced behind the nun and saw her fingers crossed.

Sister Gertrude's door was opened, but Victoria's was closed. The nun was asleep.

"Beth, I'll sit here by her bed." Sister Clare nodded to a chair by the door. "You sit over there so you can see when her visitor comes out."

They sat in silence for about five minutes. Then slowly the door across the hall opened. Beth stood.

"I'll be back again next week, Victoria. May God be with you."

The tall lanky man turned as Beth came out into the hall. His eyes widened.

"I beg your pardon. You startled me."

Beth said nothing. He turned and walked quickly away. Beth thought there was something vaguely familiar about him. She judged his age as about sixty. His brownish unkempt hair with flecks of white reached over his ears. Shabby threadbare clothes hung loosely on his thin frame. Why would a minister of the Church of England be dressed in such a fashion?

Beth knocked on the door, but no response. Slowly Beth entered the room and found Victoria in bed.

"Oh Beth. It's you. I guess I'm a little tired, even without the pills. Were you able to find out anything about my medication?"

"Yes, it's called Dalmane. Has the same effect as a sleeping pill. If you can manage not to take any, at least during the day, perhaps you can get your strength back."

"I washed it down the drain this morning. I was afraid they would find it in the trash."

"Good idea."

Beth walked to the window and stared at the smoke gray building backing up to the nursing home.

"I must leave for Llandudno, Victoria. But I'll keep in touch. And Sister Gertrude across the hall can keep you company." Beth crossed the room and took hold of Victoria's hand as she lay in bed. "Cheerio for now."

Victoria held tightly to Beth's hand, looking intently into her eyes. "I know you can help me. You're the only one who can."

Without a word, Beth turned and left the room. Sister Clare was waiting in the hall with a serving of chocolate cake from St. Winifred's kitchen.

"Come, Beth. I have a plan. Just follow my lead."

Miss Wimple was sitting at the front desk working on patients' charts.

"Miss Wimple, I brought you some cake. Thought you might need a break. Beth and I can watch the desk and answer the phone."

"How very kind. That would be lovely. I'll be down the hall in the kitchen and have a cup of tea, too."

With cake in hand, Miss Wimple exited the desk as the two visitors took their positions.

"All right, Beth, go ahead."

"And what?"

"Get Victoria's file. Find out what you can."

"I can't do that. It's against the law."

"It may be against the law what they're doing to that unfortunate woman. I'll turn on this copy machine."

Shaking her head, Beth looked at the nun, then turned to the filing cabinet. She found Victoria's file and pulled it out. The top sheet had names, addresses and phone numbers. Taking no time to read, she placed it in the copy machine. Next, sheets of medical history and daily routines.

"That should do it." She placed the file back in the proper place. Folding the papers, Beth handed them to Sister Clare who put them in her pocket.

They heard Miss Wimple coming down the hall.

"What a welcome break. The cake was delicious. Any calls or visitors?"

"Been quiet as a church mouse," said Sister Clare.

Miss Wimple came behind the counter and noticed the copy machine. "My goodness, I know I didn't turn this on."

With a sweet smile, Sister Clare replied, "Oh, I hope you don't mind. I needed to copy a dear little prayer. Our machine at St. Winifred's is on the blink. I'll be glad to pay."

"Not at all. And thanks ever so for my tea break."

As soon as the door closed behind them, Beth spoke, "Sister Clare! I can't believe you're so sneaky. And you lied to Miss Wimple."

“You think just because I’m a nun, I don’t have any faults? And besides, sometimes there’s a need for action. Little white lies don’t count too much. I’ll go to confession. Now let’s have a look at those papers.”

Unfolding the papers, the sister began reading. “Listed as next of kin, her son, Gavin. Permanent home in London, office in Paris, and a cottage in south Wales. No private physician, only the one assigned to the facility. Underlined in red – no visitors. Should not associate with other patients. Medical condition listed as suicidal, schizophrenic, not able to cope with reality. Treatment listed is Dalmane every twelve hours.”

The nun sorted through the remaining papers. “Not much else here. Just routine stuff. This certainly doesn’t add up with Victoria’s story.”

Sister Clare started the car. “Let’s go back and have tea before you leave for Llandudno.”

Not a word was spoken about Victoria’s situation as the two shared a pot of tea and scones at St. Winefride’s.

As Beth approached her car, Manna raised her head from the front seat and barked. “All right, girl, one last run and we’ll be on our way.” Beth and Manna walked a short distance down a nearby path before returning to the car. Beth started the engine.

“Beth,” yelled Sister Clare coming out the front door. She came over to the car. “I’m so glad you haven’t left yet. What are you going to do?”

“I’m going on to Llandudno.”

“No. I mean about Victoria?”

“Nothing I can do. Perhaps you and Sister Gertrude can keep an eye on her. Thanks so much. I’ll ring up next time I’m coming this way.”

“Go with God, my dear. And listen to what Our Lord has in mind.”

Chapter Eighteen

"Judge not lest you be judged."

Mist flowed in from the sea as Beth approached Llandudno. She turned down Moystyn Street, gazing at the familiar sights of shops, pubs and eating establishments. As she approached the B & B, she noticed her grandmother's well-kept flowers on the large patio in front of the house. The tables and chairs were in need of paint. That's what Grandfather used to do, she remembered. Her eyes filled with tears.

She parked on the side street and got out. Beth opened the old wooden gate and heard the familiar squeak as she entered the side yard. Grandmum's smiling face greeted her from the kitchen window. Mrs. Hughes came out and gave Beth a hug.

"Dear child. I was at the end of my tether. I thought you would never get here."

"Sorry, Grandmum. I should have called. I got delayed at St. Winefride's." For a moment she thought of Victoria.

"Come, Beth. Get yourself settled in. Supper's almost ready. Not too many guests tonight, but you never know when someone might happen by. And just where is that big friend of yours?"

"She's out in the car. Had a good run on the way up."

They went to the car and Beth opened the door. Manna almost knocked down her grandmother.

"My goodness, she's twice the size! But I must admit, I've never seen such a handsome dog in all my life."

Beth beamed. She carried her suitcases while her grandmother brought her violin.

"Adam fixed the fence for me yesterday. Some rotten boards were 'bout to give way. For sure they wouldn't hold Manna in."

"Who's Adam?"

"Nice young man. May stay for the summer if he can find enough work."

"Find work? Is he some sort of bum? How did you find him?"

"I was out front watering my plants and the cutest little mutt came up the steps. Started licking my leg. Then here comes Adam round the corner. 'Scrappy,' he says, 'leave that lady alone.' He's looking for work. Can do anything. So I mention the fence and he fixed it in no time."

"Where's he staying? In his car?"

Laughing, Mrs. Hughes responded, "Now, Beth, the good book says judge not. He has a place at Dolwen Guest House. Going to do some work for them, too."

"Now be careful. You can't be too cautious when it comes to strangers."

Beth left Manna in the yard and went downstairs with her suitcases. The feeling of going back in time surrounded her as she stepped into the room of her childhood. A single bed with a patched flowered cover occupied one corner. Beth put down her belongings and turned on the familiar pink ceramic lamp with faded azure shade. Shelves lined one wall with an assortment of old dolls, toys, and children's books.

She struggled with the drawers of the old chest. *I wager Adam can't fix these.*"

After supper Beth joined her grandmother in the parlor. She chose the old rocker covered with fake leopard fur on the back and arm rests. As a child she often sat on the matching stool in front of the brown and white tile fireplace playing with her dolls. A gold-framed mirror above the mantle reached to the ceiling.

Her grandmother sat in a comfy armchair by the bay window overlooking the street. She turned on a small lamp above a picture of her husband taken a few weeks before his death.

Beth looked up at the old chandelier holding light bulbs meant to resemble the original candles. Mrs. Hughes smiled as she watched her granddaughter examine the small tables in the room with antique lamps, statues and faded family pictures. The current magazines on the table in front of the settee looked out of place in the Victorian setting.

"Oh, Grandmum, just as it's always been. Never, never change this room. It's perfect. Just perfect."

Beth enjoyed the interesting stories about some recent guests. She noticed the added wrinkles in her grandmother's face and stooped shoulders. Snow-white hair surrounded youthful eyes. Beth loved her dearly and the grand old Victorian house. She had often thought of taking it over when her grandmother could no longer handle the work. Small glasses of sherry concluded the evening.

Back in her room Beth moved aside the childhood books and unpacked her well-worn Bible, a journal, a prayer book and several novels by her favorite author, Bala Foresight.

That should do it, she thought. Grandmum has all the old classics and the Llandudno library is adequate.

Beth settled in bed with her Bible. In only a few moments she fell asleep, with the book in her lap.

Manna's barking from the yard woke Beth. The sun had been up for some time. Surprised by the lateness of the morning, she quickly dressed and went to the kitchen. Marie, a woman who worked for her grandmother, was cleaning the last of the breakfast dishes. The smell of fried bacon lingered in the air.

"Good morning, miss. Have a good rest? Your grandmother said to let you sleep."

"I can't believe I slept this late. I must have been exhausted."

"Kept your breakfast warm. It's in the oven. And the tea's still warm."

"Any coffee, Marie?"

"Oh, yes. We have it mostly for the Americans. And our own countrymen are drinking that disgusting stuff. There's some over there," she said, nodding toward a small table in the corner.

Beth ate slowly, enjoying the breakfast. Bacon, eggs and tomatoes filled her plate. Her grandmother's homemade blackberry jam and bread melted in her mouth.

"Your grandmother's out on errands and a lunch at the church. Won't be back till afternoon. Not much work today. She said for you to take the day off. And oh yes, she fed that monster in the backyard."

"Thanks, Marie. Manna and I will hike up The Orme. Probably stay up for most of the day. After that breakfast, I won't need to eat till supper."

Out the gate, turning left, Beth and Manna started up Church Walks, passing the Victoria Tram Station. She noticed a new sign pointing to Haulfre Gardens. Before the tea house the first 'Summit Trail' waymarker directed Beth up the trail leading to the top of the mountain. After walking the steep path a short distance, she could feel her leg muscles stretching out.

"Didn't realize I was in such bad shape, Manna. Wager I'll be in better condition by the time I leave here with hikes and going up and down all those stairs. Too much studying and practice at Oxford."

Manna bounded ahead. Rounding a curve in the path the dog came nose-to-nose with a large red fox. Manna gave chase until Beth summoned her back with a sharp whistle.

"Good dog," Beth said as she patted her head.

A large jay squawked loudly at the intruders on his property. They climbed higher, leaving most of the trees behind. Enjoying the wind currents of the Great Orme, buzzards danced gracefully overhead. Quite a contrast to the feathered garbage collectors when they're busy at mealtime, Beth thought. As she climbed the familiar path, she felt at home on her mountain once again.

Chapter Nineteen

"Do not come near; put off your shoes from your feet, for the place on which you are standing is holy ground."
(Exodus 3:5)

The simple stone structure of St. Tudno's Church had stood on the wind-swept mountain for centuries. Memories of times past flooded Beth's thoughts.

It was the early summer of her twelfth year, while attending a service at St. Tudno's, she met Robin Llywelyn, a girl her own age. Their friendship was one of those once in a lifetime experiences, sharing secrets and inner thoughts.

Beth would never forget one incidence. She knew she could tell Robin and no one else. Others would laugh at her, call her foolish. It happened a few days before she met Robin.

Beth's family had hiked up on the Orme for a picnic. She wandered off toward St. Tudno's Church. Tired and hot from walking, she went inside to rest. No one was there, so she took off her shoes and socks and walked on the cold ancient stones. She opened a Bible that lay on one of the benches. She read the scripture, "Take off thy shoes. Thee are standing on holy ground."

She slammed the book shut and looked around to be sure no one was watching her. Then slowly she opened it again with eyes closed. Pointing to a page, she opened her eyes and read a verse from psalm 32. "I will instruct you and teach you in the way that you should go; I will guide you with my eye."

Beth grabbed her socks and shoes and ran out of the church into the bright sunlight. Beth recalled looking out to sea. A stunning rainbow spanned the horizon.

She told Robin every detail of that day. Remembering Robin's words always brought a smile to her face. "Do you think God is calling you to be a minister?"

They swore everlasting friendship until the end of their lives. That winter they wrote every week. Beth had saved the childhood correspondence with scrawny misspelled words all these years.

Topping the summit, Beth saw the car park contained no vehicles. She looked forward to entering the familiar surroundings of this little church, perched high upon the great rock of Llandudno. It had long been an emblem in stone to the witness of men to the Faith, first brought by Tudno, of Cyngrawdr. Beth often walked the top of the Great Orme and envisioned Tudno and his fellow monks converting the ancient pagan worshipers to Christianity. Llandudno, Church of Tudno.

"You stay outside, Manna. Perhaps you'll find one of your furry or feathered friends to chase."

Beth opened the creaking door. A man sat in the front pew facing the altar. She quietly took a place in the back. His sandy brown hair was in need of a barber. A tattered beige shirt covered his muscular shoulders. *Must be a worker from the mine.*

He sat there for a long time. Finally he got up to leave. Beth kept her head down as though in prayer. She could feel his eyes on her as he walked by. One of his well-worn work boots was laced with a string instead of a shoelace.

Yes, she thought, a worker from the mine. Outward appearance can tell a lot about a person. Beth took her small Bible out of a bag and read scripture for a while.

Going back outside to check on Manna, she saw the man walking through the graveyard, stopping occasionally at some of the oldest tombstones. She watched as he continued toward the path leading down to the ocean road.

Beth glanced out to the sea and saw a dark cloud approaching. The wind picked up. A few stubby trees and shrubs held by meager dirt and rock swayed in a distorted dance.

She turned toward the man and saw Manna standing by his side. She called and the dog quickly responded. The rain started and they went into the church to seek shelter. It was comforting inside listening to the water tapping on the roof. Manna curled up and slept. Beth wondered about the man out in the weather. He must have been drenched, unless someone happened along to give him a ride back to town or to the mine.

The rain stopped as quickly as it had started. Beth and Manna ventured out of the church. The sun came out to shine on the newly washed mountain. Even the usual gloomy tombstones glimmered with fresh drops in the afternoon sun. Birds circled overhead. A vivid rainbow dipped into the ocean.

"Come on, girl. Let's see if we can find the wild goats before we start down."

Time on the Great Orme passed quickly, as it always did, when Beth was in her element. She felt more alive and closer to her Creator when out in nature.

She walked slowly down the mountain pacing her steps with a prayer. Taking a deep breath, "Breathe in, Holy Spirit." As she released the air, she said the words, "Breathe out, Holy Spirit," repeating the words over and over as the familiar peaceful presence flowed through her body.

Looking to the west, she noticed how far the sun had advanced along the now cloudless sky. "We better get back, girl, before Grandmum sends the police up here after us."

She started down the footpath with Manna close by. Arriving at the tram tracks, Beth crossed over and decided to take one quick detour before going on. Turning right on Cromlech Road, she came to the dead end and climbed over the stile into the field. The structures of upright stones were planted deeply in the earth. They had survived since 2,500 B.C. Beth wondered if the stories were true that on All Hallow's Eve a gathering of Druids surround this prehistoric burial tomb for an ancient ceremony. She remembered asking her grandmother.

"Best not to ask such questions. Leave well enough alone."

And she remembered her response.

"Leave well enough alone! What's so well about a bunch of weirdoes having a pagan ceremony on the Great Orme? St. Tudno certainly wouldn't appreciate such behavior."

Her grandmother laughed and went on with her cooking.

Beth and Manna arrived back at the B and B.

"Beth, where have you been? I was worried when I saw the storm up on the Orme."

"We were at the church and waited there. Had a good day? Anything I can do to help?"

"We don't have any new guests for the evening. The Men's Chorus is singing at the Methodist Church tonight. Would you like to go?"

"Oh, yes, I'd love to."

"We'll have an early dinner and a walk along the promenade before the program, if that's all right with you, Beth."

"Splendid. I'll go freshen up and get ready."

Beth was glad to be back in her room. *Now what to wear?* She went over to the chest and pulled hard on the drawer. To her surprise, the whole drawer slid quickly out, she lost her balance, and fell on the floor with the drawer on top of her. The contents fell out and were strewn about the room.

"Help! Grandmum."

Her grandmother stood in the doorway, laughing at the sight.

"I don't see what's so funny. I could have hurt myself. Whatever happened to make that drawer come out like that?"

"I'm sorry, dear. I forgot to tell you. Adam came by this afternoon and fixed it. Are you all right?"

"Yes, I'm fine." Beth stood, putting her clothes back in the chest. She tried the other drawers and they slid in and out smoothly. Her grandmother watched.

"Well, Beth. What do you think? Adam did a fine job, didn't he? And he fixed my kitchen cabinets, too. He's quite handy to have around."

"I can't believe you let a complete stranger come in my room. You know I have personal things in here."

"Now, Beth. It might be a little difficult to fix those drawers if one were not allowed to open them, don't you think?"

"You're just too trusting. Does this Adam person have references?"

"Yes, Beth, he certainly does. His little dog, Scrappy. I'm a good judge of character. If a person doesn't like dogs and cats, then there's something wrong with them. That's all the reference I need. Now change your clothes. Supper's almost ready and we'll have time for a good walk before the program."

Intermission arrived much too soon for Beth's ears. The sonorous sounds of the Llanddulas Choir filled the packed sanctuary of the church. She escorted her grandmother down the balcony stairs and excused herself for some fresh air outside, leaving Her grandmother to visit with friends. She had had enough small talk on their walk about town before the concert.

Humming the tune of *Myfanwy*, the concert opener, she strolled along several blocks of Llandudno, glancing past lace curtains into the parlors of Victorian homes, where families gathered for after supper routines. A father on a red velvet settee read to attentive children on either side. An elderly couple sat in high back chairs sharing a floor lamp as they read a newspaper. A family surrounded their telly with sounds of laughter. Beth stopped for a moment to see if she recognized the show. *Keeping Up Appearances*. One of her favorites.

Arriving back at the concert, Beth could hear the chorus already singing. She slipped in the back and up the stairs. She and her grandmother had two seats on the aisle. She took her place as the audience applauded the first number after intermission.

"Beth! You should have stayed with me. Adam is here. He's sitting down stairs. I knew he was a man of culture. We'll find him after the program's over so you can meet him."

To Beth's relief, Adam was nowhere to be found. After returning home, Beth decided to take Manna for a walk along the beach. The lamps along the pier reaching out to the ocean reflected off the water, giving a magical feel to the milieu. Taking her shoes off, Beth walked slowly, the sand oozing between her toes. Manna pranced back and forth as the water swayed, attacking her paws.

Beth thought she was alone on the beach until she saw a figure some distance away coming toward her.

She called Manna and turned toward the promenade and the safety of the busy street and lights, but Manna didn't come. She ran over to the man on the beach.

"Come, Manna," Beth shouted, as she continued on her way. She stopped on the sidewalk and turned to see the man looking up at her. His frame was outlined against the dark ocean with the moonlight shining behind him. He waved, turned, and walked on down the beach.

Chapter Twenty

"For the wisdom of this world is folly with God."
(1 Corinthians 3:19)

"Beth! Get up! No sleeping late this morning! We've got work to do. Marie's not coming in. She's sick. You'll need to serve breakfast."

Beth's head was swirling and she hadn't slept well. Strange dreams all night. She couldn't remember much, except the stranger she saw the day before was in them. She lay in bed looking up at her grandmother with half-opened eyes.

"You'll have to wait until I've had my coffee before you try to communicate with me."

Shaking her head, her grandmother smiled, turned and walked out of the room. "Your coffee's ready. Now get a move on."

The day passed quickly. Beth changed beds, dusted, mopped, vacuumed, restocked tea and coffee trays, and climbed up and down four flights of stairs countless times. She didn't sit down until 3:00 in the afternoon for tea with her grandmother.

They sat at the kitchen table with hearty sandwiches and the tea tray. Beth ate her sandwich first, taking big bites. Her grandmother lifted the tea cozy off the pot and served cups of Yorkshire Tea. "Beth, thanks so much for all your help. I know you must be exhausted. Oh! I almost forgot. You have a large envelope in the mail."

Anxiously Beth asked, "Is it from Kevin? I haven't heard from him. Not even a phone call."

"No. It's from St. Winefride's. I'll get it from the parlor."

"No, you stay here. I'm almost through anyway."

Beth sat in her favorite chair with the brown envelope in her lap. Opening the seal she took out several pages, the first a short note from Sister Clare.

Dearest Beth,

Sister Gertrude and I have visited with Victoria on several occasions. In our opinion she is perfectly sane. She has written to her son and had no response. In my position, I can't get any more involved, but perhaps you can. I pray you will seek God's guidance in this matter. May the love and peace of Jesus be with you.

Faithfully yours,
Sister Clare

Putting the letter aside, Beth scanned through the copied sheets of Victoria's medical file. There must be another way to help this poor woman, she thought. There's nothing I can do. She put the papers back in the envelope as her grandmother walked in.

"Anything wrong, Beth? You have a strange look on your face. Not bad news, I hope."

"No, some news from a friend at St. Winefride's. Think I'll take Manna for a walk."

Walking down Mostyn Street, Beth and Manna passed by several shops. Manna's nose began twitching as they approached one of the local pubs known for its hearty meals. They strolled past a bookstore. Beth stopped and returned to the shop window display of a new Bala Foresight novel, *The Mystery of Laugharne.* Beth recognized the picture on the front cover, the Dylan Thomas boathouse.

She reached in her pocket and pulled out twenty pounds. Soon she was out of the shop with her new purchase in hand. The late afternoon walk along the Promenade teemed with the first summer visitors. Finding an empty bench Beth settled down for a start on her new book.

For a few moments she sat staring out to the sea. The gentle breeze lifted her hair. Herring gulls and an occasional jackdaw competed for food thrown by people on the beach. Cotton clouds decorated the sky. A small fishing boat glided effortlessly out in the water on the glassy sea. The gentle to and fro of the waves created a peaceful metronomic sound.

Beth wished Sister Clare hadn't written. She had almost managed to erase Victoria Martin from her thoughts since her arrival at Llandudno. But now the woman's distraught face was vivid in her mind. What could she do to help? A little daydreaming or reading a good book always seemed to help matters, at least temporarily.

Beth settled into reading her book. Manna ran up and down the beach, playing occasionally with other dogs along the way. The light began to dim. Beth could feel the air turning colder on her bare arms. Suddenly she realized she was not alone on the bench. She looked down on the sand to her right and saw the familiar work boots, one tied with a string. She followed the faded jeans up to a ragged plaid shirt and looked into his eyes.

"Good book?" he asked.

Beth closed the book and looked out to the water.

"Yes," she responded dryly.

"Looks like Bala Foresight's newest novel."

"Yes, it is. Have you read any of her novels?"

"Quite a few."

Beth turned and looked at the stranger. His auburn hair had golden highlights placed by too much sun. The tan face with prominent cheekbones, deep-set perceptive eyes and strong mouth caused Beth to stare. There was a ruggedness and at the same time a gentleness. The stranger smiled at her. She turned away.

"Sorry to bother you," he said.

"No bother. I was just leaving. Now where is that dog?"

Laughing, the man replied, "She's behind the bench, asleep. Mind if I walk with you?"

"If you like," she said.

As they stood Beth, was surprised to discover that he was well over six feet. They walked along the beach in silence with Manna between them. Beth felt uncomfortable. She would be glad when they reached the street. He certainly wasn't going to walk her home. She would see to that. But he was quite handsome in a rough sort of way.

"What's your dog's name?"

"Manna."

"Interesting name for a dog."

"Yes, it is."

"Have you read the Foresight book that was set in Paris?" he asked.

"Yes, she's my favorite author."

"Personally, I think she's rather good, but sometimes a little too sentimental. Like that scene at the top of the Eiffel tower with the two lovers."

"I think that was the best part of the book. It was so real."

"Well, maybe it's a girl thing."

Reaching the street, Beth faced toward the stranger and responded indignantly, "Well, if more of you men would try to understand about love and romance, this would be a much better world." She turned and walked down the street with Manna in tow.

Chapter Twenty-One

"For we are his workmanship, created in Christ Jesus
for good works, which God prepared beforehand,
that we should walk in them."

(Ephesians 2:10)

Marie called on Thursday and said she had a virus. Grandmum woke Beth early every morning to serve breakfast, clean rooms, shop, and run errands. By the time the guests were settled in, the day was almost gone. Beth often glanced up at the Great Orme, longing for the steep rocky hillside, feeling the fresh ocean wind dance across her face. She daydreamed of the solitude of St. Tudno's church, wondering if the stranger had ventured into the church again. The man kept creeping into her thoughts and she enjoyed fantasizing about him. Perhaps he was secret agent or a spy hiding out in Llandudno.

He resembled one of Bala Foresight's characters in one of her earliest books. Beth remembered every detail of the plot. A mysterious stranger came to a small town in France. He was the illegitimate son of the mayor, who never knew of his existence. When the mayor had a serious accident, the stranger, a skilled surgeon, saved his father's life. After confessing his true identity, he gave the mayor a letter from his mother written before she died.

One evening after supper Beth and Manna ventured out to the long pier. The relentless waves beat against the

Great Orme cliffs on her left. Turning to her right she watched the gentle rolling waves of Llandudno Bay. Quite a contrast, she thought. Like life.

She looked back at the water pounding the cliffs and spoke, "The other side of my life. A minister? An uncertain life." She sighed. "And Victoria. What to do about Victoria."

Taking a deep breath cleared her head. Manna nudged her leg. "Yes, girl, we'll go down to the beach for your run in a few minutes."

They walked along, reaching the deserted children's carousel. Beth closed her eyes and thought back to those childhood summer days of picnics and sand castles, riding the white horse with the golden mane and her friend, Alice, on the black horse. She hummed the carousel tune from those happy years.

Opening her eyes, she was startled to see a man standing a few yards away. The lights of Llandudno were behind him shadowing his face. Manna barked and then wagged her tail.

"Stay," Beth commanded. The white mass of fur stood attentively at her side. The man turned and walked away without saying a word. Strange, she thought. I'm sure that's the man I talked to the other afternoon.

The next morning Beth woke to the sound of a bird singing outside her window. The sun was well on his way to warming her side of the planet.

"Brother Sun, Sister Moon." she said, thinking of the words of St. Francis. "Make me an instrument of Thy peace."

After dressing she hurried to the kitchen where she discovered the familiar sight of Marie standing in front of the stove. Her shabby housedress was partly hidden by one of Mrs. Hughes' aprons. Turning around she smiled.

"Have a good sleep, Miss Beth?"

"Much better than usual. I slept heavy all night."

"Haven't been sleeping good around here?" Marie asked.

"Too much on my mind, I guess. Can I help with breakfast?"

"No, some of the guests have already left. There's one couple waiting for the full English breakfast. You sit and drink your coffee. That coffee's what's hurting your sleep. Our Welsh stomachs don't take kindly to it. Herb tea is what you need. I'll bring some tomorrow."

"That's very kind of you, Marie, but I may not drink it. How about you? Feeling better? We missed you around here."

"I bet you did. Your grandmother told me about the work you did. I thank you for it. Won't be so much for me to do today. I am feeling better, but still a little tired."

Marie returned to her cooking while Beth sipped her coffee and started eating a currant scone. After a few minutes, Marie turned around and stared at Beth.

"Man trouble? Is that what's bothering you? You're too young for such foolishness."

"Oh no, I've a wonderful boyfriend back in Hawthorne. In fact he's the son of Lord and Lady Gately. We plan to be married," Beth responded proudly.

"Well, Miss hoity-toity! Good for you!"

The women laughed. Beth almost choked on her full mouth of scone and coffee.

"What's going on in my kitchen?" Grandmum shouted while coming down the stairs. She came in the kitchen with the morning mail. "Someone's got a letter from her sweetheart."

Beth read the letter from Kevin and after studying an enclosed photo, she handed it to her grandmother.

"Well, that's a fine looking young man standing in front of the Eiffel Tower, but who's that shriveled old prune with him?"

"That's Lady Gately, Kevin's mother."

"My goodness! If she were to smile I believe her face might crack."

Mrs. Hughes handed the picture to Marie. "And this might be your mother-in-law?"

"She's not as bad as all that," Beth said.

"Is your good man coming to see you?"

"Not sure. As usual his mother has him scheduled for social obligations, as she calls it. But he's back in Hawthorne by now and will probably call sometime today. Says he may come over for a day."

"That would be nice," said Grandmum. "I'd love to meet him." She put her hand on Beth's shoulder. "You look a little more rested this morning. I've been a little worried about you."

"I did sleep much better last night. Tried something a little different and it worked."

Marie finished cooking the breakfast and started to take the tray up to the breakfast room. She turned to Beth. "I hope you're not taking those sleeping pills. I read how your generation just lives from one pill to the other."

"No, Marie. I tried something much more radical."

"And just what might that be?"

"Prayer."

Marie turned and left the room.

"Well," said Grandmum. "That's the first time I've seen her at a loss for words and I've known her many a year. Prayer, Beth?"

"Yes, prayer. It's amazing how often I forget to pray. I mean really pray."

"What do you mean, really pray?"

"I do my prayers and Bible reading every morning and evening. But I've been going through the motions. Saying words but thinking of everything but the words."

"That's understandable, dear. After spending all that time at school, it's no wonder you're all prayed out."

Beth smiled at her grandmother's way with words. "All prayed out. That's a good way to put it. At school I was surrounded by grand buildings, sacred texts, religious art, and learned theologians. But the times I felt spiritual was when I got out of Oxford."

Grandmum got up, poured another cup of tea and more coffee for Beth, and then sat back down. "You've always loved the country, even as a child."

"Grandmum, do you think God gets tired of all the church doings?"

"I don't know, dear. Sometimes I do."

"You should see how stressed out everyone is if the bishop or some other church dignitary is coming. They wouldn't get that excited if Jesus himself came to call. In fact, they would send him off to the Salvation Army."

"My goodness, Beth! Best you not speak your mind around certain people, or you'll never be a minister."

"You know, Grandmum, I'm not sure that's the direction I'm going. If Kevin and I get married, it wouldn't make any sense anyway."

"What do you mean, if? I thought it's definite. Your mother told me not long ago you two were about ready to set a date."

"Well, not exactly. I want to be married in my parish church with my vicar performing the ceremony. His mother insists on St. Paul's Cathedral with the Bishop of London performing the ceremony, and a fancy reception, of course."

"Best for you two to elope. Mark my words, Beth, if this woman gets her way with this, she'll get her way with the rest of your life. You've got good stubborn Welsh blood flowing through your veins. Remember that!"

"Yes, Grandmum. Stubborn Welsh blood."

"Tell me about the prayer that put you to sleep last night. I may need it sometime."

"First I sang "Nos Da."

"Aye, yes. Nos Da. Good Night. I remember singing that to you when you were just a wee one."

Beth's grandmother began singing the tender song of evening time. "To them who sails the ocean deep, come favoring winds and peaceful sleep. And may the billows gently flow to rock her cradle as they go."

"I remember, too, Grandmum."

"You couldn't. You were just a baby."

"But I do. I remember the sound of your singing."

Grandmum beamed. "Well, isn't that something. And the prayer?"

"I couldn't sleep for several nights. I've been worried about some things. Last night I got up and wrote down the concerns on paper. Then prayed to God His will and not mine be done in each of the situations."

"Good, Elizabeth. We can look back on problems that took a lot of worry time. When the air clears, we're given a different view, and then we usually find something else to worry about."

Grandmum took Beth's hand. "And so then you were able to get some sleep?"

"I got back in bed and started saying the Lord's Prayer, pausing after each phrase. I was sound asleep before I got to the amen. Didn't wake up until I heard that feathered alarm clock singing this morning."

"Yes, he stays around here most of the time. I always throw him breadcrumbs after breakfast. Any plans for today? Marie and I can take care of things around here."

"Manna and I will go up on the Orme."

"That sounds grand. Sorry you won't be here though. Adam is coming this afternoon to redo the number 5 bathroom. He did such a good job on number 3. Such a nice young man."

"Yes, Grandmum," Beth responded with disinterest.

"Before you venture off for the day, I want to talk to you about something. Do you remember your aunt, uncle and cousin down in Laugharne?"

"Yes. I remember Ann quite well. Especially the Christmas when we all came here, one of the best holidays ever. And one summer we spent a week together, except that wasn't as much fun."

"Now, Beth, it seems to me that you two girls kept getting into trouble that week. I had never had any problems with either one of you before. You both were to stay for two weeks, but I called your parents after one week.

Beth responded in a playful sarcastic tone. "Well, it wasn't my fault."

"Just whose fault was it? The devil?"

"No, actually it was Ann. You remember Alice and I were the best of friends. We did everything together. Then Ann came to town. She didn't like Alice at all. I think she was jealous."

"Beth, you can't blame her. She was looking forward to being with you, especially after the good times you two had here at Christmas."

"Ann kept calling her Alice in Wonderland. My friend was sick and tired of hearing the Alice stories. She could care less that Alice Liddell was Lewis Carroll's inspiration. I remember her telling me her life was more like Alice in Horrorland."

"My goodness! I had no idea."

"That was obvious. You had the grand idea of taking us to tea and the Alice in Wonderland shop one afternoon."

"I remember that, Elizabeth. Thought it was a grand idea. Perfect for three little girls. Interesting how we adults think we understand children."

"And how children think they understand adults. When I visit old folks in nursing homes, the contented ones are to me more like unspoiled children."

"What do you mean by that?"

"They're content with the way things are. Not necessarily their physical condition, but a way they view life. One woman told me she would much rather have a visit from a child than an adult."

"Why would she say such a thing?"

'Because,' she said, 'I'm getting ready to go to heaven and children just came from there. We're kindred spirits."

Mrs. Hughes put her chin on her hand and looked out a window. "I never thought of it that way. But I do know the only thing for sure in life is death."

"Yes, Grandmum, but not in a negative way. I like the word transformation. Our physical body dies, but our spiritual body continues on."

Beth got up, cleared the table and started doing the dishes while her grandmother sat at the table sipping her tea. "My vicar asked me to visit a lady in the hospital last month and she told me quite a story. The woman remembered having severe pain. All of a sudden the pain was gone. Her body felt like it was floating and she saw relatives and friends who had died. Moving her hands about up in the air, she described a fluttering of light around her. When the woman felt something warm on her forehead, she opened her eyes and there stood the vicar, anointing her with oil."

"My goodness, Beth. Sounds like she died and came back to life."

"Who came back to life?" asked Marie as she entered the kitchen with a tray of dirty dishes.

"Just someone Beth was telling me about. Are the Jones ready to check out?"

"Will be about half past. I'll go up and start the cleaning. Beth, you better get out of here before the prime minister puts you to work."

Beth started making a sandwich to take on her hike.

"I never did get around to why I wanted to talk to you about your relatives in Laugharne. How would you like to ride the train down to visit them?"

Turning around with a surprised look, Beth responded, "Great, I'd love to."

"I'd like to give you the trip as your birthday present. I talked with my brother last night and mentioned the possibility. He talked to Ann and she's quite agreeable. Doesn't have a job at the moment either."

"But don't you need me around here?"

"Not for the next week. Marie's sister is coming and she's going to help around here, so this is the perfect time."

"That's super! I've never been to that part of Wales. Dyfed is so different from the country here in the north. And a visit to Dylan Thomas' home. Thanks, Grandmum. But that's quite an expense. I could drive my car."

"Wouldn't you rather take the train?"

"Oh, yes."

"Then it's settled. I'll check on the schedules. Ann can pick you up in Carmarthen. Now you go on and have a good day on the Orme."

Chapter Twenty-Two

"The Lord is my strength and my song."
(Psalm 118:14)

Beth and Manna arrived back at the B and B as the sun hugged the horizon. They entered through the front door and when she turned toward the stairs leading down to the kitchen, a small brown dog came running up to her. Manna cocked her head and began sniffing the new acquaintance. The dog stood on his hind legs, stretching as tall as he could, but barely reaching above Beth's knees. Picking him up, Beth started down the stairs.

"Grandmum." she shouted. "We're home. Hope you didn't worry. This little dog is so ugly, he's cute."

Walking into the kitchen Beth was startled to see a man sitting at the kitchen table with her grandmother. For a moment the two stared at each other. Then at precisely the same time they both said, "It's you!"

Mrs. Davies looked from one to the other several times. "Well, come sit down, Beth. This is Adam, the young man I've been telling you about. Adam, this is Beth, my granddaughter. Have you two met before?"

Neither Adam nor Beth spoke.

"Well, one of you say something. I might as well be talking to these two dogs."

Beth looked down at the floor and recognized the familiar boots. Adam spoke. "So you think my dog is ugly?"

"Not really. I didn't mean it that way. Perhaps eclectic would be a better word." She put the dog down. "He's cute. What's his name?"

"Scrappy."

Beth sat down at the table across from Adam. "Where did you get him?"

"I found him in London or you might say, he found me. I was walking back to my flat late one foggy evening. Heard a whimpering sound from an alley and went to investigate. I found this little lump of wet fur barely alive. Been with me ever since."

Glancing over at Manna, Adam continued, "I'm sure my dog food bill isn't as high as yours. Where did you find such a handsome looking creature?"

Beth smiled at Adam. "That's quite a story. Perhaps another time."

"I'll be looking forward to hearing it. Perhaps over dinner tonight?"

Beth could feel her face warm. Was she blushing? Surely not. She got up from the table and went over to the sink to get a glass of water. Adam stood.

"I'd like to take you girls out to the King's Head for dinner tonight. How about it?"

Grandmum smiled. "I haven't been there since my husband died. That sounds grand. How about it Elizabeth?"

"Why don't you two go on? I'm pretty tired after that hike. And besides, I'd have to freshen up."

"Nonsense! We can go just as we are, except for my apron. It's not a dress up place. The boys from the mine go there right after work. And I'm not going if you're not going."

"O.K. I'll go. Just be a minute."

Beth retreated to her room. She sat on her bed looking out the window and thinking. *Why do I feel strange? I certainly have no interest in him. A handyman. I'll make it clear at the first opportunity I'm engaged.*

Beth changed and met her grandmother and Adam outside. Grandmum was busy examining her flowers and shrubs while Adam stood by the railing looking out to sea.

"Let's be off," Beth said.

The two women started up the sidewalk. Suddenly they realized they had left Adam behind.

"My goodness!" Grandmum exclaimed. "He's still standing there like a statue. Adam," she shouted. "Are you coming?"

He quickly turned around, startled by her voice. A sheepish grin appeared on his face as he joined the women.

"Sorry, guess I was lost in thought."

"Care to share your thoughts?" questioned Beth.

"Perhaps another time. But they might seem rather dull to such an educated young woman as yourself."

Grandmum grinned. "Now you two behave yourselves."

Smoke filled the bar area of the low-beamed pub. Animated conversations bounced about the room. Several of the occupants nodded or waved at Beth's grandmother. The bartender waved and pointed up the half flight of stairs to the back dining room. Hanging ale tankers from the low timbered ceiling intrigued Beth. Walking over to the side of the crowded room she examined one of the old photographs. Adam touched her arm.

"Now it's you who's being left behind."

After quite a discussion of the lengthy menu, each decided on a different selection. Beef and Ale Pie for Adam and Tikka Masala for Beth.

"I'll have Bangers and Mash," said Grandmum. "Just like your grandfather and I would have on a Saturday night." She looked around the walls. "Still the same old pictures. You know this is the oldest pub in Llandudno. It was right here that Edward Mostyn and his surveyor mapped out the town." She pointed, "There's his picture right over there. It was quite the seaside resort in its day."

Looking at her grandmother as she reminisced, Beth tried to picture her and her grandfather forty years ago. She remembered the family stories of their close relationship. Adam's voice brought her back to the present.

"Penny for your thoughts, Beth"

"I just hope my marriage will be half as good as my grandmother's."

"My goodness, granddaughter. What a lovely thing to say. I thank God everyday for my husband. But each relationship has a life of its own. A marriage should be forever, but there are times when we choose for the wrong reasons. There was no question with your grandfather and me. A love that was meant to be."

Tears came to her eyes. She looked away. Adam and Beth smiled at one another and changed the subject.

While they ate their bread pudding, the owner joined them at their table with his pint of Newcastle Brown ale.

"Tis a pleasure to have you in my establishment, Mrs. Hughes. And with such a fine young couple."

Beth quickly responded, "Oh, we're not a couple. I'm Mrs. Hughes' granddaughter and this is …is…a…"

"I'm a Jack of all trades, out on the town with a couple of lasses. We'll probably be up all night carousing and end up in jail by morning."

Even Beth got a chuckle out of Adam's remark, thinking about her matronly grandmother behind bars.

After arriving back at the Hughes' home, they sat in the parlor for a glass of sherry.

"Beth, I've got everything arranged for you to take the train down to Largharne."

"But, Grandmum, I forgot about Manna. I would hate for you to have to take care of her."

"Not to worry, Beth," responded Adam. I'll be in town a while longer and would be glad to come by. I go up the Orme at least every other day, so she would have a good run. And I'll take her down to the shore on the other days."

"Are you sure? She seems to like you." Beth stretched and yawned. "Excuse me, but I'm a bit tired and I have only a few pages left in a Foresight book."

"Which one are you reading?"

"The Mystery of The Druids' Circle."

Adam chuckled. "Don't you think it's a bit hokey? Borders on the supernatural a bit too much for me."

Beth stood up, folding her arms over her chest. "No, I don't. A good story often involves imagination. Some of our holy shrines were originally Druid places of worship. I find it all quite fascinating and interesting. Bala Foresight is a craftsman at bringing her stories to life. I'm glad we've got some good female writers."

"I didn't mean to upset you. I'm just a little surprised at your interest in this sort of fiction. Your grandmother told me about your theological education."

Beth looked at her grandmother and rolled her eyes. "Why is it people think that anyone who has a religious education has to be boring and stuffy? Although I must admit, most clergy are. But I know a few that aren't, like the vicar at St. John's in Chester. He's a breath of fresh air to the Church of England. We just need a few more like him."

"Like you? Are you planning on becoming a minister?" he teased.

"Not tonight!"

Turning, Beth walked out of the room. "Good night, Grandmum. Good night, Adam."

Beth heard the front door shut when Adam left. She thought of their first meeting at St. Tudno's chapel. From the conversation at dinner it was obvious he was well educated. A man at the pub came over and asked when they could play golf again. He mentioned Adam's handicap of four. Something didn't fit. Getting into bed Beth said her evening prayers, but afterward, she couldn't quit thinking about Adam.

Chapter Twenty-Three

"Let the children come to me, and do not hinder them;
for to such belongs the kingdom of heaven."
(Matt.19:14)

"Beth, your young man is on the phone," shouted Grandmum early the next morning. "Says he can call later."

"No, tell him I'll be right there." Beth sat up on the edge of the bed rubbing her eyes. She grabbed a robe, hurried to the kitchen and picked up the receiver.

"Kevin, is it really you? It's been forever. Are you back in Hawthorne?"

"Yes, tried to call last night, but no answer."

"We were out to dinner," Beth said.

"Thought I'd come over Monday for a few days."

"Oh no, I'm going on the train down to Largharne to visit relatives for the week. My grandmother has already made all the arrangements. But there's a change of trains in Chester for about an hour. Can you come in and meet me?"

"I suppose, better than nothing."

Beth listened as Kevin told about his travels in Europe. Her life sounded rather dull in comparison.

"Sorry, Beth, but I've got an appointment in Chester, so must ring off. See you in Chester for an early lunch on Monday. I've missed you so much. Love you, dear."

"Love you, too, Kevin."

As Beth got dressed for the day, she thought of their conversation. She had a slight smile on her face as she thought of the meeting in Chester and the possibilities of her future life with Kevin. *At least we'll have an hour together. This time I'll be the one leaving.*

The next few days passed quickly as Beth prepared for her trip to visit her relatives in south Wales. On Sunday morning, as usual, she went to church with her grandmother. Once a year The Church of the Holy Trinity held an annual flower festival with other Llandudno congregations displaying twenty-five biblical scenes. While Grandmum visited with friends before the service, Beth had time to enjoy the exhibit.

One scene showed an off-balanced house sinking into sand, while the house above it was built on a substantial rock looking surface. A Methodist church was responsible for this display. She thought of the combined efforts of women and men from different denominations. Barriers that separated neighbors on Sunday mornings were brought together in the visual presentations of scripture.

Beth ambled along, reading each scripture and viewing the exhibits along the side aisles of the church. One was a scene of Jesus surrounded by children and wild flowers of northern Wales. Beth stopped and stared at the presentation. All of a sudden she felt transported back in time, becoming one of those little children listening to the simple, yet profound words of The Great Teacher. *Jesus teaching me, teaching the world. The way of truth so clear, so uncomplicated.*

Beth blinked her eyes. She heard the first notes of the opening hymn. She said a silent prayer as she walked back down the aisle to join her grandmother. *Be with me as I try to walk in your Way and not mine. Amen.*

The minister made his point in the sermon after about ten minutes, but he chose to continue for fifteen more. Beth had made excellent marks in homiletics and had prepared a sermon on the same scripture.

As Grandmum and Beth left the church, the vicar invited them to lunch in the parish hall. He made a point of sitting next to Beth. Obviously Grandmum had told the minister all about her.

"Yes, your bishop and I were classmates at Cambridge. Fine churchman. Knows the liturgy like no one else. And just how do you two get along?"

"Well, sir. I haven't had much opportunity to visit with the bishop. He certainly has a lovely voice for chanting, don't you think?"

As the two women were leaving, the vicar called out, "So glad you could join us. Perhaps next time you come to town, you'll be ordained."

From the doorway Beth responded, "What a lovely invitation. I would be delighted to celebrate the Lord's Supper at the altar of Holy Trinity."

Beth turned to leave, then glanced at the vicar's wide eyes and red face.

Grandmum shook her head. "Well, Beth, you got the last word this time. But mark my words, you best be careful. He's probably calling your bishop right now."

"Sadducees and Pharisees. Some things haven't changed in over two thousand years."

Beth woke up early on Monday morning. She put on a flowered Laura Ashley dress, anticipating her lunch with Kevin. After placing her bags in the parlor, she joined her grandmother for breakfast in the kitchen.

"Thought I'd go down to the main street and get a cab to the station."

"No need for that. Adam will be here to take you."

"Adam! Why on earth did you ask him to take me?"

"He offered. Said you might have last minute instructions for Manna."

"Oh, well. It'll save me a pound or two."

Just as they finished breakfast, the front door opened.

"I'll wait up here," Adam shouted. "Came a little early. No rush."

"Nonsense," said Grandmum. "Come down. There's tea, coffee and plenty of tea cakes."

Adam walked in the kitchen, dressed in a handsome tan sports jacket, dark brown pants, well-polished shoes and white shirt.

Mrs. Hughes handed him a cup of tea. "My goodness, look at you. Off to a fancy occasion?"

"I'm going to Bangor for the day. Thought I would drop Beth at the junction on the way. Would save her at least one change of trains."

"I don't mind changing. You can give me a ride to the Llandudno station."

"No bother. And don't you look lovely this morning."

"Thank you."

Adam gulped his tea. "Ready to go?" Turning to Mrs. Hughes, "Need anything from the big city?"

"Not a thing. I'll feed Manna tonight."

"No need. I'll be back before dark. And we can have a run on the beach."

With a jovial laugh, Grandmum replied, "I'll be sure to have my running shoes on."

The back of Adam's old Ford Courier had carpentry tools, scraps of lumber and opened paint cans, but the front seats were clean and neat. The road to Llandudno Junction was crowded.

"Must be the Scottish pensioners going back up north for the week," Adam said. Your grandmother told me there's quite a lot who come for weekends."

"Apparently she told you quite a bit. But we don't know much about you, do we?" Beth said, studying the rather expensive clothes. "This must be a business trip to Bangor."

"Some business, some pleasure. I'll spend most of my time in the library. And I'm meeting some friends for lunch."

"Friends in Bangor? How did you meet them?"

"Oh, by chance."

Beth folded her arms determined to find out more about this so-called handyman.

"And where exactly do you come from?"

"Here and there."

"No, I mean, where were you born?"

"London."

"Where in London?"

"Hard to remember. I was so young at the time."

"Oh, Adam, you're so exasperating!"

"Why, thank you, Beth. That's about the nicest thing anyone's ever said to me. Say, speaking of nice, you do look jolly nice today."

"I'm meeting Kevin Gately for lunch in Chester," she responded with an air of smugness.

"Kevin Gately? Son of Lord and Lady Gately?"

"Yes, how do you know them?" she asked.

"Probably saw something in a newspaper or magazine."

"Kevin and I are engaged. We'll probably be married by this time next year."

"Um, interesting match," said Adam.

"What do you mean by that?"

"We're almost to the station. Any other instructions for Manna? I'll stop by morning and evenings. And also look in on your grandmother. Thought I'd take her out to dinner again this week."

Adam pulled up in front of the station and insisted on carrying Beth's bags onto the train. Beth settled into a window seat, looked out and saw Adam standing alone on the platform staring up at her. She stared back. Neither lifted a hand.

Chapter Twenty-Four

"Does the clay say to the one who fashions it,
'What are you making?"
(Isaiah 45:9)

Beth collected her luggage before the train arrived at Chester station and waited. She didn't want to waste a minute of her time with Kevin. It had only been a fortnight since last she saw him, but it seemed like forever. She stepped over the freshly painted *Mind the Gap* sign as she descended the train stairs.

Kevin was standing at the far end of the platform near the first class rail car. They saw one another at the same instant. Beth dropped her bags and ran to him. He held her close, kissing her several times.

"You look wonderful, dear. But where are your bags? You know you have to change trains here."

Beth turned to see a station attendant standing over her luggage examining the tags. "Those are mine. I'll be right there," she shouted.

"No need." Kevin waved to a man and nodded his head. "I've arranged for someone to put the luggage on your train with a reserved seat. That'll give us more time to visit."

"You certainly know how to spoil a girl. Isn't there a Fish 'n Chips close by?"

"We have a table waiting for us at the Queen Hotel."

"Lovely," Beth responded. "At least it's just across the street."

The old Victorian Hotel was definitely not her 'cup of tea.' Beth had dined there with Kevin's parents the year before. Lord and Lady Gately were always given the best of service.

Weaving hand in hand through the crowded station, the couple hurried across the busy Chester street in front of the train station. The proud statute of Queen Victoria stood guard over the entrance.

"Are we eating outside in the garden area on this beautiful day?"

"No, Mother doesn't like to eat outside."

"Mother?"

"Yes, when she found out I was meeting you for lunch, she insisted on coming along. Said she missed seeing you. I think she may be coming around a bit. Didn't want to ruffle those matronly feathers, you know."

Beth smiled in spite of her frustration. At least she dressed up a bit. But she would have preferred the Grosvenor, if they were to have a fancy lunch. At any rate some of the clientele there would be under fifty.

Lady Gately, beautifully dressed, sat in the formal dining room overlooking the garden. A member of the staff led Beth and Kevin to her table. Glancing at Beth from top to bottom, Judith Gately surveyed Beth's clothes. "So sorry Kevin didn't inform you we would be having lunch here. I've taken the responsibility of ordering. The head waiter was quite helpful," she said with an air of authority. "He has children about your age."

As soon as they were seated, the waiter brought Coke for Kevin and Beth. Lady Gately sipped daintily on her glass of sauterne.

"So Kevin tells me you're going to visit relatives in south Wales. What part?"

"My relatives live in Laugharne."

"Well, my goodness. I have some very dear friends who have purchased property in that area. They already have a home in Paris and London. Can't imagine anything too grand in the Welsh countryside. Saw the Martins at a party in London just last month."

Almost choking on her drink, Beth exclaimed, "Gavin Martin!" Her eyes widened.

"Beth," said Lady Gately. "What's wrong? You look rather disquieted. Do you know Gavin Martin?"

Beth couldn't answer at first. She thought of Victoria and remembered the form that gave a location in Wales as a second residence. "I've seen his name, but can't remember where," she said.

"Well, Elizabeth," said Lady Gately, "I'm sure you'll have a most delightful time."

The waiter arrived with lunch. Lady Gately's ornate salad looked almost too good to eat. The waiter proudly placed over-cooked hamburgers with greasy fried potatoes in front of Kevin and Beth.

"Cook usually doesn't prepare such food, but for you, Lady Gately, nothing is too much trouble. It's always a pleasure to serve you."

He walked away with his nose slightly elevated. Beth wished he had asked her if everything was satisfactory. She would have ordered exactly what Lady Gately was having for lunch.

"Let's enjoy our meal together. You young folk don't have much time before the train departure. Elizabeth, tell me what you've found amusing in Llandudno. Any interesting visitors or concerts?"

"No, Lady Gately. It's still a bit early in the season for much activity."

Beth attempted to eat some lunch while Kevin's mother went on about their travels in Europe. She brought pictures of the two of them with friends at impressive locations. Pointing out each stranger's face with an explanation of his or her importance, added to the boring conversation. Next Lady Gately gave the same talk Beth had heard the last time she dined there.

"Built in 1860 and they still use some of the items from that time. For the convenience of passengers the porters would meet every train dressed in their bright gold and scarlet livery."

A server came to the table and replaced Lady Gately's empty wine glass with another full one. "It's such a shame that we've lost a great deal of our civilized manners. And the celebrities and dignitaries that have slept under this very roof. Charles Dickens, Lily Langtry and Cecil Rhodes."

"Yes, Lady Gately. I so appreciate the writings of Charles Dickens that made society aware of the abuses of his day."

Kevin gave Beth a nudge under the table. On the surface Beth seemed quite interested, but all she could think of was Victoria and Gavin Martin.

"Sorry, Mother," said Kevin. "But it's time we were off. Don't want Beth to miss her train. You stay here and order some dessert for me."

Graciously thanking Lady Gately for the lunch, the young couple hurried out of the dining room.

"So sorry, Beth. Couldn't get out of it, but at least we've got a little time before you leave. Let's get on the train and get you settled."

"Grand idea. In fact, why don't you just go with me? Have you ever thought of running away from home?"

"Believe me, many a time."

A station attendant escorted them to the waiting train. The seat next to her reserved seat was empty. Kevin and Beth sat and talked about plans for the future. He would come to Llandudno as soon as she arrived back at her grandmother's. Looking out the window they suddenly realized the train had started to move. Kevin jumped to his feet and started laughing. "I guess Mother will have to eat my dessert. She'll think I did this on purpose."

"Not a bad idea, if you ask me."

"I'll get off at Wrexham and take a taxi back to Chester."

Kevin called his mother on his cell phone. Beth watched as he explained the situation, trying not to laugh.

"Yes, Mother. I'll meet you at the cathedral gift store in about an hour or so. Yes, Mother. Yes, Mother."

He put the phone back in his pocket and looked intently at Beth. "Now, what's this about Gavin Martin? That was quite a reaction you had when Mother mentioned his name."

"Nothing really. I visited a convalescing home in Hollywell with Sister Clare and happened to meet his mother. She's a resident there."

Beth took Kevin's hand. "Now let's talk about us. Do you have any more trips planned the rest of the summer?"

Wrexham came into view much too soon. After Kevin had kissed her goodbye, Beth sat by the train window, watching Kevin as he waved. She read his lips. "I love you." She responded in silence, "I love you."

Settling back in her seat, she thought of the explanation she had given Kevin about Gavin Martin. She hadn't lied, but she hadn't exactly told the truth. No need to worry Kevin about the matter.

Gliding effortlessly along the continuous track, the train swayed gently on an occasional curve. Beth saw old churches with moss eaten stones and spires green with mold, wooly sheep in need of a clip grazing in fields surrounded by rock fences, white and black cows, no two alike. Emerald vines grew out of bricks on walls along the track.

All the while her restless mind kept wandering, staying on no one thought for any length of time. She felt depressed. Probably her short time with Kevin and the unexpected lunch with Lady Gately and the uncertainty of a week with relatives she barely knew. Victoria. And again the words of the vicar, "Be open to possibilities."

Slowing down, the train stopped at a small, dirty, antiquated station. Reaching out of the soot-laden brick was a delicate white flower encompassed by a few green leaves.

The sight reminded Beth of a program she saw on television about Mother Teresa. The nun in white lived in the midst of filth and dying in the streets of Calcutta. This simple woman, winner of the Nobel Peace Prize, was riding a train looking out at the people of India. God spoke to her of an eternal vocation here on earth. Beth fell peacefully asleep as the train pulled out of the station.

An abrupt stop woke Beth. Realizing it signaled another change of trains, she grabbed her bags, exiting just before the train departed.

Reading the schedule and track numbers, she realized she would have to climb the far stairs to reach the platform for the connecting train to Carmarthen. As she struggled with her luggage up the stairs, a voice came from behind.

"Hey, luv, let me give you a help."

Before she knew it a muscular young man had grabbed her bags and was two stairs ahead of her.

"Where to, my luv?"

"Platform three."

"Bloody good, that's my train. Going to Carmarthen?"

"Yes."

The train was just pulling in.

"Got a ten minute wait before we leave." Eyeing a refreshment station close by he asked, "Care for a beer or coffee?"

"No, thank you, and thanks for helping with my luggage."

Beth watched him as he walked away. His royal blue jogging suit didn't hide the obvious fact he spent time lifting weights. She wondered if he might be a professional rugby or soccer player. Not anxious to hear the word "bloody" in every other sentence for the remainder of the trip, she picked up her bags and boarded the train. Relieved to see a crowded train with no two vacant seats next to each other, she settled into a place next to a matronly lady.

If she had driven her car from Llandudno, she would be in Largharne by now, but she rather enjoyed the train and seeing the interesting mix of people who chose this means of transportation between the smaller towns of Wales. She noticed the young man who carried her bags didn't get on her car, or perhaps missed his train, because he was sitting at the station counter drinking beer.

The lady next to Beth was absorbed in her book for several miles. Closing her book, she sighed. "Those poor dear people."

"I beg your pardon," said Beth. "Did you say something, ma'am?"

"Oh dear, it's this book. I get so involved in their lives. I'll probably not sleep tonight if I don't finish it."

Beth looked at the cover. Danielle Steel! She looked away so the lady wouldn't see the amused look on her face. At the next stop the lady got off. Before Beth could settle back into her own thoughts, she heard a familiar voice.

"There you are, my luv. Lost track of you. Glad there's a place here. Some girl in the back car changed her baby's nappies. Enough to bloody well gag you," he said as he plopped down in the vacant seat next to Beth. "So, my luv, business or pleasure?"

"Going to see relatives in Laurgharne," Beth replied. She wished he would go away.

"Going to Dylan's place?" he said. "Never cared much for his writing. Have a pint for me at the Brown Hotel. They say that's where he got a lot of his inspiration. Drinking a few pints of Newcastle Brown always gives me inspiration, that's bloody well true."

Getting no response, he carried on. "And so do you work or in school?"

"I just graduated from Oxford."

"Well, ol' gal, I'm quite impressed. What in?"

"General Studies." Beth didn't see any need to tell him her main concentration was theology, although she certainly wasn't worried about this man wanting to engage her in a theological discussion. Steering him away from any more questions about herself, she asked in disinterest, "Business or pleasure in Carmarthen?"

"Going to a book signing."

"Whose?"

"Mine."

"Yours? What kind of book?"

"The history of physical culture with illustrations. Goes back to the Romans. Sold a good number on the net. Coming down for the games in Cardiff next week, had an invite from this bookstore in Carmarthen, so decided to give it a go. Probably not anything you would be interested in."

"Well, I might enjoy looking at the pictures," she said.

They laughed. How many times had Beth thought she had someone figured out by appearance and surface conversation? Add another to her list.

She pulled a book out, pretending to read. He got the hint and started reading a sports magazine. A few miles from Carmarthen, Beth went to the lady's room and changed into casual clothes.

Beth tried to imagine Ann's appearance after all these years and remembered her as rather plain. At least she was sure they would enjoy hikes around the area like they did in Llandudno.

The train pulled into the Carmarthen. Beth's traveling companion carried her bags through the small station and put them down in front.

"Sure you have a ride, my luv? I think I see mine coming just over the bridge. We can take you wherever you want to go."

"No, thank you. My cousin will be here shortly."

Beth looked around for a woman her own age. She saw a young woman walking across a car park across the street. She was dressed in black stretch pants, a tight flashy sweater, leather jacket, and clunky shoes with two-inch soles. Her make up was heavy, complete with eyeliner and dangling earrings, all topped in dark red, spiked hair. The bright sunlight caught the shine of a variety of ear studs climbing up each ear.

"That your cousin?"

"No way," Beth smirked.

A black Mercedes came down the road and stopped in front of the station. Dressed in the latest conservative fashion, a plumpish young man got out of the car.

"Alan, glad you made it. Your books arrived last week. Already sold a bunch. Ready to go?"

"Hold on. Want to be sure this young lady has a ride."

"Beth?"

Beth turned to see the flashy dressed woman. "Ann?"

Alan grabbed Beth's luggage. "Where to, ladies?"

"Just over there, deary," Ann replied, eyeing Alan up and down. "Appears you've lifted a bit more than a little luggage."

Beth followed the two as they chatted on the way to Ann's car. Shocked by her cousin's appearance, she didn't hear a word they were saying, wondering if her visit with her relatives would be as dull as she had anticipated.

Chapter Twenty-Five

"He who is faithful in a very little is faithful also in much."
(Luke 16:10)

Ann's car turned left out of the car park and crossed over the River Towy Bridge onto the main road.

"What are those weird looking boats on the river?" Beth asked.

"The coracles. A bunch of daft people, if you ask me," Ann sighed. "Floating around in those silly boats. The Coracle Centre is over at Cenarth Falls. Went over with some friends one day to watch the salmon leap. Cheering them on until some stodgy old coot came over and made us leave. Said we were disturbing the surroundings."

"I've heard about coracles, but never saw a real one. They date back to the Ice Age, if I remember right. I wrote a paper comparing the coracle with the spiritual life. They say the early Celtic monks would get in their coracles without oars and let the currents take them to where God wanted them to go. A letting go of control. Thy will be done."

Ann rolled her eyes in response. "My car may be old, but I'll stick with it, thank you very much."

Twisting through the narrow back streets of Carmarthan, the cousins rode along in silence.

"Want to stop in for a pint before we go on to Laugharne?" asked Ann.

"That's fine, if you like," said Beth.

"No, do you, yourself, want a drink? Makes me no difference."

"Well, I am quite tired. I could have been here in half the time, if I'd driven. But I did enjoy the train ride."

"We got a dear of a granny, don't we?"

"Yes, we certainly do."

Pulling into a parking space on St. Catherine Street, Ann stopped the car. The girls got out and started walking down the street.

"I called up Granny today to find out what you were like. Said you liked to read and hike. So I'm going to give you a quick tour of Myrddin, in case we don't get back to town."

"Myrddin?"

"Yes, named for our own Celtic wizard, Merlin. Carmarthen's Welsh name is Caerfyrddin, the town of Myrddin, or Merlin."

Pointing to a large building on their left, Ann informed Beth, "That's the cattle market. Not much going on today. I like to come in with girl friends and hang out. There's definitely not much to see in Laugharne.

Beth smiled. "You mean cattle or boys."

"You've got my number, for sure. This is market day, so we'll stop off. Got this top here last week, but they've got a lot of rubbish, too."

"Any used books? I'm always on the look out."

"Probably not your kind of books. Mostly common stuff. Not much religious tripe, but then I wasn't looking for any."

The girls laughed. Walking in fresh cool air revitalized Beth after sitting most of the day. The market was much bigger than she expected. Tables and booths spilled out into the parking area. The girls found little of interest as they strolled up and down countless aisles. They went outside.

Beth spied a bookstore on a corner of a side street and pointed. "Mind if we stop in over there?"

Ann followed Beth into the shop past the newer books. The dimly lit rear of the store was filled with old dusty editions. Beth looked at the titles until she picked out a large navy book with gold lettering on the well-worn cover.

"John Keble's *Christian Year*. Printed in 1827 with illustration. And only five pounds. A steal!" she exclaimed gleefully. "You'd never find this in Oxford."

"Looks like a dirty old book to me."

"Oh! Just listen," as Beth opened the book. "This is from his morning poem."

Old friends, old scenes, will lovelier be,
As more of heaven in each we see.
Some softening gleam of love and prayer
Shall dawn on every cross and care.

"Isn't that just wonderful?" Beth flipped through several pages. "And listen to this from his evening poetry."

Only, O Lord, in thy dear love
Fit us for perfect Rest above;
And help us, this and every day,
To live more nearly as we pray.

As Beth was walking to the counter with her prized possession, she noticed a display of newer used books.

"Here's a Bala Foresight book. This is one of my favorites." Beth picked up the book and they walked toward the counter.

"Bala Foresight?" said Ann. "Never heard of her. Interesting name, Bala. Is that her real name?"

"Don't know. Why do you ask?"

"In Welsh it means the place where a stream or river flows out of a lake. So I would think that if an author had that name it would mean she had all these ideas, like a big lake with boundaries, and when she gets ready to write, it just flows right out at the bala. Like from the brain to the computer keys."

"Um. Interesting," said Beth. She studied her cousin. *There's a lot more to Ann under all that make up and crazy hair.*

"Ann, do you speak Welsh?"

"Oh, yes, most do around here, especially in the small villages and countryside. Still have all Welsh schools in some spots. Those bloody Englishmen have tried to fight it. Fine with me if they go back to England."

"Now hold on," interrupted the shopkeeper. "We're not all that bad. In fact, I'm taking Welsh lessons right now."

"Sorry, sir. Didn't mean to offend."

Taking the books out of Beth's hand, he looked up and smiled. "Interesting combination. Both for you?"

"The Keble, yes. I already have the Foresight, but that's for my cousin. It takes place close to here."

"Yes, I rather like her books, too. Have you seen the latest edition of *The Sun*? Has her picture on the front cover."

"No, I never buy that trash," Beth responded arrogantly. "But I am curious to see what she really looks like."

"Well, I just happen to have a copy behind the counter. Think some customer must have left it here," he said, smiling at Ann. "But you probably wouldn't want see it."

"Well, maybe just a peak or two," said Beth curiously.

The creature on the front cover barely resembled a human being. The badly scarred face was surrounded with tangled gray hair. The caption under the picture read, "The Real Bala Foresight." Beth opened the paper and read the entire article. She finished and laid the paper on the counter.

Shaking her head, Beth looked up. "Do you really believe this garbage? Her husband threw acid on her face. She's hiding out somewhere in Africa. I don't believe any of it."

"Who's to say," he said, "but it sells a lot of papers. She's one of the most popular writers nowadays. Fun to read and interesting. Good plots. Not much in this Keble book, but eloquent words. You a fan of his, too?" he asked Ann.

"No, but my cousin is. She's a graduate of Oxford University. Plans to become a priest, too," Ann responded proudly.

"Is that so?" He smiled. "One of those uppity liberal females. Never gone to a church with a woman vicar. Still not sure how I feel about it. But you can't be too bad, if you like Keble and Foresight. Two of my favorites."

They walked out on the street, busy with late afternoon shoppers. Beth noticed the venders were hard at work tearing down their displays.

"I'll show you Guild Hall and Nott Square."

"Nott Square. That sounds familiar."

"Believe it or not," Ann said, "I remember a bit of history. Drummed into our heads by old lady Evans." Ann continued in a sarcastic tone. "Nott was the victor of the First Afghan War. The dates are 1841-1842. Also there's the monument of Bishop Ferrar, Bishop of St. David's. Burnt at the stake at the very spot by Bloody Mary in 1555. Wouldn't be my choice as a way to go."

"Well, Ann, I'm quite impressed. Had to learn a lot of dates at Oxford, but I've forgotten most of them."

"I'll be repeating those dates on my death bed. Asked old lady Evans when we were going to talk about our own Dylan Thomas. Her face got red as a tomato and said she didn't approve of his life style. Then she marked me down for being uppity."

After visiting Guild Hall and Nott Square, the girls turned on to King Street. An imposing church steeple a block away pointed to the sky. Beth quickened her step. Ann grabbed her arm.

"Hold on, girl. St. Peter's goin' nowhere. Been there for over 900 years.

"Sorry, must be automatic reflex."

"Knew you would want to see the church. After you're ordained, you can come down here and be a vicar. My cousin, the vicar. Who knows, someday, my cousin, the bishop."

"Now hold on, Ann. The church authorities haven't accepted me yet. And there's other considerations that you don't know about."

"Other considerations?"

Beth didn't answer.

In front of the church stood a weathered sign listing the services. Beth glanced at her watch.

"What luck! Evensong. And we're just in time. Do you mind if we go?"

"How long does it last?" asked Ann.

"About twenty minutes."

The girls hurried into the church, picking up a leaflet by the door announcing the psalms for the service. A dozen or so people stood in the front pews. The choir began processing in from the south side of the nave, singing the hymn, "The day thou gavest, Lord, is ended."

Beth and Ann took seats mid-way back. The ornate stained glass colors were beginning to fade as the sun receded. Beth experienced a tranquility and comfort that had escaped her for some time.

Glancing at Ann, she noticed her cousin focusing on the procession. Behind the ornate, hand-carved wooden cross came angelic choirboys and men dressed in red cassocks partly covered by chalk white surplices. A handsome young priest walked at the end of the procession.

Arriving at their appointed places they sang the final words of the hymn, "Thy kingdom stands, and grows for ever, till all thy creatures own thy sway."

Standing in front of the altar, the minister opened the service with a loud authoritative voice, "We have all strayed like sheep, each of us going his own way."

Ann whispered, "Boy, he can say that again."

Leaning over, Beth spoke softly in her cousin's ear, "Yes, but he probably won't."

An elderly lady a few pews ahead of the girls turned and peered at the late arrivals.

"Never been to a service like this," said Ann.

Opening the Welsh Prayer Book, Beth led Ann through the service of Evensong. She found it interesting to follow the words on the left pages in Welsh, but relieved to read the prayers and psalms in English on the right pages.

After the service Beth and Ann departed the silent church. Street lights illumined the darkened streets.

"Best we go on to Laugharne," said Ann. Mum will have supper waiting."

They walked in silence back to the car. Out on the main highway, Beth was the first to speak.

"Thank you, Ann. I really enjoyed seeing Carmarthen and attending Evensong. I hope we're not too late."

"No, I told Mum I'd give you a tour. She said, 'Show her more than the pubs.' Wait till she hears we went to a church service."

In a short time the car was off the A 40 and passing through St. Clears. Quite an assortment of sights met Beth's eyes. One sign announced an Antiques Fair at Civic Hall. The Black Lion Hotel boasted their delicious bar meals. The sign, Pizza Point! brought a faint smile to her face.

Next they drove out into open countryside. High hedges hid rolling hills, as Ann's car followed the curving road. A sign announced riding stables off to the left. There the road began leading gradually down toward the water, into the town of Largharne.

The first noticeable landmark was St. Martin's Church, surrounded by ancient tombstones and dwarfed by gigantic trees reaching heavenward. Ann pointed, "See the foot bridge going over to the modern cemetery? That's where Dylan Thomas hangs out these days."

As they drove down into Largharne with homes and businesses sharing common walls, they passed Brown's Hotel on the left. Ann nodded, "Dylan's watering hole. If there are any tourists in town, that's where they'll be."

Turning left at the Three Mariners Pub, the girls passed the darkened bakery. A faint light showed empty display counters in the window awaiting fresh baked goods for the next day. Ann pulled her car halfway up on the sidewalk of the narrow street past the bakery. A stout round-faced woman with gray hair pulled back in a bun greeted the two girls at the doorway.

"Beth! You're finally here," she said, as she came out and opened the car door. Beth got out and gave her Aunt Bessie an embrace and kiss on the cheek. "Been worried sick. Supper's on the stove and ready. Where have you been? The train late?"

"No, Mum. Showed Beth around Carmarthen and then to a church service at St. Peter's."

"Church service, is it? Why Beth, perhaps you'll have a good effect on my girl. Would do her no harm to go to church now and then."

Beth and Ann smiled. "Mum, you should see the minister. Looks like a movie star. May bloody well go back."

Aunt Bessie shook her head. "Ann, watch what you say."

They went inside. Saturating the air of the tidy Welsh home was the fragrance of the early morning bread from the adjoining bakery. Familiar family photos adorned the mantle piece. Beth spied the picture of the two sisters some forty years ago standing on the beach at Llandudno with the Great Orme in the background. The table leading into the kitchen was set for four. Beth wondered if the fourth was for Uncle Hugh or cousin John.

"Your Uncle Hugh isn't home yet. Always stops off at Brown's for a pint or two. I told him to come straight home, but knew he wouldn't." She smiled and shook her head. "Your cousin John lives in Tenby. Ann, show Beth to her room. Used to be John's. Clean, with a good hard bed, but you'll see it's still a boy's room."

As the girls put the luggage down in John's room, they heard the front door slam shut.

"Smells like lamb stew, Bessie. Where's the girls?"

"Da's a dear, but a bit crusty," Ann said. "Doesn't talk much, except down at the pub. Use to go with him when I was younger. I'd sit in the corner at Dylan's table. Heard more tales than I would care to remember. Those old codgers!"

Beth followed Ann into the living area. Uncle Hugh was already seated at the table with his steaming stew in front of him. His massive shoulders extended well past the back of the large chair. The faded brown work shirt was missing a button or two. A wide smile appeared on his sun worn skin as Beth entered the room. Standing, he held out his hand and vigorously shook Beth's hand.

"Well, Elizabeth. You've turned into a pretty lass. I remember a scrawny kid with long braids. Sit yourself down and have some of your Aunt Bessie's stew. Best there is. *Eilfam yw modryb dda.* Aye, a good aunt is a second mother."

As soon as all were served and seated the four took hands. Hugh Griffith said a prayer in Welsh. The only word Beth understood was her own name. Savoring the tasty stew and brown bread was a relief to her empty stomach after the long train ride. Aunt Bessie started speaking in Welsh in seemingly endless sentences.

"Hold on, Bess," Uncle Hugh said. "I don't think our Elizabeth understands what you're saying."

"No, I don't. Just a few phrases. You don't hear it much up North like you do down here. *Amynedd yw mam pob doethineb.* Patience is the mother of all wisdom."

With a hearty laugh, Uncle Hugh responds, "I've got a better one. *Heb wraig heb ymryson.* Without wife without strife."

"Behave yourself, Hugh. Now tell us about your day."

"Just 'bout finished with this job. Got a farmhouse with a leaky roof out a ways, so may be home a little later tomorrow evening. How's your day been, Bessie?"

"Sold out of everything but a few Welsh cakes. Had to go down to the market to buy back my own bread." They all laughed. "If I bake extra tomorrow, they'll be leftovers."

"I'll eat any leftovers you have," said Beth, reaching for her third piece of bread.

With a sly grin, Uncle Hugh directed a question to Beth. "So, Beth, best you be calling yourself Elizabeth around here."

"Why do you say that?"

"Well, you know what Beth means in Welsh."

"What?"

"You mean you don't even know what your name means?"

"What?"

"What do you want to know, what?"

"Oh, Hugh. Stop teasing the girl. She knows that Beth means 'what' in Welsh."

Lively conversation continued as they finished the meal with blackberries and cream.

Chapter Twenty-Six

"For God alone my soul waits in silence."

Loud rock music from outside woke Beth the next morning. She opened the window and saw a young mailman going from door to door. Every time he returned to his mail car and opened the door, the noise blared out into the street. Surprised at the time, she dressed and ventured out to the kitchen. The smell of fresh baked goods filled the air. The door leading into the bakery was opened. Aunt Bessie was serving customers while Ann stood at the cash register. Ann gave a quick wave. She looked quite different without the mod clothes and heavy makeup.

"Coffee's on the stove. Come on in and take your pick," said Ann. "No breakfast served around here."

"Can I help?" asked Beth.

"No, take it easy. As soon as the morning rush is over, we'll be off to the cartref."

Beth wondered what the cartref was. After two mouth-watering Welsh cakes, a cream cake and coffee, she ventured out to walk around the town. Her first instinct was to walk up the hill to inspect the church and check the service schedule. *There's more to life than church.* She turned left toward the sea.

The cobblestones under her feet felt like the familiar streets in the walled city of Chester. Beth remembered a quote from a Samuel Taylor Coleridge poem about

Laugharne her mother would often repeat when talking about Bessie, her younger sister. Saying it in a whisper she walked slowly towards the estuary.

"The hills high, not unwooded
Castle close upon the sea.
Barking, yelping, whining, wailing
Of the various sea fowls."

Squawking gulls and crows gathering on tops of chimneys demanded Beth's attention. Turning the corner at Town Hall, the ruins of Laugharne Castle with two 12th century towers overtook the landscape. She stood motionless, impressed by the massive structure. "Castle brown as owl." Beth remembered a Dylan Thomas quote. The massive iron gates were closed to morning visitors.

Across the main road a large Celtic cross atop a round stone structure stood guard over a parking area with surrounding shops and eating-places. The local market had the most business. A fat Cheshire cat stood guard on her perch by the front door. Nearly every customer gave her a few strokes.

"*Bore da,"* said a passing stranger.

"Good morning," replied Beth.

Passing over a footbridge she stood alone and looked out on low tide. A few fishing boats lay resting in the mud. Unaware of the noise of morning traffic or walkers, she retreated to her own world. She kept repeating in her mind a sentence from a psalm. "For God alone my soul in silence waits."

"Beth! Beth!"

She turned to see her cousin standing beside her.

"Hey, you were lost in space. I'm through helping Mam at the bakery, so we're off for the rest of the day. Want to visit Dylan's first?"

"That sounds grand. Ann, have you heard of a place called Pentowyn?"

"Pentowyn? You're looking right at it. It's that house across the way," she said pointing to a large white house surrounded by smaller buildings on a hill across the estuary. "Put on your wellies and we'll walk across."

"Really?"

"No," said Ann laughing. "Just teasing. How do you know about Pentowyn?"

"I know of the owners. Is there a way we can find out if they're there? I might like to pay them a visit."

"Not a problem. Mam knows the caretaker's wife. She comes over here about once a week to see relatives. Always stops by the bakery. I hear they're fancy folk from London. Hey! Let's go on to Dylan's and then walk up and see the horses. Might get to ride if they're not too busy. The stable boy and I are kind of like friends," she said with a sheepish grin.

"Oh. I see."

"Not what you think. Well, at least not yet. But maybe someday. At least that's one Mam would approve of."

The girls walked back past the Griffith's home, turning down a narrow road. Two signs at the intersection marked the way. "No Vehicular Access" and "Dylan's Walk." Golden flowering shrubs cascading over rock walls on either side decorated the path. Singing male robins announcing their ownership of certain trees added additional entertainment.

Around a curve a blue garage perched on the side of the cliff faced the water. A glass window cut out of the boards allowed visitors to peak inside. Dylan's work place. A gas stove, curling photographs, pens and numerous scrunched-up balls of paper on the simple desk suggested Dylan Thomas would return any minute. Two empty beer bottles reminded visitors of his love of drink.

"Right here's where he did most of his writing," said Ann with an air of authority. 'Under Milk Wood,' being his most famous. It's really about Laugharne. And at Richard Burton's funeral, they read Dylan's poem, 'Do not go gently into that good night."

"It's so peaceful here," said Beth. "And the view is inspiring. No wonder he chose this place."

"The quote I like best is about Laugharne," said Ann. 'And some, like myself, just came, one day, for the day, and never left; got off the bus, and forgot to get on again."

Walking down the path a short distance, a small iron gate opened to stairs leading down to the boathouse. A variety of trees and plants on either side showed someone's determination to plant every possible kind of vegetation that would grow in the area. Here and there darted half-wild cats, playing hide and seek with visitors and each other.

A woman greeted the girls at the door. She gave Ann a wink. "No charge for today, girls."

Some of the original furnishings adorned the simple living area. Over in the corner a period wireless set played with the voice of Dylan Thomas reading his own creations. The view out a window to the ever-changing water and light of the estuary created an ambiance of going back in time.

On the second floor, two rows of benches sat in front of a video screen. Ann and Beth watched a presentation of the life of the poet and playwright. In the downstairs kitchen turned into a simple tearoom, the cousins enjoyed a cup of tea and then went outside to a terrace overlooking the estuary. They stood in silence for several minutes. Beth stared at the stark white of Pentowyn against the rolling emerald hills across the water. Ann noticed.

"What's the deal with Pentowyn?"

"Oh, nothing really. I happened to meet a Mrs. Martin at a convalescing home in Hollywell. Her son has a second home and it just happens to be Pentowyn. Small world isn't it?"

Cocking her head with eyes narrowing, Ann replied, "I think there's more to the story than you're telling me, cousin. But that's fine. So do you want to pay him a visit if he's there? No trouble to drive over."

"I would, but I don't, but I should. So I guess the answer is yes."

"Fine. That's settled. Now I'll treat you to a toastie at Brown's. Might as well have a Dylan Thomas day. Then up to the stables to check things out."

Stopping by home, the girls freshened up a bit. Aunt Bessie informed Beth that the new owners of Pentowyn had arrived a few days before and would be there for a couple of weeks.

Stale cigarette smell wafted through the air of the pub. Sooty walls held pictures of days gone by. The bay window on the front gave a good view to the street. A bus to Pendine roared past just as the girls closed the door. Except for a couple of men at the bar, the place was empty. Ann led Beth over to a round table half-enclosed in a side alcove. A wrought iron frame supported a well-worn rough wooden top. The legs rested on wooden tips.

"You sit here at Dylan's table. Tom's been offered over a thousand pounds for that old thing, but won't sell," Ann said smiling. "I'll go order the toasties."

Beth sat and listened to the flowing Welsh language. Coming in the front door, a stranger nodded at the pub owner standing behind the nicotine-crusted bar.

"The usual, sir?"

"Yes, Tom." He took a long look at Beth. Then he said something to Tom in Welsh.

Ann turned around quickly from leaning on the bar and said in English, "Now watch what you say. That's my cousin from up north. And she'll have nothing to do with the likes of you."

Everyone laughed, especially Beth. Ann returned to the table with a couple of pints of ale.

"Had to get you this ale from Kent. Has a mild taste, but the name is the best part. Knew you would want some."

"And just what is the name?"

"Called Bishop's Finger. A bit mild. Good for an afternoon drink. Do all bishop's have big fancy rings? One came to visit the church here in Laugharne. Mam dragged Da and me with her. We had to sit and listen to the longest, most boring sermon ever. Then afterwards, there was a "do" for him.

Everyone got in a queue. He stuck out his hand with that big gaudy ring and expected everyone to kiss it. We don't know about such fancy things around here, so we all just shook his hand, except the vicar. He knelt down and kissed the bloody thing. It's all we could do to keep from laughing. Looked kind of silly to me."

Beth shook her head smiling. "Sorry I missed the occasion."

"Tom said the cook was sick, which is a good thing. He makes better toasties than she does any day."

Tom came to the table with lunch. The homemade wheat bread toast encased a warm melting concoction of country ham, local cheese, country tomatoes and mushrooms. Watercress decorated the side of the plate.

"Hope this is to your ladies' satisfaction," Tom said, as he ceremoniously put the plates on the table.

"Why this is lovely, Tom. Think I'll suggest the church ladies come here for afternoon tea."

"Be glad to serve them some stout ale. Would do them good," he replied with a broad smile.

Ann laughed. "Now behave yourself, Tom."

Returning to the bar, he resumed the men's conversation in Welsh.

Beth felt like she was in a foreign country. She studied the memorabilia and tried to imagine Dylan sitting at this very table, writing his words and watching his world go by.

Chapter Twenty-Seven

"God is our refuge and strength,
a very present help in trouble."
(Psalm 46:1)

Early the next morning Beth stood alone at the water's edge in the fog. A faint glow from the yet rising sun gave a soft radiance to the Largharne Estuary. Rising from the water, the far hills seemed to move as the light changed. The harsh white of Pentowyn stood out against the emerald land and yellow primrose. No light shone in the sizeable farmhouse. Beth stared at the tranquil scene and wondered what the day had in store.

Large birds glided above the water in search of a morning meal, creating a ballet in the sky.

The squawk of crows interrupted Beth's serenity. She remembered one of her grandfather's Welsh sayings.

"*Melysaf y can eos, ond nid erchis, Duw I'r fran dewi.*"

"Sweetest sings the nightingale, but God did not command the crow to be silent."

I seem to have a few crows in my life, she thought. Or could it be as Grandfather used to say, "Watch out, my dear. Anytime you speak ill of others, you may be looking in the mirror."

More land appeared as the tide receded. Gulls swooped down into the newly exposed salty mud and marshes searching for food. A gray heron glided effortlessly in the distance. Floating balls signaled the deep channel passage for small boats.

Beth's eyes traveled again to her mission for the day. "Lord, help me to say the right words," she whispered, turning away from the peaceful scene while the first rays of sun broke forth to dispel the morning fog.

After breakfast the girls left for Pentowyn Farm. Beth gazed out the car window deep in thought. Suddenly Ann hit the brakes when she came around a curve. Beth hit her head on the windshield.

"You all right?" asked Ann. "It was you or them."

Horses from the nearby stable filled the road.

"I'm fine. Just a tap."

The early morning bus from Carmarthen waited on the other side.

"I bet Winky is fit to be tied," said Ann. "I can hear him going on." She mimicked a man's low voice. "What right have those bloody hoofs to be on my road. It'll run me late to Pendine. And Flouncy havin' me breakfast ready. I've got a mind to run 'em over."

Beth watched an amusing collection of city riders and dogs pass in front of their car. As soon as the road was clear, Winky gave a disapproving honk and continued on his way.

"How long will it take to get there?" asked Beth.

"At least thirty minutes or more."

"Thirty minutes? Why so long when it's so close?"

"Because this old car won't float. We have to go up to St. Clears, get on the A40 and then down the road to Llanstephan. We turn off to Pentowyn before we get there. There's a cut off that could save us a few minutes, but I got lost last time I tried."

"There's a castle at Llanstephan, isn't there?"

"Yes, and would you believe I've never been in it? Want to take a look after your visit?"

"Yes, I love to wander about old castles. Takes me back in time. Seems like such a romantic era. Knights in shining armor. Damsels in distress. One of Bala Foresight's books took place in a medieval castle." Beth sighed. "Some of the romance scenes were so dreamy."

"Dreamy! Romantic! If we lived back then we would be emptying chamber pots. How would you like to take your monthly bath in freezing water? I'll take this century, thank you very much."

The narrow country road leading to Llanstephan was bordered by high growing hedges most of the way. Occasionally a scene would open up over the stone fences made years ago by farmers clearing the earth for planting. The rock boundaries on the hills presented a green checkerboard, dotted with cows on some and sheep on others.

"I never tire of looking at these hills. It's so peaceful here," said Beth after a lengthy silence.

"Too peaceful for me, cousin."

Taking another turn down a narrow side road leading to Pentowyn, Ann responded, "Hope we don't meet another car. There's places where one of us would have to back up a ways."

Ann slowed. A sheep dog stood in the middle of the road.

"That's ol' Maggie. Everyone around here knows her. Gets out in the road every time she hears a car coming." Ann stopped. "Come on."

Beth and Ann got out and greeted Maggie. A large break in a rock fence showed a road leading to an old farmhouse in need of repair. Ann picked up a stick and threw it. The dog retrieved it, ready for another throw. Beth joined in the game.

"Quite a dog," said Beth. And quick on her feet. How old is she?"

"Older than you think. She's still a good sheep dog. Won a few trials in her younger years. But the owners don't pay her much mind. Named her Maggie after Margaret Thatcher. The caretaker at Pentowyn keeps her supplied with scraps."

Scraps, thought Beth. Scrappy, Adam's dog. *I wonder what he's doing right now. Repair work or hiking The Orme.* Things didn't fit together where he was concerned.

Beth was startled by a loud horn. She turned and saw a car behind Ann's.

"What right have you to block my way?" shouted a woman in a silver Mercedes.

Ann went over to the car.

"Sorry, we'll pull in the drive so you can be on your way. It's best to slow down because of the dog. She tends to get out in the road when she hears a car."

The woman had her window up before Ann could finish her apology. Beth and Ann returned to the car and drove off the road.

"Beth, I'm afraid that may be who you're going to see. No one else drives a car like that around here. Has a London plate and some sort of official sticker on it."

The girls continued on the road that sloped down toward the water hidden behind oak and ash trees. *Pentowyn Manor House* read a large ornate sign around the next curve.

"What a bloody ugly sign!" said Ann, as she turned on to the freshly surfaced driveway. The Mercedes was parked in front of the house.

"This place has changed. Painted over the stone, added pillars and a new front entrance. The caretaker told me, but I didn't think it would be this different. A proper English manor house. Doesn't fit here, that's for bloody sure."

Beth and Ann sat in the car for a few moments. Beth took a deep breath and sighed.

"What did I tell you? It's her," said Ann.

"Well, maybe not. Perhaps a visitor from London."

"Don't you ever get tired of being so optimistic? If you were more like me, you wouldn't be disappointed." Ann patted Beth on the shoulder. "Now get on with you."

Beth got out of the car and straightened her clothes. She ran her fingers through her hair in a half-hearted attempt to look a little more presentable. Turning back around to Ann, "Wish me luck."

"I have a feeling you'll need more than luck for this expedition."

"Okay, then. Say a prayer."

"Jolly good. That would guarantee a catastrophe."

As Beth walked up the stairs, a chill shot through her. She looked around at her cousin. Ann waved with a smile, nodding her head. Beth reached for the elaborate brass doorknocker. The sound reverberated through the still Welsh air.

After a few moments, the door opened. A maid dressed in a proper uniform greeted her.

"May I help you?"

"Yes, I would like to see Mr. Gavin Martin, please."

"Won't you step in? Who shall I say is calling?"

"My name is Elizabeth Davies, but he doesn't know me."

The approach of clicking high heels came from the back of the house.

"Who is at the front door?"

"Someone to see Mr. Martin, madame."

"You can go, Nancy. I'll take care of this."

Beth recognized the disgruntled woman who had passed them on the road. She stood staring at Beth until the maid left. The well-tailored blouse and skirt, perfectly applied make up and well-styled hair looked out of place in the country farmhouse.

"What is this about?"

"Personal business."

"And what kind of personal business might you have with my husband?"

"I beg your pardon, ma'am, I didn't know Mr. Martin was your husband."

"Well, what exactly do you want? My husband is quite busy and doesn't have time for idle chat and neither do I," she said, folding her arms and tapping her foot impatiently.

"I'm a friend of his mother's. I'd like to talk with him about her situation."

Margaret Martin's eyes narrowed as she studied Beth. The tapping foot stopped.

"You can discuss anything that concerns Victoria Martin with me. I'm in charge of decisions about her care. It's too painful for my husband. The whole situation made him physically ill."

"But I'd appreciate talking with him," Beth insisted.

"Well, that just won't do. He's quite busy with business matters and can't be bothered. Now say what you have to say. I'll discuss it with him later. If he wishes to see you, he can give you a call. Now get on with it. I don't have all day."

Margaret Martin's lifeless eyes stared past Beth as she gave details of Victoria's situation. She left out any mention of Sister Clare and Victoria's story about the vicar. As soon as she finished, she waited for a reply. Margaret Martin moved a hand to her chin, shifting her mouth around in nervousness. Her eyes stared to the side, looking at the floor.

"I don't quite understand how you have made yourself an authority on Mrs. Martin's illness. In the first place, she is restricted from having visitors. My husband keeps well informed about his mother's illness. Just what is your interest?"

"I happened to meet her one day while visiting a friend there."

"I'll give my husband your message. If you don't hear from him, I suggest you allow the matter to drop."

"Yes, ma'am."

Beth wrote her name and Ann's telephone number on a piece of paper. Mrs. Martin snatched it from her hand. Beth turned, opened the front door and went outside. The door slammed behind her.

Walking slowly back to the car she turned once more to look at Pentowyn Farmhouse. A movement caught her eye from an upstairs window. A man stood there, looking down at her. Must be Gavin Martin, she thought, as she got into the car.

"Well, looks like you certainly weren't welcomed with open arms."

"Not in the least. I don't trust that woman. Wouldn't let me talk with her husband. I gave her your number. She said she would relay the information." Beth stared at the front door of Pentowyn. "Guess I've hit a dead end."

"You've done the best you can. Let's go visit the old castle, then on in to Carmarthen for lunch and take in a movie. I want to show you a good time while you're here."

"You already have. I do enjoy being with you and your family. And Largharne is so different from any other town I've been in."

"Yeah, different and boring."

The toasties at the pub in Carmarthen were tasty and the chips soaked in oil. The noisy bar bustled with lunchtime visitors. Ann and Beth sat at a corner table. Ann waved at a couple who came in. They spotted Ann and came over to the table.

"Alan and Denise, this is my cousin, Beth Davies, from Hawthorne. Have a seat."

"No, we can't. Looking for a couple of blokes. Thought they might have slipped in for a pint. Better be on our way," said Alan, surveying the room. "Going to hike the coastal path at St. David for a few days."

"That sounds like fun," said Beth. "Never been to that part of Wales."

"Why not join us?"

Beth looked at Ann with anticipation. A smile and a shake of her head "no thanks" was the only answer.

Alan and Denise left in search of their friends.

"If we were to go to St. David," Ann said, "it wouldn't be with those two. Definitely not your cup of tea or mine."

After the movie and shopping, the girls stopped by a pub for dinner. A local Celtic band started setting up their gear while Ann and Beth finished their supper.

"Let's stay and hear their first set," suggested Beth.

"If you want to hear good music, I know a band just a few blocks from here. Good hard rock. Best in these parts."

"How about we stay here for a while and then go over there?"

"Sounds like a plan. But I can't take too much of this folksy music. Sounds all the same to me."

"Ann, funny you should say that. I was just about to say that about hard rock!" Beth laughed.

Chapter Twenty-Eight

"Women are like tea bags. You don't know how strong one is until it's in hot water."
(Eleanor Roosevelt)

Ann and Beth slept late the next day. At eleven o'clock the cousins sat at the kitchen table staring at their coffee cups.

"Think we should go back to bed, Beth?"

"Heavens no. I think we should go out for a hearty breakfast and then take a long hike."

"Hike! Not on your life!"

"Well, maybe not too long a hike. How about *The Owl and the Pussycat Tearoom*? You keep talking about that place. It'll be my treat."

"Okay. Sounds good. Their Welsh rabbit is delicious. Made with our local cheese, it is. Best I've ever had."

A plethora of owls and pussycats decorated the tea-room. Some were on shelves in a display case shaped like a boat. A large carved wooden owl and pussycat stood guard on a sign noting the sweet selections for the day. The menu was on a chalkboard with a variety of choices from crawl to Shepherd's pie plus a variety of salads. Small vases on each table held fresh flowers. Beth and Ann selected a table to the side, looking out on the street.

A carpeted area in another part of the large room was the owner's sitting room. Beth admired the antique furniture.

An embroidery hoop waited for more thread to finish the design. A large stuffed owl and pussycat sat high up on a china cabinet. Beth noticed a man who came in with his delivery tray of brown eggs.

"Usual order?" he asked the owner's wife.

"Yes, but I'll need double on Friday."

"Right, I'll be sure to tell the chickens."

Beth enjoyed every morsel of her Welsh rabbit and salad.

"Any dessert for you ladies?" asked a waitress.

"Let's split one, Beth. They're big portions."

"Sounds good. You order."

"Fresh Blackberry pie with coddled cream and two spoons."

The dessert arrived just as the door swung open. In walked Margaret Martin with another woman.

"Well, dear," said Mrs. Martin, "you've seen the castle and this dreary village. No place decent to eat, but this establishment is rather amusing and the food satisfactory. Better to eat here before we go on to Carmarthen."

The two women took a table in the opposite corner. Beth leaned over to Ann in a whisper.

"There she is. I bet she never told her husband I came by the other day."

"Why don't you go back over? She won't be there to interfere. Here's my car keys. I'll stay here."

"Oh, you just want all the dessert."

"Go on, Beth. You'll never know if you don't give it a try. When the waitress goes over to take their order, you can slip out without her seeing you."

Beth saw the silver Mercedes parked in front of the tearoom. She hurried out of town to St. Clears, on to the main highway and then the road to Llanstephan. She had no trouble remembering the side road to Pentowyn. Beth slowed down as she neared the home of the friendly dog. There was Maggie waiting by the side of the road.

Beth felt her heart beat faster. Did Mrs. Martin tell him about her visit? She said the situation made him ill. What if he's mentally ill and Victoria is, too?

A Rolls Royce was parked in front of the house. Knocking on the front door several times brought no response.

"What luck. Not even here," she said with disgust. Going back to Ann's car, Beth retrieved her camera. "Might as well go round back and see the view from this side."

The back of the house had a large recently added addition. Across the estuary, the castle towered over the town. Small fishing boats rested in the mud at low tide.

Dylan Thomas' white boathouse and bright blue workshop stood out against the seashore. She looked up to the far left at the dots she knew must be the horses from the riding stable.

As she snapped her last shot, something moved in the lens. Beth was startled to see a man walking toward her. He waved and yelled, "I'll be right there."

Beth watched as he got closer, a tall man with a deliberate long stride. He was dressed in jeans and tee shirt, wearing rubber boots and carrying a jacket.

Must be the groundskeeper, she thought. Perhaps he can tell me when Mr. Martin will return.

As soon as the man reached Beth he said, "Gavin Martin. How can I help you young lady?"

Not at all what she expected. He had a kind face and Beth felt comfortable for some reason. Quite in contrast to his wife.

"My name is Elizabeth Davies. How do you do, sir."

"Are you lost again?"

"Lost? I haven't a clue what you mean."

"You came yesterday, didn't you? I saw you from the upstairs library. My wife said you had stopped to ask for directions."

Beth looked away, took a deep breath, and said a silent prayer for courage. She turned and looked straight into his eyes with determination.

"Mr. Martin, I came by to talk to you about your mother."

Gavin Martin gasped. His face turned pale. His eyes widened.

Slowly he asked, "You…you know my mother? Do you work at the, the facility?"

"No, but I've met her."

He looked out at the peaceful scene of Largharne. Tears welled up in his eyes and he reached for a handkerchief.

"Must be the salt air. Always makes my eyes water. Let's go inside and have a talk."

Beth and Mr. Martin walked side by side without a word. She held back the temptation to look at him. She glanced at the handkerchief clutched tightly in his white knuckled hand. How she wished she had never met Victoria.

What in heaven's name was she doing here, walking beside this stranger? His wife had lied to him and to her. Reaching the back door, he sat down in a chair, taking off his muddy wellies. Beth took the cue and sat in another chair to take off her shoes.

"No need, my dear. Your shoes are fine. But if I were to wear these wellies into the house, Margaret would have my head."

They entered the back porch of the house. An array of tools, lumber, paint cans, and assorted brushes in disarray filled a large portion of the area.

"Sorry about the mess. This was intended to be our quiet residence. There's more activity in this house than Victoria Station. I sent the servants home as soon as my wife left."

"Sir, I'm sorry I've come at such a bad time."

"Probably the best time you could have come. No one to interrupt us."

He stepped into some slippers in the kitchen, and then led Beth into the dining room. The crystal chandelier caught the afternoon sun, reflecting on the walls. The sizeable dining room table held an arrangement of dried flowers. Gavin Martin pointed to an elaborate empty sidepiece.

"Margaret is awaiting a shipment from London of Royal Doulton and Waterford for that monstrosity."

An Oriental rug covered a good portion of the freshly refinished oak floor.

"What a lovely room," Beth remarked, "Especially the chandelier."

"Yes, I suppose. Between you and me, I'd rather eat in the kitchen."

"Let's go into the front parlor. It's a little more put together than the rest of the house. Care for something to drink?"

"No thank you, sir. I don't want to take too much of your time."

"As you could see, I certainly wasn't busy at my desk."

"Sometimes the best work we can do for ourselves is no work at all," said Beth.

Gavin Martin looked at Beth. "Perhaps you are wise beyond your years, young lady."

She followed him into a room filled with plush furniture and antiques. The bay window on the side looked out to a smooth hill leading up to a forest. Beth knew from her view across the estuary that some high cliffs dropped down to the open sea. She walked over and looked out the window.

"Have you walked through the woods, over to the cliffs?"

"Yes, several times. There's an open space just as you reach the cliffs. With my binoculars I can see Caldey Island."

"Can you see the monks?"

"No, but I hear they're always praying."

Beth laughed. "Well at least you can go inside the monastery."

"Can't you?"

"They don't allow women inside. I find it interesting that they busy themselves making fudge and perfume. Doesn't seem monk-like to me."

Gavin Martin stood beside one of the chairs facing the window. "Elizabeth, let's sit here for our visit."

After Beth was seated, he sat and stared blankly at the bottom of the windowsill. Beth waited for him to speak. The silence was interrupted by Gavin Martin's shaky voice.

"When you came, you told my wife you wanted to talk with me about my mother?"

"Yes."

"And she told you I was busy?"

"Yes, I gave her my name and number. She said you would call if you wanted to talk with me."

"Sorry about that. The situation with my mother is quite painful. Margaret has been taking care of the details for some time. I think of her often, but at times it seems like she doesn't exist, at least, not the mother I used to know. When I visit her, she's incoherent. But I don't understand. If you don't work there, how do you know my mother?"

"I was visiting a friend and happened to meet her."

"Well, it's nice of you to come by."

"Sir, it's not exactly what you might call a friendly visit."

"What do you mean?"

Beth gathered her courage. "Your mother is being overly medicated."

"Overly medicated? How do you know? Are you a nurse?"

"No, sir."

"My mother is not well. She had a nervous breakdown some years ago. Went off the deep end. Poor woman couldn't cope with the sudden death of my father," he said, shaking his head.

"Yes. I know."

"But how could you know? A complete stranger."

"I've talked with your mother."

"But my mother is not in her right mind. I'm just thankful she's in a safe place and being taken care of properly."

Beth stood up almost knocking over a small table between the chairs.

"Being taken care of properly! You call giving the poor woman strong sleeping pills to knock her out twenty four hours a day being taken care of?"

"Sleeping pills?" Holding up his hand, Gavin Martin motioned to her. "Calm down, Elizabeth."

Beth sat down, folding her hands in her lap, trying to relax. She looked out the window.

"How could a son treat his own mother is such a way."

He straightened up in his seat.

"You've met my mother once and you act like an authority on the matter. I admit that I haven't been involved with her treatment. I rely on my wife to update me on her current condition. She's told me there hasn't been any change in her and she has no concerns."

Beth jumped up again. "No worries! They give her Dalmane every morning and night. So strong they make her sleep all the time."

"How do you know such a thing?"

"Never mind. I just know. And she's not allowed visitors."

"No visitors? That's not true."

"Well it is. Except for one priest who comes once a week."

"Probably sent by the Bishop. Such a kind man. And after the way my mother treated him. Such stories she told. But of course she was ill."

Beth collapsed back into the chair with a look of disbelief. Her hands held tightly to the arms of the chair.

In almost a whisper, "Bishop Dakyn. He was her vicar, wasn't he?"

"I've said more than I should. I hope this conversation will go no further, but it might help if I explain some things about my mother's condition. You know, I think we could both use a good cup of tea."

Gavin Martin got up and hurried out of the room. Beth walked over to the window.

Wish I'd never come, she thought. Closing her eyes, she took several deep breaths. Come Holy Spirit, come Holy Spirit, she prayed over and over again. As she began to relax, the whistle of the teakettle startled her.

In a few minutes Gavin Martin appeared with a tray complete with a teapot covered with a lavish tea cozy, embroidered tea napkins, Staffordshire china, and a plate of tea biscuits. He placed it on the small table between the chairs. After offering sugar, lemon and milk, he served Beth her cup of tea.

"Perhaps if you have a cup of tea in your lap, you won't be able to jump up again," he said with a smile.

Trying to sound calm, Beth replied, "Well, sir, I'm quite impressed with a prominent London solicitor serving tea."

"How do you know so much about me?"

"Your mother told me quite a bit about you, your father, the circumstances of his death and the incident."

Gavin offered Beth some biscuits.

"No, thank you."

She remembered the difficulty in balancing a cup, saucer and biscuit on formal occasions.

"The times I've visited her, she hardly recognized me. The doctor said it was part of an emotional reaction. Not wanting to accept reality. I'm rather surprised you were able to have such an involved conversation."

"That's because the nurse was late with her pill the day I met her. When she didn't take her pill, she started improving."

"Not taking her medication? Is that wise?"

"Haven't you been listening to me? The pills make her sleep constantly. And there's no need. She is perfectly sane. And I believe the story about the vicar."

"But why do you believe that?"

"I have my reasons."

A loud phone ring caused them both to almost drop their teacups. Gavin went to the entrance hall to answer.

"Yes, Margaret. You and Vivian on your way to Carmarthen? No, I'm fine. Sound funny? Must be the connection. Had a nice walk to the water and now having tea. There's plenty in the fridge for dinner and I've work to do. Why don't you and Vivian make a day of it and have dinner in town? Yes…bye, Margaret."

Returning to his chair he filled the teacups. Then in a business like tone Gavin said, "All right, Elizabeth, I want you to tell me everything that pertains to my mother. Don't leave anything out."

When she told about seeing the records, he responded, "You know that could be construed as a criminal offense."

Beth did not mention the involvement of Sister Clare or the girl working at the nursing home. But she did inform him that some who knew Bishop Dakar did not perceive him as the perfect example of sainthood.

After she finished, he carried the tea tray out to the kitchen. Beth could hear the running water and clatter of dishes. She walked to the kitchen and found him standing at the sink staring out the window. She grabbed a tea towel and dried the dishes. He put everything back in its place without speaking a word. Then he turned to her with a stern look.

"I'm going to look into this situation on my own. I have a private investigator who executes discretion. I was so overcome by my own feelings, I completely ignored Mother. Left it to Margaret and her doctor and psychiatrist. Such a mistake," he said, shaking his head.

Going over to a small table he picked up a pencil and paper and handed it to Beth.

"Please write any information I may need to contact you."

After Beth wrote down addresses and phone numbers, she left it on the table and followed Gavin Martin to the front door. He handed Beth his business card. "This is my number in London. Don't call here at Pentowyn or speak to anyone about our conversation. If you see Mother, please continue to be her friend. I'll be in touch within a fortnight. If you discover anything else, don't hesitate to call."

He walked Beth out to Ann's car. She extended her hand. Gavin Martin wrapped both his hands around hers.

"Thank you for coming. I know this must have been difficult for you."

Gavin Martin kept holding her hand. Beth couldn't find words to console him about his situation. They stood there for a moment until Beth pulled her hand away. As she turned out the drive, she glanced in the rear view mirror, seeing Gavin Martin walking slowly up the stairs of Pentowyn. *I have a feeling this situation concerning Victoria isn't over yet.*

Chapter Twenty-Nine

"We are like a puff of wind; Our days are like a passing shadow."
(Psalm 144:4)

Beth found the Hughes home empty when she returned to Largharne. She left a note: "Going out for a walk."

A short distance away, she ventured into a graveyard on a cliff overlooking the water. Newly formed clouds blocked out the sun. Persistent rays of light penetrated through the vapors, glistening on the water. Walking to the back of the small, antiquated burial site, she admired the sizeable ornate Celtic cross on the edge of the precipice. Golden primrose clung to the ancient stone barrier built to protect visitors from the sheer drop. Stately ash trees shaded the old gravestones. Clumps of sea aster and thrift added color.

Beth closed her eyes and felt the lowering temperature penetrate her skin. Standing there for some time, she took deep breaths and repeated her breath prayer over and over. Visiting her prayer world was a frequent tool during the hectic days of Oxford, but she hadn't felt need of it lately--not until her visit to Pentowyn.

Slowly, she breathed in three words, *Come Holy Spirit.* Slowly, she breathed out, *and flow through me.*

Beth embraced the silence. A sentence from scripture entered her thoughts. "Come away, by yourselves to a lonely place, and rest awhile." Surrounded by the quiet, she could feel the steady rhythm of her heartbeat. The only sound was her breath, in and out, in and out.

The sudden squawk of birds in the estuary below broke into her reverie. Two gray herons fought over an unlucky fish. Others stood close by, waiting their turn for scraps. Redshanks, waders and oystercatchers scurried about as the low tide surrendered its bounty.

Occasionally a shaft of sunlight caught a hunter darting from the broken clouds, momentarily setting its wings ablaze. A flash of dull orange in an overhead branch marked the presence of a robin. He joined in the entertainment of the late afternoon with a tuneful song.

Glancing around at the diversity of tombstones, Beth realized, life does go on. All the dreams and aspirations of these have died. We all live with restless souls, until we rest eternally.

Thinking of a portion of a psalm that had been an Oxford assignment, she repeated the words in a whisper, "Those of low estate are but a breath, those of high estate are a delusion. In the balances they go up, they are together lighter than a breath."

Beth wandered back and forth between the unkempt, uneven rows and read some of the chiseled names and dates. One of the newer ones read, "George Tawe Williams, son of Rees and Mary Williams of Banister Farm, Laugharen, who died Sept. 10th, 1906, Aged 4 years. Suffer Little Children to Come unto Me." Tears filled Beth's eyes as she read of the several children in the area who died long before their parents.

Looking at her watch she realized she had been there for over an hour. Almost at the entrance she turned to read one last stone that appeared to be the most recent in the graveyard. Glancing down to the middle of the large gray-pink granite, Beth read the words, "In the midst of life, we are in death. Elizabeth Davies, who died July 1, 1924, aged 73 years. Thy Will be Done."

She stared, overwhelmed at her own name on the stone. She read the words over and over again. She knew in her mind it was time to leave, but her feet felt cemented to the spot.

What regrets will I have at the time of my own death? "Thy will be done." God, what is your will for me? Looking over the myriad of tombstones, her thoughts persisted. *And my life? Ministry? Marriage?*

Beth sighed and whispered, "I do feel called to the priesthood. It's easy to say here, in front of you silent witnesses. Pray for me, all who have gone before. And you, Elizabeth Davies, who lies cold in the ground. You had your challenges and I have mine. May you rest in peace."

Slowly Beth turned and walked past the iron gate that guarded the entrance. The sun was setting, giving a crimson glow to the sky. She turned for one last look, surveying the silent remembrances. "May light perpetual shine upon you and give you peace."

Beth opened the door of the Griffith home. "My goodness, where have you been?" Aunt Bessie exclaimed "I was almost at the end of my tether."

"I'm so sorry, Aunt Bessie. I lost track of time."

Aunt Bessie smiled. "That's all right."

"Mam was about to call out the police," Ann chimed in. "When someone's missin' round here, you can always find them at the pub." She glanced over at her father. Uncle Hugh replied with a nod and a sheepish grin.

"Dinner's ready. Fixed crawl tonight," Aunt Bessie said. She served large bowls from the stove. "Mary 'cross the way brought over extra fish. Had fresh leeks and potatoes from her garden, too. Threw it together, so here 'tis."

"My Bessie makes the best crawl in all the country. Different every time, but always the best," Uncle Hugh beamed, rubbing the ample stomach protruding over his belt.

Beth sat at her assigned place, wishing she were having fish 'n chips instead. The crawl looked and smelled awful. Gingerly she took a first spoonful. In no time she was ready for a second bowl of the delicious concoction.

Beth's aunt and uncle had lively stories to tell about their day. Quite a few folk in Laugharne made for interesting tales. Beth's week with her relatives was almost over and she wished she had a few more days with them.

"Mam has a big order in the morning," Ann said. "Some fancy do up at St. Clears. I'll be helping her most of the morning. Thought you might want to take the hike up the Carmarthen Bay Coastal Path."

"I'll be glad to help, too," Beth said.

"No thanks," Ann shook her head. We've got a routine. Besides, I'm afraid you'll want to drag me up there. After lunch we'll go to Carmarthen for the evening."

Aunt Bessie nodded. "Sounds like a good plan to me. Maybe someone will ask me out to dinner as well."

"Meet me at Brown's for a toastie, me Luv," Uncle Hugh said in a gruff voice.

"It'll not be a toastie at Brown's. You'll come straight home and clean up. Then it'll be a proper dinner at The Stable Door Restaurant. And I'll be having spinach cannelloni with feta cheese, thank you very much."

"You see how I'm treated, Beth? Outnumbered by these women. It's enough to do a man in," he grinned.

"Oh, Hugh. Go smoke your pipe."

After Beth and Ann cleaned the kitchen, they went out for a walk toward the estuary.

"All right, Beth, tell me what happened at Pentowyn. I didn't want to ask in front of Mam and Da."

Beth told her every detail.

"So what are you going to do now?" Ann asked.

"I have no idea. God only knows."

Beth woke early the next morning. The aroma told her Ann and Aunt Bessie had been up for some time. She put on her jeans, an old plaid shirt and tied her hair back with a favorite blue ribbon. Lacing up her hiking boots, she glanced at her small travel Bible. *I'll stick that in my jacket pocket. No time for morning prayers.*

Beth went in the kitchen and gulped down some coffee. Stuffing some wrapped pastries in her pocket, she opened the bakery door and bid farewell to Ann and Aunt Bessie.

She walked out onto the silent street heavy with light mist. Past the town clock striking six, she saw Largharne castle looming through the fog like a medieval painting. The town looked deserted in the gray dawn. As she crossed the wooden footbridge above the clear fast-moving stream from the north, she thought of how the water would mingle with the estuary and then out to the ocean to become salt water. *Our lives mingle together as does nature.*

She saw a young couple on an inlet waiting in their wellies for the receding tide and the promise of a bucket full of cockles. She waved. They returned the gesture.

Beth walked along the water's edge past a large estate. Two Welsh Corgis ran up to a fence and barked at her. She went over and petted them. As she continued on her way, she saw a sign marking the beginning of the coastal path. The fog began lifting as the sun chased away the clouds. The purplish-blue sky with hints of gold gave the promise of a clear day.

Beth entered a tree-shaded path with heavy undergrowth on either side and crossed a threshold into a different world. The dead leaves on the ground obliterated any sound of footsteps. She stopped for a moment to listen to the nothingness. Holding her hands together, she said a Celtic prayer her grandmother had taught her many years ago.

"I will walk secure and blessed
In every clime and coast,
In name of God the father
And Son, and Holy Ghost."

Smiling, she could hear the familiar words of her father spoken each time they went fishing,

"A poor life this if, full of care
We have no time to stand and stare."

Beth hadn't thought much of her parents back home in Hawthorne. About this time, her mother would be scurrying about the kitchen making breakfast for herself and her husband. The teakettle would be whistling away and Mum would scold it. "Oh, be quiet you noisy thing. You're worse than those squawking birds who won't keep their mouths shut every morning."

Since it was Saturday, the weekly kippers would be dancing in the pan and the currant scones would be baking in the oven. Her father would be busy in the corner checking his fishing gear.

Growing up, Beth considered her parents' life quite mundane and tedious. Now she understood. Her parents' lives were so meshed at times they lived as one, knowing one another's thoughts without speaking. She wondered if she and Kevin would ever have such a relationship.

Beth used to go with her father on his weekly day of fishing. But now her busy schedule left no time for such outings. Fish 'n chips were her kind of fishing expedition. She vowed to join her father the next time she was at home on a Saturday.

The sun crept further up the horizon as she continued on the steep shaded path, humming *Be Thou My Vision*, an ancient Irish tune. Stretching her leg muscles felt good. She lifted her hands high up to the sky and then off to the side, touching the sides of the taller bushes and an occasional tree branch. *I must look a funny sight, she thought. Glad this trail is deserted.*

Just as she rounded a sharp curve, she collided with a disheveled bearded man. Eying Beth up and down with a leering yellow smile, he spoke, "Haven't seen the likes of you around her. Got a fag, me luv?"

"No, I don't."

He was gone as suddenly as he had appeared. Beth retraced her steps and watched the stranger until he was out of sight. Turning, she continued slowly on her way.

A clearing gave way to a panoramic view of Largharne, the castle and estuary out to the sea. She gazed at the distant shore. Pentowyn stood out against the tranquil scene. *I've done what I can.* Beth remembered her grandmother's words, "Mae'r Arglwydd yma. Mae ei Ysbryd gyda ni." The Lord is here. His Spirit is with us.

Along the path, vines of raspberries begged to be picked. By the time Beth had one hand full, she saw a substantial bench facing a large sign.

Settling back in comfort, she brought out her breakfast wrapped in napkins. Plopping a few raspberries into her mouth, she sensed the slight crunch as the morsel's sweet tartness exploded in her mouth.

After finishing her picnic breakfast, she studied the sign. Amazed at the detail and information, she wished she had brought along pencil and paper to make notes. Laughing at herself, she thought, just like a student. It featured a detailed colorful drawing of the countryside with illustrations of all the trees, plants and birds. The variety of life inhabiting the Carmarthen Bay Coastal Path amazed her.

"So that's the name. A cormorant." Beth smiled as she remembered seeing the dark feathered creature on a hike above the Dylan Thomas' home.

From the high overlook, she watched a large bird diving into the water below. The bird reappeared with a wiggling fish in his beak. Flying over to a sand barge, he quickly devoured his meal. Then spreading his wings as though in flight, he strutted around drying himself in the sun like a proud peacock. A chunky oystercatcher provided further entertainment with laterally flattened, heavy bill reaching into a mollusk and prying the shell open.

Beth studied more of the sign. The familiar herons mentioned by Dylan in his poems were easy to spot, as well as the shelducks, geese, waders and plovers, but there were quite a few unfamiliar birds. Resuming the walk she went for some time until she noticed the sun straight above her head and knew it was time to return.

The solitude had been a literal "God send" for her. Beth hungered for this time without knowing it. She remembered a paper she had written while at Oxford. Her friends had dared her to turn it in, so she did. She had used the term, recreation, to write on the value of re-creation.

She wrote that the spiritual life is in constant need of becoming new, while embracing the old. All that is good is a creation of God. We find Him with our eyes as well as our hearts, souls and minds. He speaks to us in silence, in the setting sun, in a thunderous storm, in the gentle breeze. The air that touches us touches others. The Holy Spirit as a gentle breeze passes to become a part of us. Then moves on to others. Miles away. Continents away.

By including St. Francis and a few of her favorite Celtic saints, she thought it was quite well written. The red pen in bold letters stood out at the top of the cover page. *Unacceptable! Pantheistic!*

The next day she turned in the conservative, boring paper that would satisfy her professor's dusty, predictable approach to religion.

"Yes, I learned to play the game. If God chooses to ordain me, she thought, perhaps I can draw back the curtains of some dark protected rooms of our church and bring in some light, clear away the cobwebs, and open the windows to the fresh loving air of Light.

Domine in lumine tuo videbimus lumen.' Lord, by Thy light shall we see light."

Refreshed and re-created, Beth walked back down the path returning to civilization.

"You missed a call from Kevin," Ann said, as soon as Beth walked in the door. "Said he had to go to London for something and would ring back tonight."

"Probably one of those social engagements his mother arranged for him. Wait till we're married. I'll tell the maid to inform Lady Gately we're not at home every bloody time she calls."

"Why, Beth. What a thing to say about your future mother-in-law."

Beth smiled and nodded.

"Now change and we'll be off for your last night. There's a super band playing at the Boar's Head Pub."

Chapter Thirty

"For where your treasure is, there will your heart be also."
(Matthew 7:21)

Beth dozed a good bit of the way on the train. The late night in Carmarthen with Ann and her friends had left her exhausted.

"Llandudno Junction!" shouted a voice, waking Beth from a deep sleep. Grabbing her bags she got off a moment before the train departed for Bangor.

Five minutes after Beth's train pulled out of the station, she saw the Great Orme rising from the water. *Hope there's not too much to do at Grandmum's. Want to go up there tomorrow.*

Beth thought of Adam and the first time she saw him at St. Tudno's church. He had entered her mind on more than one occasion this past week in Laugharne. He had come into her life by accident. Years from now she probably wouldn't remember his name, and yet....

The train came to an abrupt halt at the end of the line in Llandudno. Beth looked out her window. Adam stood on the platform with Manna. As she stepped off the train with her bag, she lost her balance and fell into his arms. He held her for a moment, until she pulled away. She felt a warm redness in her face and kept her head down.

"Thank you for coming, but it wasn't necessary," she said as she knelt down and gave Manna a hug.

"Manna couldn't wait one more minute for your return, so we walked down to meet you. Here, I'll take your bag," Adam said, taking her suitcase and handing Manna's leash to Beth. "She's had a good run along the beach before we came. Didn't know if you would want to get out tonight or not."

Beth thought of the words, get out tonight. Did he mean with him or with Manna? As they walked along the street, she tried to look at him out of the corner of her eye. He wore the same old scruffy boots, work shirt and jeans.

"Been busy with odd jobs this past week around here?" she said.

"Not too. Hiked up the Orme with Manna a couple of times. We walked back on the coast road one afternoon. Stopped in at the lighthouse. Interesting structure, especially for 1862. One of a kind."

"And did the owners invite you in for tea?" Beth said, smiling.

"As a matter of fact, they did. There're dog lovers and quite taken with Manna. Gave me a tour and invited us to come back. I could take you up there, if you'd like."

"Oh, probably not. I've had enough musty old buildings to last me a lifetime. Oxford was full of them."

"Ah yes. The stodgy old ivory towers. But if you change your mind." Adam continued in a mysterious tone. "A setting for a Foresight novel. A remote cliff with thunderous waves lashing the rocks below. An ancient lighthouse haunted by a crazed lighthouse keeper. A young girl's car breaks down on the desolate road. She stumbles through the storm to the distant light for shelter. What danger lies ahead!"

"Bala Foresight isn't that melodramatic."

Beth and Adam turned the corner to Mostyn Street. Locals and tourists out for late afternoon shopping and pub visits filled the main street. As they were crossing the street with baggage and dog in tow, a large tour group came across from the opposite direction. Beth and Adam were pushed into one another and the suitcase fell out of his hand. The latch flew opened. A few items fell out.

Getting down on their knees, they stuffed the articles back into the suitcase. Adam's hand touched Beth's when they attempted to fasten the latch. Beth looked into his eyes. Neither moved, as pedestrians passed by on either side.

Adam smiled. Beth looked away and saw Manna looking from one to the other. An impatient car horn blasted their silence from the noisy world surrounding them. Beth scrambled to her feet and they continued walking.

After a few moments Beth spoke. "How is Grandmother doing? Many guests this week?"

"Not many. I was able to finish the work around her place."

"Does that mean you'll be moving on?"

"Not just yet. I have other work in the area."

I think I'm glad he'll be around longer. Or am I?

They walked the rest of the way in silence.

Opening the front door, Beth called out, "Grandmum! I'm home."

The fragrance of lamb stew and homemade bread filled the air. A note on the table in the entrance area read, "Will return soon."

"No doubt about supper for tonight, Adam. I'm sure there's plenty."

"Best check with your grandmother. You girls may want some time together."

Reaching into his pocket, he brought out a business card, wrote a phone number on the back and handed it to Beth.

"Just ring me later, if it's convenient. Take your bag to your room?"

"No thanks. I can get it."

Adam turned and walked out the door.

"Thanks again," Beth called out, but no response. She watched as he hurried down the street. Strange, she thought. Turning the card over, she read the name of a London solicitor with an exclusive address.

I knew it. Adam's a private detective working undercover. Who could he be spying on? Llandudno would be a good place to hide out. Think I'll do a little detective work on my own.

After putting her bag away, she left a note for her grandmother with Adam's card.

> Going to the library. Will be back by 6:00. Here's Adam's number. Ring him up if you want to invite him to dinner.

The Internet at the library gave Beth little information, only the fact the firm on the card was one of the prestigious ones in London. Apparently the solicitor's specialty concerned legal business matters.

When she returned to her grandmother's, she learned Adam would join them for supper.

Beth attempted to examine her feelings about him. *He's just some drifter, a handyman. Don't know why I should waste my time thinking about him.* But she couldn't deny her curiosity.

During dinner that night, Beth told Adam and Grandmum about her trip to Largharne.

"Your grandmother was quite nervous about you and your cousin getting along," Adam said. "I told her not to worry. I knew you would have a meaningful experience."

"Now, Adam, that sounds a bit heavy," Beth said.

Handing Beth and Adam generous portions of gooseberry pie, Grandmum asked, "And did you have any meaningful experiences?"

"Never thought to describe the trip that way," Beth said. I did enjoy Ann immensely, although we're opposite in many ways."

Adam smiled and nodded. "Often we can learn from those who are quite different from us and from our concepts of life."

"Why, Adam," Beth said, "you sound like a philosopher. Have you studied philosophy?"

"I've dabbled a bit."

"Have a favorite author?"

"Several. Pascal, Kierkegaard, Teilhard de Chardin, and Hemingway, to name a few."

"Quite impressive for a handyman, I must say."

During the dinner conversation Grandmum mentioned one of her frequent guests. Beth noticed Adam's interest and he asked several questions about him. The guest had business in Llandudno and would stay at the B & B almost every week. His stylish black BMW looked out of place parked on the side streets of Llandudno.

Beth helped her grandmother clear away and wash the dishes while Adam went out in the backyard to feed Manna and Scrappy some leftovers.

As the women were finishing their task, Grandmum whispered, "You certainly seem to be interested in Adam."

"Not the least bit interested, just curious."

"You know, dear, I hesitate to say it, but you're almost rude to him sometimes."

"Oh, Grandmum, he's got a tough skin. Besides, I think he enjoys my comments and questions. Like a game between us."

Adam was waiting for them outside the parlor.

"Mrs. Hughes, mind if I leave Scrappy here while I go to the library?"

"Not at all. As a matter of fact, Beth said she needed to go to the library. You young folk can go along together," she said smiling.

On the way Beth tried other questions that might give her some additional clues to Adam's real identity, but he evaded the questions or changed the subject.

At the library Beth observed him as she sat at a computer. Walking over to the drinking fountain at the same time, she noticed he had selected books about Stratford-Upon-Avon, a collection of Shakespeare's plays and a travel book centering on the area northwest of London.

Returning to her computer, she continued a name search. No success, so she decided to go and look over Adam's shoulder at his screen. "Current Plays at Stratford."

"Going to the theater?"

Adam jumped at the sound of her voice. "Not any time soon. Ready to go?"

"No, you go on. I've got some more work to do," she responded, not wanting to walk back with him.

"I'm not quite ready either."

She returned to her computer and decided to check the Bala Foresight web page. Not much new except promotion of her new novel. Beth enjoyed reading the fan mail. It resembled the *Dear Abby* newspaper column that one of her American friends at Oxford had shared with her.

Bala encouraged aspiring new writers. Beth wondered if the author should give out too much information. *Doesn't she know she's helping her future competition?*

Engrossed in reading the web page, she forgot to keep an eye on Adam. Glancing over, she noticed he was concentrating and typing at lightning speed. As soon as she got up, he glanced over at her. Typing a few more words, he exited the site before she could see the screen.

Looking at his watch, Adam smiled. "About time for the library to close. Walk back along the beach?"

"I suppose. It's on the way home."

Few people were on the promenade in the late evening. Beth and Adam strolled along in silence for some time, then climbed down the stairs onto the sand. Adam put his books on a bench.

"Beth, let's take our shoes off and walk in the water."

"How did you know I was thinking the very same thing and didn't want to say it?"

"Why not?"

"Because you would think it childish."

"We worry too much about what others think. Gets in the way of living life."

Beth and Adam ran in and out of the water, teasing the tide as it approached dry sand. Neither noticed the lateness of the hour until a policeman walked up and mentioned the time. Laughing, they returned to the bench and put on their shoes.

Beth looked at his books.

"Stratford. Going there next to do some work?"

"You seem curious about me, Beth."

"You're not a handyman, are you?"

"Well, I am right now."

"But you haven't always been a handyman, and I don't think you are right now. I think you're up to something," she challenged, with a slight smile.

"Perhaps."

"And I think I know what your real profession is. You're some sort of investigator, private detective or undercover agent."

"My goodness. You're quite perceptive to surmise that possibility."

"I'm right, aren't I? But I hope it doesn't involve anything dangerous or unscrupulous."

"No, no danger at all. Most would call it a quite boring vocation, but I do enjoy the travel and meeting interesting people, like you, Beth."

He reached over and put his hand on hers. "I hope we will be friends for some time."

Beth could have drawn her hand away, but she left it there. It seemed right. Almost comforting. Staring out at the water, the couple sat a foot apart with hands touching. An almost moonless sky accentuated the stars. A shooting star captured Beth's attention. She wondered what Adam had wished.

Back at the B & B, Beth found her grandmother asleep on the sofa in the parlor.

"Grandmum, wake up. I'm home."

"Heavens! You young folk were out late. The library closes at nine."

"We walked on the beach for some time and then just sat."

"Just like your grandfather and I use to do. How romantic. I do like Adam. He's a fine young man. A good match for you."

"Grandmother! Have you forgotten? I'm engaged to Kevin."

Grandmum smiled. "As your grandfather use to say, 'Let's go turn up our toes. Busy day tomorrow."

That night brought restless sleep and incoherent dreams. First she heard the sound of surf relentlessly beating against a rocky shore. Next a scene appeared with a man looking over a vast expanse of rolling hills with mountains in the distance. Beth felt herself walking toward him. One moment it looked like Kevin dressed in his casual Oxford clothes. Then the man turned into Adam wearing his work clothes and old boots. As soon as she got close enough to see the face, he vanished. She was left alone on the hillside.

She woke with a start. 2 a.m.

Beth fell back asleep. Another dream. She was alone in a deep forest with trails going in four directions. Which one to take? Night began to fall and she was hungry and cold. She turned, facing each path, saying a prayer. Finally making a decision, Beth took a few steps down the chosen path. The faint sound of church bells behind her interrupted the silence. She turned to follow the bells and awoke at 5 a.m.

"That's it," she said in disgust. "Might as well get up and get some work done."

The aroma of breakfast filtered up to the top floor just as she finished cleaning one of the unoccupied rooms. Going downstairs, Beth joined her grandmother for breakfast.

"My goodness! You've already done a full day's work. Marie and I can take care of the rest. Why don't you take the rest of the day off?"

Beth welcomed the opportunity. Perhaps a hike up the Orme with Manna would clear her head and get things in perspective.

Selecting a different route, she walked down Church Walks past the row of Victorian B & Bs facing Llandudno Bay. The deserted pier stretched out to a calm sea. Blue water and sky almost matched. Beth usually avoided this way because it seemed so touristy.

Happy Valley and *Ski Llandudno* looked like a Hollywood movie set. The garden area held an odd assortment of trees, shrubs and flowers imported from other lands. While walking through the grape arbor, she noticed some fruit that looked ripe for picking. Not able to resist she grabbed a few, putting them in her mouth. The sour taste exploded as she bit down. Running over to the side of the walk, she spit out all she could.

Up the side of the grassy ski slope, absent of manmade winter snow, she remembered the fun one Christmas when she and her cousins skied for the first time. They went down the hill more on their bottoms than on skis. To a child's eyes, the hill gave the impression of a gigantic mountain. Now it was just a small hill. Wild Kashmir goats coming down into the valley dotted the hillside. In the summer months they usually roamed the Great Orme, hidden from view. Strange, she thought, and continued on her way.

The fresh air invigorated Beth. She was thankful to be out in nature again, chatting with Manna as they climbed side by side.

"I'm engaged to Kevin. The church thing can take a back seat until after the wedding. I have a great life ahead of me. As far as Adam, he's just a curiosity. I'll see nothing more of him. If he persists in any way, I'll just explain how things are and that will be that. Tonight I'll sleep like a baby."

As she topped the rise of a hill, Beth noticed an ominous cloud some miles out over the Irish Sea. Quickening her walk, she gauged she had just enough time to reach the shelter of St. Tudno's Church. The cool moist wind increased. The top of the few trees that insisted on living on the summit of the rocky mountain came into view as the rain hit her face. She saw something small and furry coming towards her. Scrappy leaped into her arms. Beth looked up and saw Adam standing near a tall Celtic cross.

"Hurry or you'll be soaked," he shouted as he ran to the church door. She ran as fast as she could, holding Scrappy under her jacket, but the heavy torrent of rain attacked her. She reached the church, drenched. Adam held the door open.

Leaning over his backpack he took out a towel and old work shirt.

"Better take off those wet socks and shoes before you catch cold." He looked at Beth and laughed, "You look like a drowned rat. The water soaked through that flimsy jacket of yours." Holding out the shirt, he said, "Take off that wet shirt and wear this one."

"I will not!"

"You'll catch cold in this freezing church if you don't. He turned and walked down the aisle facing the altar. "I promise I won't peek, so help me God."

Beth couldn't help but be amused at his serious oath, as she changed into his shirt.

"Okay, you can turn around."

She sat in a back chair, stripping off her shoes and socks. Grabbing the towel, Adam knelt down and began drying her feet.

"That's not necessary," she said, standing and walking a few steps away. He followed with the towel. She could feel his gentle touch as he dried the back of her hair.

"Thank you," she said, turning around. Their eyes met as he continued to dry her hair. She wondered what it would be like to kiss him. One little kiss would do no harm. Their lips were about to touch when suddenly the wind blew the door open. Adam rushed to close it.

Not knowing whether to be disappointed or relieved, Beth sat down in a pew. Adam joined her.

"Beth, I didn't think you'd be up here today. Didn't you have a full day of work at your grandmother's?"

"Yes. But I couldn't sleep. Kept having dreams and waking up, so I got up extra early and got everything done."

"Couldn't sleep? I'm a good listener."

"Well, you know how dreams are. It's amazing how often you can't remember them."

"Took a class once on interpreting dreams. Quite interesting. It's important to write them down the moment you wake up."

No need to write those dreams down. I remember every detail.

"Adam, do you have a university degree?"

"No, didn't see any need. I do enjoy studying a variety of subjects and people. Makes life interesting. I think too much emphasis is put on a degree, social status, and wealth. What's vital is the soul of a person."

"Those are commendable comments for someone who doesn't have a family to support. But certain professions require training, education. I need my degree if I'm to..."

"To what?"

Looking up at the cross of the ancient church, Beth said in a whisper, "To become a minister."

Adam also stared at the cross. He turned toward Beth, took her cold hand and held it in his warm hands. Beth couldn't turn and look at him.

"Beth, I think that's great. The church needs more like you. You could bring some light into the dark places like you do into this shadowy building."

"You really mean it? About me becoming a minister?"

"Yes."

They sat in silence with faces toward the altar, listening to the gradual decrease of the rain. Rays of sun gave color again to the windows and filtered into the building.

"Care for a ride home? I drove my car up after I checked the weather."

"I know now why the goats were seeking shelter down in *Happy Valley*. Somehow they knew the storm was coming."

"Interesting how often animals can sense certain things before we humans."

"Now don't tell me you took a course in animal behavior."

"Not yet, but not a bad idea."

As Beth got into Adam's car, she noticed a laptop and a box of files. "Strange tools for a handyman," she said.

Adam smiled, but said nothing. The dogs settled on an old blanket in the back seat.

"Mind going along Marine Drive the long way?"

"Not at all. Haven't taken the drive all summer. Always walk up with Manna."

Driving past the lighthouse, Adam said, "A shame it's been converted to a B & B, but the owners have done a grand job. From the looks of the cars, they must have a full house. Every time I venture up on the Great Orme I try to imagine what it must have been like to live here hundreds of years ago."

"Me, too," Beth nodded. "Wish we could step into one of those time machines, but only if we could be back in time for supper and a good night's sleep."

"Well said! I'll wager you'll sleep well tonight, Beth."

Back at her grandmother's, Beth and Manna got out of the car and shut the door. She leaned over and looked through the window.

"Thank you for the ride, Adam. There's something I need to remind you. I'm engaged."

Smiling, Adam replied, "No problem," and then drove off.

Beth watched as his car turned the corner. *I wish I'd never met him.*

Chapter Thirty-One

"But I have calmed and quieted my soul, like a child quieted at its mother's breast."

(Psalm 131:2)

"Beth, I've been so worried, especially with the storm."

"Sorry, Grandmum. Manna and I were almost to the top when it came in. Adam gave me a ride home."

"Adam?" Grandmum noticed her shirt, "Looks like he gave you more than a ride home. Nice color."

"Oh, Grandmum! I got soaked. He and Scrappy were up there, too. We waited out the storm in the church."

Smiling, Grandmum replied, "Interesting how things work out, isn't it dear."

"Just a coincidence, nothing more."

"You've got two letters. One from London and one from Holywell."

Beth changed and went to the parlor to read her mail. The envelope from London had Brigid's name on the return address. Beth hadn't heard from her Oxford friend since graduation. The first two pages of the letter described her East End flat in detail. The last page surprised Beth.

> I have the most fantastic job working for Stockton Publishing Company. Hard to realize that I'm having such fun and

getting paid for it. And now for the great part. My boss is the editor for Bala Foresight! I told him you are her biggest fan. When the time is right, I'll ask if there's a chance for you to meet her. Have included my phone at home and work. Let me know when you can come.

Love,
Brigid

The letter from Sister Clare contained news about Victoria. A new medication forced her to stay in bed constantly. A large sign posted on her door announced no visitors. Sister Gertrude had improved and she would soon return to the convent. The nun concluded her letter by encouraging Beth to take some action about Victoria.

Beth stared at the letter without seeing the words. She didn't hear her grandmother come into the parlor.

"Elizabeth! Are you sleeping with your eyes opened? From the look on your face, must be bad news."

"It is, but I don't know if there's anything I can do."

Grandmum sat beside Beth on the couch. She put her arm around her. The grandmother's loving presence said far more than words to Beth. After a while, she spoke.

"Grandmum, mind if I make a call to London?"

"Not at all dear. Do what you need to do."

Hurrying to her room, Beth located Gavin Martin's card and called the office number. His secretary was quite formal until Beth gave her name. She said Mr. Martin would call back within a few minutes.

Shortly, the phone rang. The voice of Gavin Martin dredged up memories of their conversation at Pentowyn. Beth read the portion of the letter that contained information about Victoria's condition.

"I was told that her medication would be changed! And I requested a different doctor. This is inexcusable. I had planned to go for a visit next week. I'm leaving London immediately. Elizabeth, any chance you can meet me at Holywell?"

I'll check with my grandmother, but I can probably arrange it."

Later that evening Beth skimmed through a recent London paper. A picture caught her eye. The caption underneath read, "The Bishop of Chester out for a stroll with his spiritual director."

The man standing beside the bishop wore a monk's habit. She reached for her grandmother's magnifying glass on a side table. Focusing the glass on the picture, Beth exclaimed, "I knew it! That's the priest who comes to visit Victoria every week."

Manna and Beth were on the road by midmorning the following day. She planned to stay at home in Hawthorne that night. When she called the Gately Estate, Sybil, a maid, informed her Kevin had left for a boating excursion with classmates from Oxford, but would return the next day.

A large group of tourists had arrived for lunch when Beth drove up to St. Winefride's. She found Sister Clare in the kitchen with some of the sisters preparing food.

"Elizabeth, good to see you." She motioned for Beth to come out in the hall for privacy.

"Mr. Martin came by early this morning," the nun said. "He looked a mess. Drove from London last night and stayed the night with his mother. You are to go over and meet him there."

"Can I leave Manna in the back yard?"

"Certainly. Mind if I take her for a romp after lunch? She's so well behaved. Better than some humans I know."

Beth found the front door at the nursing home unlocked. The friendly nurse, Miss Wimple, greeted her with a smile from behind the front desk. Apparently expecting Beth, she nodded toward the hallway of Victoria's room.

Beth opened Victoria's door. Gavin Martin, his face unshaven, wore wrinkled clothes. He sat by his mother's bed. She was asleep. He stood and motioned for Beth to follow him out into the hall.

"Elizabeth, so good to see you. Thank you for your help. After our talk last night, I instructed the doctor to stop the medication. I've had some investigating going on about this place, but it takes so long. Following our conversation yesterday, I had a friend from Chester come over and stay with Mother until I could arrive. Another doctor has been assigned and the head nurse put on leave. I hate to tell you, but my wife is behind part of this mess. She and the bishop."

"I'm so sorry, Mr. Martin. I know that must be difficult for you."

"I've had my head buried in the sand long enough. We seem like the ideal couple, but we've been living apart under the same roof for a number of years. I was a fool to put Margaret in charge of my mother's well being. And to think I believed that vicar and the psychiatrist."

"Gavin! Gavin! Where are you?"

"Coming, Mother."

Victoria's face lit up when she saw Beth.

"My friend, my dear friend. Wonderful to see you," she said with outstretched arms.

Beth went to her bedside and gave Victoria a hug.

"You two visit awhile," Gavin said. "I have some calls to make."

Victoria told Beth about her son's plans. The new doctor who visited that morning expected a full recovery; only it would take some time for her to regain her strength. In a matter of days, she would be moved to a facility near London that would aid in her rehabilitation

"Isn't it wonderful?" Victoria took Beth's hand. "And I know it's because of you. Gavin told me the details. One might say you stepped in where angels fear to tread."

Beth laughed. "I wouldn't go as far as to say that. I do have a tendency to speak my mind. Sometimes at the right times, but more often at the wrong times."

"Gavin is quite impressed with you, young lady. I can assure you if there's ever anything we can do for you, don't hesitate to ask."

Gavin Martin walked in carrying a tray with adequate provisions for afternoon tea for three.

"Afraid they don't have any Royal Doulton at this establishment for you ladies, so this will have to do. This time next year, we'll have afternoon tea at the Georgian."

Beth told about Llandudno and her trip to Laugharne. Gavin described future holidays with his mother. Mention of a cruise on the Mediterranean caused Beth to reveal her knowledge of the travels of St. Paul to Ephesus, Rhodes, and Athens. "Be sure to visit the island of Patmos where St John wrote the book of Revelation. I hear the monastery and icons are fantastic."

"The what?" asked Victoria.

After an explanation of icons, the Martins invited Beth to join them as their tour guide. A woman coming in with Victoria's dinner signaled the time. Beth and Gavin stood.

"I really should be going. My parents are expecting me home for supper. But I can stop by on my way back to Llandudno, if you like."

"That would be wonderful." Victoria smiled. "I'll look forward to your visit."

Gavin stood. "I'll walk you to your car, Elizabeth."

The late afternoon sun couldn't reach the dreary part of Holywell. They walked in silence until Gavin opened Beth's car door.

"I can't thank you enough for all you've done. Isn't there something I can do for you?"

"Seeing your mother is thanks enough. Such a shame she had to go through this horrible ordeal. And all because of one person."

"My wife?"

"No! The Bishop."

Gavin shook his head. "I pray she will someday be the mother I knew long ago."

Taking Gavin's hand, Beth said, "Your mother is quite a different person now. I have a feeling she may come out of this a stronger woman. Be patient as you both go through this healing time together."

Beth got in her car and drove off. She looked in her rear view mirror and saw Gavin walking slowly back into St. Beuno's. After retrieving Manna at St. Winefride's, she continued on her way to Hawthorne.

Chapter Thirty-Two

"Oh what tangled webs we weave,
when first we venture to deceive."
(Shakespeare)

The next day after breakfast with her parents and a walk with Manna on the Gately Estate, Beth decided to go into Chester to shop. Seeking the peacefulness of the Cathedral from the crowded city streets, she entered by one of the side doors. The somber stillness brought welcome relief.

Down the south choir aisle, she entered the Chapel of St. Erasmus, a quiet place for prayer, undisturbed by visitors. Her prayers centered on Victoria and her recovery. She thanked God Gavin had taken charge of the situation. But when she thought of the bishop, she felt anger instead of forgiveness.

As she was leaving the chapel through the ornate 16th century Spanish iron gate, Beth saw the Bishop of Chester coming toward her.

"Excuse me, Bishop. Would you have a few minutes?"

"Why, Elizabeth Davies. I've thought of you often. Of course. Come with me to my office. Perhaps a change of heart?"

"Yes sir, you might call it that."

Neither spoke until they reached the reception area.

"Mrs. Richmond, show Miss Davies into my office. I'll be with you in just a few minutes."

Mrs. Richmond glared at Beth as she led her into the room.

"Have a seat. The Bishop will be with you shortly."

The door closed behind her with a thud. *I feel like I've walked into the lion's den.*

Going over to a window, she looked out on the cathedral grounds. Movement on the other side of the glass pane caught her eye. A spider had woven an ornate web in the bottom corner of the window and a fly was entangled in the snare. Beth watched as the spider approached his next meal.

"What tangled webs we weave when first we venture to deceive," she sighed.

"Tangled webs, my dear?" came the bishop's voice a few feet away.

Startled, she turned, facing him. He approached Beth and put his arm around her shoulders.

"Come, dear, and sit. We'll have a chat."

She pulled away, choosing a chair opposite his desk. He sat behind his desk and seriously eyed Beth. "You seem a bit out of sorts, Miss Davies. How can your bishop be of assistance?"

Beth stood defiantly. "Help me? I'll not have you helping me like you helped Victoria Martin."

The bishop's face turned ashen white. "I have no idea what you're talking about."

"Oh yes you do."

"I think it's best you leave my office immediately," he said reaching over to an intercom.

"Not until I've had my say, preferably in confidence."

He withdrew his hand.

"You lied about that poor woman to protect yourself. Ruined her life when she counted on you for help and convinced her son she needed psychiatric care." Beth knew her face was flaming.

"I have nothing to say to you." He stood, clutching the edge of his desk. "You have no proof. My word against hers. Someone like you couldn't possibly understand how decisions must be made for the good of the church. Besides, the matter was closed long ago."

"Not long ago. Not for a woman confined to a nursing home because of your lies. And it does no good to confess to your spiritual director and receive absolution."

Fists clenched, he shouted at Beth. "You have no right to talk to me in such a manner! I am your bishop!"

"You have the audacity to call yourself a man of God? You are not my bishop!"

Beth turned and stormed out of the office, before he could reply. She walked through the cathedral and into the crowded streets of Chester. She couldn't believe what she had just done.

Reaching Grosvenor Park, she walked down a familiar path. Sitting on the hill where the grass reached down to a small lake, she watched the ducks swimming lazily on the water. Instead of feeling remorse at her outburst, she felt relief.

That takes care of any possibility of ordination. But what's right is right. What's done is done. So be it.

Beth drove back to Hawthorne. When she saw Kevin sitting on her front porch, her heart skipped a beat. She could tell him all about Victoria and the bishop. It would be such a relief. He walked over and opened her door.

"Beth, I thought you'd never get home."

After they kissed, they went over and sat on the porch steps. She told him the entire story about Victoria, her meeting with Gavin Martin and the scene with the bishop. After she finished, Kevin stared off into space, shaking his head. "I can't believe you said that to the bishop. It's so inappropriate. Somehow, you'll have to apologize."

"Apologize? What about that poor woman? And there have probably been others from what I've heard."

"Oh, he's just a harmless old chap. But he is a bishop and that means you must respect his position, Beth."

Beth stood and walked a few feet away, looking off into the distance. She couldn't believe what she just heard.

Kevin came over and put his arms around her. "Let's go out for dinner tonight. The Grosvenor? It's one of your favorite places."

"Kevin, don't you understand? I can't apologize. He did a horrible thing." Beth pulled away.

"After you've had some time to think about it, I'm sure you'll reconsider. Now how about dinner?"

"No, not tonight. And perhaps not any other night."

"What do you mean?"

"We may be different in too many ways, Kevin. I need some time to think."

Beth turned and climbed the stairs into the house, leaving Kevin. She went to her room, looked out the window and watched him walking down the road toward the Gately Estate. How many times had they walked that same road together, sharing their hopes and dreams for the future?

The knock on the door interrupted her thoughts.

"Beth, are you and Kevin going out for dinner or should I set an extra place?"

"Only a place for me, please. Be down in a minute."

At supper, Beth described her trip to Largharne and how much she enjoyed visiting her relatives. Her father stood as soon as he finished his pudding. "Think I'll go down to the pub. You girls visit a while."

"Da, are you going fishing tomorrow?"

Before he could answer, her mother spoke, "Now where else would the likes of him be going? Shopping at Harrods?" Pointing her finger at him she continued, "And don't you dare bring home any of those slimy bodies for me to clean. I'll get my fish from the market, thank you very much."

"Nice to know who's in charge of this establishment," he said, smiling at his wife. "As I said, I'll be at the pub. Beth, did you need me to stay home tomorrow?"

"No, thought I'd go with you, if that's all right."

"Why you haven't been fishing with me since you were a wee one. Be glad to have the company."

Beth's father gave his wife the expected goodbye kiss. She watched with a look of comfort. Ever since she could remember, he never left or arrived home without a kiss.

Beth started washing the dishes. Her mother fixed a pot of tea and set it on the table with two cups.

"Come, sit. Dishes can wait. Now tell me, what's bothering you."

"I don't want to go into all the details now, but I think Kevin and I are calling it off."

Her mother paused. "I see. Do you think it's for good, or is this a lover's spat?"

"I think it's for good," Beth said, "but it would have helped you and Da. Neither of you would ever have to work again."

"Oh Beth! We have a good life. I ask for nothing but your happiness."

"It's strange, Mum. I feel like I've lost my best friend. I do care for Kevin, but I'm not sure I've ever really been in love with him."

They sat at the table for over an hour reliving family stories. Beth was anxious to hear every one her mother could remember, especially about her grandfather.

"Now what's this about you wanting to go fishing with your father? That nearly knocked me off my chair."

"You know, Mum, sometimes we don't spend time with those we love and then…" Beth held back her tears. Her mother patted her hand.

Beth excused herself and called Llandudno. After hearing her grandmother didn't need her help at the B & B for a few days, she decided to stay at home in Hawthorne.

Chapter Thirty-Three

"Thou desirest truth in the inward being; therefore teach me wisdom in my secret heart."
(Psalm 51:6)

A few days later on her way back to Llandudno, Beth stopped at Hollywell to visit Victoria Martin. She walked down the hall to Victoria's room, passing a woman walking with a cane.

"Beth, it's me, Victoria."

"My goodness! I didn't recognize you. And such a pretty frock."

"Gavin arranged for some new clothes. I'll be leaving in a few days. Any chance you ever get to the London area?"

"As a matter of fact, I have a very good friend who has just moved there. When I come down for a visit, I'll get in touch."

"That would be splendid. And you can always call Gavin's office to find me."

Beth drove out of Hollywell more convinced than ever she had made the right decisions. Manna leaned her head out the car window further as the Great Orme came into view. The dog began wagging her large tail, almost hitting Beth in the face.

"Settle down, Manna," Beth scolded. "We'll have our time. I wonder if Adam's up there."

Pulling up in front of the B and B, Beth hurried inside. "Grandmum, I'm home."

Walking past the parlor, she noticed a large bouquet of flowers on the table.

"In the kitchen, Beth," her grandmother shouted.

After giving her grandmother a hug, she asked, "Where did those flowers come from? One of your guests?"

"No, read the card," she replied with a grin.

Beth tried to act disinterested. Mrs. Hughes told about the recent guests and a chorus concert. Beth had trouble listening to her grandmother because she kept thinking about the flowers. She left and went to the parlor. A card was pinned to one of the pink ribbons.

> To Two Special Ladies.
> Must be gone a few days.
> Will call when I return.
> Love, Adam

Beth almost dropped the note when her grandmother walked in.

"How long has he been gone?"

"A few days."

Beth heard a knock on the front door. "Maybe that's him. Why don't you answer?"

Grandmum walked back into the room followed by Kevin Gately.

"If you young folk will excuse me, I'll be down in the kitchen finishing my baking."

"Beth, I called your home and your mother said you had left, so I decided to drive over. Any chance we can have dinner? We need to talk."

"I suppose," she said.

"I'm staying over tonight at Bodysgallen Hall. We could have dinner there."

"Would you mind going up to the King's Head? I don't feel like anything fancy."

"Fine. What time?"

"Seven."

"See you then."

Kevin left without another word.

Beth and Manna walked to the shore. She sat on a bench, watching Manna romp back and forth into the waves. She wished Kevin hadn't come to Llandudno. Perhaps he had a change of heart about the situation with the bishop. But after examining her feelings for him over the past several days, she wasn't sure if it would make any difference.

Manna came running over, nudging her. Looking at her watch, she realized she had just enough time to change for dinner.

The King's Head Pub was crowded for a weekday. Its owner showed them to a corner table in the back room that had flowers and a large "reserved" sign on it.

"You must have called ahead, Kevin."

"Yes, I think it's the first time anyone has made such a request at this establishment."

After ordering, Kevin talked about his boating expedition and how much he thought Beth would enjoy such an excursion. She talked of her fishing day with her father, which appeared pale by comparison. While waiting for dessert, Kevin finally approached the subject.

"I'm sorry I upset you the other day. I didn't mean to," he said, taking her hand. "Have you come to terms with the problem?"

"What do you mean, come to terms?"

"I mean do you realize that we need to smooth over the situation?"

Beth looked away, trying to think of how to respond. The owner walked in the back room followed by a customer. It was Adam. As soon as he saw Beth and Kevin, he turned and walked out.

"What's wrong, Beth? You're as red as the roses."

"Nothing, nothing at all," she responded, drinking some water.

"Kevin, I'm sorry. I appreciate your coming all this way. But I haven't changed my position. I care for you a great deal, but ..."

"Beth, I love you. I thought we would get married, have a wonderful life together."

"I did, too, at one time. But we're from two different worlds that don't fit together. You're a wonderful man, Kevin. I care a great deal for you." Tears filled Beth's eyes. "It's for the best we go our separate ways."

Kevin looked away. "I'm afraid you're right, Beth. I've seen it coming for some time and didn't want to face it."

The waiter arrived with the desserts. Beth stared at her bread pudding.

"Anything wrong, sir? This is what you ordered."

"Everything is fine. The bill, please, if you don't mind."

Beth and Kevin didn't speak as they walked the few blocks back to the B and B. Beth reached in her pocket and handed Kevin the engagement ring.

"No, I want you to keep it."

She smiled, shook her head and placed the ring in his hand.

Kevin kissed Beth on her forehead, then got into his BMW convertible and drove off. Standing on the sidewalk, she watched as his car turned the corner. The ocean breeze cooled as she walked along the beach that evening. Returning to her room she slept a peaceful, dreamless night.

The next morning Beth asked her grandmother if Adam had called. Not a word.

"Are you and Kevin spending the day together?"

"No, Grandmum, we broke it off."

Her grandmother asked nothing more. She gave Beth a list of errands and chores. By the time Beth had finished them all, it was time for supper.

"That's the best stew I've ever had, Grandmum" Beth said, rubbing her stomach. "Worked up a real appetite. After the dishes, I'll go down to the shore with Manna. She could use a good run. Want to go?"

"No, dear. You and your furry friend go along. I can finish up these few dishes. And besides, *As Time Goes By* is on the telly tonight."

Manna barked as soon as she reached the shore. A familiar yap answered her. Adam sat on a bench they had occupied several times that summer. He stood as Beth approached.

"I'm just going," he said. "Good to see you again."

"Please don't go. Sit with me for a while."

Adam sat down at the far end of the bench. Beth sat in the middle. Her heart beat faster, as she tried to think of something to say. She wanted to tell him everything. About Victoria, the bishop, Kevin. But she didn't know where to start. She looked down at her shoes making patterns in the sand. Adam's hand was resting on the bench. She moved over and touched his hand.

"I'm not engaged anymore."

He looked at her and smiled. "That's the best news I've heard in years. Let's take off our shoes and walk."

All the problems of her life could wait. She wanted to live in the present moment. That's what life is really about, she thought.

The next several days passed quickly. She and Adam spent every moment they could together. He came over for breakfast nearly every morning and helped with chores and errands, so they would have time for picnics on the Great Orme and walks on the beach in the moonlight. Beth felt as though she were living in a dream world. She had never been happier or really in love, she realized.

Once in a while she wondered about Adam's real profession, but she knew that in time he would tell her. When she told him about Victoria and the bishop, his response was, "Bully for you! That calls for a celebration!" That night Adam took Beth and her grandmother out for dinner at one of the nicest restaurants in Conway.

A smaller number of guests were booked the next few weeks as the summer season was coming to a close. Beth hadn't thought much about it until her grandmother asked one morning, "What do you plan to do this fall, Beth?"

"I'm not sure, Grandmum. Adam and I haven't talked about it either."

"You and Adam are quite a pair. I've never seen a happier two, except your grandfather and I. Knew it was a good match the moment you met."

"Well, you certainly saw more than I did. But perhaps I should think about the fall. I do need to make plans. A job or something."

"I love having you here. Stay as long as you like."

The phone rang. Beth answered it. "Brigid? Is that really you? I'd love to come sometime. Day after tomorrow? Bala Foresight? Really? Wouldn't miss it for the world. Yes, I know where that is. I'll take the train, then taxi to your office. Be there at five? Right. I understand. I can keep a secret. See you then."

Sitting on their favorite bench that evening, Beth told Adam she would be gone for several days to visit a friend in London. She didn't want to tell him about the opportunity to meet Bala Foresight. Besides, it might not work out.

"Why don't you get in touch with Victoria Martin while you're there?"

"That's a grand idea. I'll call her son's office in the morning. I'll stay in Hawthorne overnight and catch the express to London from Chester."

"Beth, I'll be gone for a few days, too. I'll miss you."

"I'll miss you, too. We've never been apart, I mean...since we've...."

"I know, Beth. I'd like to ask you one question before we both leave Llandudno tomorrow."

He took her hand in his. "Will you marry me?"

Beth couldn't believe the words.

"What?"

"Will you marry me?" he shouted.

"Yes, Adam. Yes!" she said, laughing and crying at the same time. "But remember, you could end up married to a vicar."

They stood, holding one another for a long time and kissed. Hand in hand Beth and Adam walked along the shore, stopping now and then, looking at one another. Beth wanted to make sure her world was real.

Adam walked Beth to the front door of Mrs. Hughes B & B. "When we both return, I'll explain about my job."

"Tell me now, Adam. Please?" she said.

"Just a few more days," he replied.

After one more lingering good bye kiss, the couple parted.

Chapter Thirty-Four

"For still the vision awaits its time."
(Habakkuk 2:3)

Beth sat on the log overlooking the Gately Estate. The sound of bleating sheep startled her. How long had she been here reliving her life? Glancing at her watch, she realized she had just enough time to catch the express train to London. She wasn't going to miss this opportunity to meet Bala Foresight.

She and Manna ran down the hill, dodging the multitude of sheep droppings. She stopped suddenly, remembering her book left on the log. *It'll be there when I get back in a few days. No time now.*

Beth decided on a dress, then struggled into pantyhose, groaning as she put on heels. She shook her head as she emptied the contents of her backpack on the bed: a half-eaten crusty sandwich, an empty water bottle, rain hat, one of her father's old jackets, a pair of heavy socks and an assortment of dull pebbles that had looked stunning when she fished them out of a stream. Grabbing a few essentials, some casual clothes, and her make up bag, Beth packed quickly. Her unopened letter from the bishop was the last to go in.

The express to London held few passengers at mid-day. Beth settled into a window seat with her backpack beside her. The countryside rushed past as she stared out the window. She reached over, unzipped a front compartment of her pack and took out the envelope. For a few moments she stared at the bishop's seal guarding the back. Breaking the seal, she took out the letter.

Dear Miss Davies,

I hope you will keep this letter in strictest confidence. Next week I shall announce my retirement from the Office of Bishop in the Church of England. I am aware Mrs. Martin is well on her way to recovery. I wrote to her asking for forgiveness. By the grace of God, the lady in question responded with a quite amazing acceptance. I cannot undo the wrongs I have done to this merciful lady, but I pray, with God's help, I can do something of value in my remaining days here on earth.

Our mutual friend, Bishop Short, has invited me to South Africa for a visit. I shall be well on my way before the official announcement is made public. In time, I shall return to England. Thank you for confronting this sinner. Our church is indeed quite fortunate to have you as a member. It would be a travesty if you were not allowed to continue on the path God has chosen. I have taken the liberty of sending letters of recommendation to colleagues who might assist you in your endeavors.

I still have reservations concerning the ordination of women to the priesthood, but you have caused me to reflect on the matter. Kindly come by the cathedral office at your convenience. There is a package for you I pray you will accept with my gratitude. Let me assure you my assistant checked with the authorities and there is no need to return the object in question to Greece.

May God's peace and blessings be with you.

Faithfully yours,
The Right Reverend John Daykn
Bishop of Chester

Beth reread the letter several times. Her emotions were mingled. Sad and relieved. Excited about the possibilities, not only for herself, but for the bishop as well. And the gift. *He's given me that exquisite icon! It's more than the gift. It's what it represents.*

Beth arrived at Victoria Station as she finished a stale sandwich purchased on the train. Her taxi delivered her at the prestigious office building and she punched the number on the lift for the top floor. With each passing floor, anticipation increased.

What do I say? I love your books sounds so trite. Should I ask for an autograph? She may be a crotchety old bag who doesn't want to be bothered with the likes of me. I promised Brigid I wouldn't reveal her identity. Maybe her boss won't let me meet her

The door of the elevator opened. The foyer of the office was filled with lavish antiques and floral arrangements. Brigid looked quite comfortable behind a large oak desk neatly arranged with a computer, a phone with an array of separate lines and an assortment of secretarial supplies.

"Beth! Right on time."

"Yes, Brigid. I hate to tell you, I almost missed my train. Went out for a walk."

Laughing, Brigid responded, "Like those walks you took at Oxford and always missed an important lecture. You know you'd still be there if it weren't for my notes."

Beth giggled. "Is she here yet?"

"I'm not sure," Brigid said in a whisper. "Always comes in a different way. We have a secret back entrance."

"No you don't."

"Well, actually we do. It's really the freight elevator around back. Bala always comes up that way. Prefers to stay away from the public."

"Brigid, did you read the article about her in The Sun? It stated she was badly scarred. That's why she's in hiding."

"It's not true."

"So, you've met her?"

"No, but my boss told me for some reason she's coming out in public in two weeks. Until then, you must keep her true identity a secret."

"I promise."

"So how's Kevin. Have you two set the date?"

"We've broken up. And I'm in love with someone else. And I mean really in love."

Brigid's eyes grew round. "Beth, I can't believe..."

A buzzer sounded.

"Yes, sir?"

"Has your friend arrived?"

"Yes, sir."

"Bala Foresight is here, Miss Seymour. You may both come in now."

"I'm so excited." Beth put her hand on her heart. "I can't believe I'm going to meet Bala Foresight."

"Calm down, Beth. If you get any more excited, you'll pass out."

Brigid walked over to an enormous wooden door and opened it. Beth followed close behind. Brigid's boss stood behind his desk. A large window framed the blue sky with Big Ben as the centerpiece.

"Mr. Hill, this is my friend, Elizabeth Davies."

Promptly walking from behind the desk, he extended his hand. "How do you do. Miss Seymour tells me you are quite a fan of Bala Foresight."

"Yes, sir. I appreciate the opportunity to meet her."

Mr. Hill peered over his reading glasses with a slight twinkle in his eye. "I can assure you, Bala is not going to be what you expect. Do you understand the conditions? You are not to disclose the author's identity."

"Yes, sir."

"Our author is in the adjoining room." Nodding to Brigid, he looked toward a wall. "Miss Seymour, if you would be so kind."

Brigid walked over, opening a door camouflaged by a false bookcase. Beth could hear footsteps on the wooden floor of the next room approaching the doorway. She held her breath in suspense. A man in jeans and plaid shirt stood in the opening.

Beth gasped. "You can't be Bala Foresight."

Adam laughed, "Well, I didn't know you were Miss Seymour's friend. Yes, Beth, I am Bala Foresight."

Beth shook her head. "That explains your behavior. But I still can't believe it."

Mr. Hill looked from one to the other. "It's obvious you two don't need an introduction."

"Beth," said Brigid, "I don't understand. How do you know him?"

"I not only know him, I love him."

Adam walked over to Beth. "I've always written under a pen name, so I could blend in and absorb locations and people. But when I met you, I knew my life would change."

Adam held Beth in his arms and kissed her. She felt the promise of a lifetime of love.

"May the God of hope fill you with all joy and peace
in believing, so that by the power of the Holy Spirit
you may abound in hope."

(Romans 15:13)

Made in the USA
Lexington, KY
09 September 2018